The Brookfield Daughter:
Sanctuary

Richard Douglas Taylor

Jer-Ben Publications, Inc.

Published in the United States by: Jer-Ben Publications, Inc.

Library of Congress Cataloging-in-Publication Data

Taylor, Richard
The Brookfield Daughter: Sanctuary

   ISBN-13: 978-0978923853 (trade pbk)
   ISBN-10: 0978923855 (trade pbk)

Printed in the United States

Email comments or queries to rdtaylor@mediacombb.net
Web site: www.primetimes2.com/books.html

10 9 8 7 6 5 4 3 2 1

To all you beautiful aliens.

Chapter 1

Against the pool's tropical backdrop, from nose to foot she looked every bit the island native, her wet, tanned skin glistening in the mid-morning sun. As she ascended the curved, marble steps, the mother of two wanted to look back to see which sibling was winning *king of the raft*, or in this case, *king of the raft that emulated a giant slice of pepperoni pizza.* It was delivered at the front gate just this morning by Amazon drone, and the kids were fighting over it even before Dad blew it up. Suzy knew the novelty would wear off before lunch.

She was also curious if her husband was still lounging in his patio chaise over there under the big umbrella. Was he doing the same thing as when she left him, reading his BassMaster magazine? He said he didn't want to swim this early, because the heater hadn't warmed the water enough yet.

Yes, Suzette Marie Brookfield-Jackson wanted to see what the rest of her family was doing at this very moment. They meant the world to her.

But first things first.

Using her fingers as combs, Suzy pushed her dripping bob away from her face, at the same time craning her neck to scan the cloudless sky. She couldn't help looking up. It was a habit developed years ago, when it was crucial to keep a close watch on the heavens.

Satisfied nothing was there, she returned her attention to the earth and her present reality. Jax appeared to still be reading, although Suzy thought it odd he was now wearing his amber-mirrored Oakley's. He usually wore sunglasses outdoors, but never while reading. He was probably sleeping.

Her nine-year-old Nicole and seven-year-old Nathan were still fighting over dominion of the pizza slice rubber raft. They didn't seem to mind that the pool's heating system had kicked on only ten minutes ago, leaving the water a bit crispy. But Suzy minded. She should have listened to Jax. So, that one fast lap around the pool was enough, and that two-layered hot tub with its bubbling, one hundred and ten degrees was calling her name.

The transplanted farm girl cherished every minute she could spend with the family in the open air, what with all those things they had to hide from in the sky. A decade ago it was the Reggs, with their infrared scanners and dogged determination to locate and capture anyone with a hint of Mejan DNA. That threat was mercifully long gone. But it was replaced with a different one...not as dangerous, but annoying enough to keep one eye on the sky anytime the family was outside here at The Mansion.

The airborne enemies these days were humans, using whisper drones, hot air balloons, and an occasional news helicopter to buzz the two hundred-acre estate—hoping to learn who the richest man in southeast Iowa might be dating at the moment. They had no idea Suzy and Patrick (Jax) Jackson had been married for ten years with two children. It was imperative to keep the public in the dark, for many reasons.

So, security was a top priority here, as evidenced by the louvered metal roof that could snap shut to cover the entire backyard pool area in less than a second, if and when the radar hidden in the children's three-story playhouse detected anything larger than a crow coming within a hundred yards of their airspace. And good luck to anyone trying to climb over the electrified front gate or ten-foot-high, chain-link fence running the entire perimeter. The Jacksons had always cherished their privacy, even when Jax was a boy living here with his now-deceased parents. Today, the thirty-five-year-old was worth four times his age in millions, and was married to a beautiful woman who was part alien. Privacy was more than essential.

"You guys hungry? Suzy called to the kids, although she doubted they heard her. "Need a snack?" It didn't matter; when it was time, their insatiable appetites—coupled with the sight and smell of whatever Odett and Loretta had whipped up—would get them out of the water faster than a close lightning strike.

Something was caught in Suzy's wedding/engagement rings. She brought the guilty hand up for close inspection to discover it was a hair, one of her own. Angling it in the sunlight, she hoped it was a solid brown, like it was supposed to be. But there was no mistaking its solid whiteness, like the streaks that had

8

been gracing her temples for years. She hated the gray, considering she was only twenty then and barely thirty now. But being abducted by hairy, smelly ETs with shiny, sharp instruments can do that to you.

That gray hair reminded Suzy why she had worn her beige, skin-tight one-piece today: she had worn it just for him. Jax always liked it, saying it complimented her bronze skin and perky curves just right. Well, he didn't *always* say that. In truth, he said it only once, the first time she wore it. That was six years ago, a few months after Nathan was born and she had lost all her baby fat for the second time.

But the object of today's fashion choice didn't seem to be looking at her. He was still engrossed in his fishing magazine. He hadn't noticed her at all. Actually, he hadn't said anything complimentary about her looks in two years, seven months, and four days.

Chapter 2

Pretending not to be watching from behind his amber-mirrored sunglasses, Jax Jackson marveled at how his wife didn't look a day older or a pound heavier than the day they met at the Brookfield's farm pond ten years ago, almost to the day. Despite all they had been through during the clandestine war with the Reggs, plus Suzy giving birth to those two golden gremlins splashing out there on the pizza raft beside the waterfall, she was still a vision, as lithe and attractive as ever.

Still, there was that oversized cranium and those larger-than-normal, copper-brown eyes, all three seeming more pronounced these days. Was that even possible? Jax remembered that day when she purposefully removed those big sunglasses and beach-comber straw hat to reveal her alien features. She was afraid he would find them hideous, yet he remarked they were quite attractive. And as time went by, he'd gotten so used to them, he hardly noticed the abnormalities anymore.

But lately he found himself wishing his wife was closer to ordinary. He felt bad for thinking that way, but he couldn't help it. It severely limited their social circle to the immediate family, some of whom were part Mejan like Suzy. Her mother—Mary—was a full one-quarter Mejan, having a brainpan and peepers so large she could never hide them with a bobbed haircut or floppy hats like Suzy could. Poor Mary had been a virtual shut-in at The Farm her entire life. At least Suzy could take the kids and venture out among the populous now and then. But never with Jax. They couldn't be seen together.

Jax glanced down at his own midriff, the muffin-top of too much rich-living and too little exercise peeking over the waistband of his white trunks. Being in his mid-thirties, wasn't he was allowed some love handles? They hardly detracted from his six-two frame with broad shoulders and jawline. Just the other day in the shower Suzy said he was sexy. She wouldn't lie. Suzy couldn't lie.

"Who was that on the phone a minute ago?" asked Suzy, crossing the marble slabs to grab the towel from the chaise lounge next to her husband's.

"Your mom," Jax replied, automatically handing up her black Tiffany sunglasses, "inviting us for dinner tomorrow evening."

"Oh, good," she said, twirling the Tiffanies, in no hurry to put them on. "That okay with you?"

"Sure," he said, arching his own sunglasses long enough to look up at her. "We haven't been out there for a while." Hoping his enthusiasm didn't sound too forced, Jax quickly drained the last of his breakfast orange juice and set the plastic cup on the round, slatted, cedar table. The Farm. Her family. The sum total of their social life.

Suddenly from the breezeway, Loretta announced her pending arrival, exactly as she and her mother, Odett, were required to do. From day-one they knew the Jacksons were a secretive pair, especially the missus, what with her always wearing hats and sunglasses, even at the dinner table. The Jacksons said they worked for a government agency and didn't like people sneaking up on them, even here in The Mansion. Odett and Loretta had no idea what the real truth was, and weren't about to pry.

At the sound of Loretta's voice, Suzy quickly slipped on her sunglasses and white, floppy beach hat. Counting to three, the nanny exited the house and approached with a pitcher of OJ at the ready. Coming up beside the table, she asked if anybody needed refills. His train of thought now completely derailed by the distraction, Jax okayed half a glass. Suzy said she was fine.

"There still be a couple waffles left over, if you wants 'em," smiled the lanky, Columbian woman in her early-forties, as she poured Jax's glass. "I could heat 'em back up."

They both shook her off. "You eat them," smiled Jax. "You could gain a few pounds. But keep them away from Odett. She doesn't need the carbs."

"Mamma left to go to the sto," said Loretta, "and I already et three."

A whining protest from Nathan turned Loretta's attention toward the pool. "Nicole, honey" Loretta called, "you share the raft with yo little brother. Take turns if yose have to." Loretta

11

stood fast until her order was obeyed, then she turned and glided back into the house.

A little embarrassed for not keeping a better maternal eye on her two offspring, Suzy strolled back to the edge of the pool. "Kids," she called. "You want to go out to The Farm tomorrow afternoon?"

"Yeah!' yelled Nathan, letting go of the raft and starting to swim toward his mom in anticipation. Nicole echoed the affirmation, then took advantage of the abandoned slice of pepperoni pizza to climb aboard. They both knew The Farm meant all kinds of fun things to do, from spearing the pigs with corn stalks to bowling in Grandpa and Grandma's super-cool rec room. Nathan especially loved to fish for those big bass in their capsule-shaped pond on top of the hill in the north pasture. He had gotten his first spinning rod for his sixth birthday last year, and he and his dad were having some good times up there. Nicole liked to fish, too. But she took more after her mother and two uncles, being captivated by anything digital. She was already writing code.

Neither kid, however, knew anything about their own home's secret communications room, let alone The Farm's, or what the big silo was really for, or what lay hidden beneath that pond. They were still too young. And since the Regg threat had been eliminated a decade ago, there was a chance they would never have to know…or learn about their family's connection to that covert agency known only as *The Desert*. Of course, Nicole and Nathan's enduring innocence would hinge on the outcome of certain global affairs, which currently were volatile at best.

Sitting on her lounge chair, Suzy spun to purposely face Jax, who was still pretending to read his magazine. She might have paid more attention to the fact his Oakley sunglasses were now up on his forehead, not on his nose. But Suzy was more involved with silently rehearsing her next words, while studying Jax's semi-supine form for any clue to his present mood. Even if that mood turned out to be good, she knew this conversation was not going to end well. But so what? She had nothing to lose.

"What say we go shopping this morning?" she grinned awkwardly. When there was no immediate response, she added, "We need to pick up some wine for tomorrow night, and I'd like to look for something new to wear...something casual. You know how hard it is to find my size. You could use a couple new shirts."

Jax stirred a little. "Both of us?" he snorted, without looking her way. "*Together*?"

"Sure. Why not?"

Jax dropped his magazine to his lap. He sat up and looked curiously at his wife. It was just what he had been musing about minutes ago. They were certainly on the same wave length. But, as much as he would love to go out in public together, it had to remain in the dream world, as always. "C'mon," he scoffed. "You know why not."

Suzy folded her arms across her stomach. "Yes, I *do* know," she whispered, yet her tone was determined. "I've known it every day for the past ten years."

"Then why are you bringing this up now?"

Suzy fidgeted, gathering her rehearsed words. "I guess I'm getting tired of it, Jax," she sighed. "I wish we had a normal life. I wish we didn't have to home-school the kids. I wish I could walk down the street on your arm. I wish we could all go to City Park, go out for dinner at a restaurant as a family." Suzy paused, keeping the final and most important complaint to herself: *I wish you'd look at me the way you used to, as if my Mejan features were fascinating instead of repulsive.*

"We do all that when we go to the Caribbean or Mexico twice a year," said Jax dismissively.

"Sure," groaned Suzy. "After you've gone ahead on the corporate jet, and the kids and I come later on a commercial flight. We feel like terrorist...or drug mules. And while there, I still have to keep my head and eyes covered like I'm a leper."

A dripping-wet boy suddenly sloshed up beside them. Like his sister, Nathan was a scant, one-sixteenth Mejan. They were human enough that their heads were only slightly oversized, as were their round, brown eyes. Neither feature drew scrutiny from adults or teasing from other children. But then, they weren't around that many *normal* people anyway.

"When did you say we are going to the farm?" Nathan asked, wiping his nose on the back of his hand. "Was that tomorrow or today?"

"Tomorrow, sweetheart," replied his mom, handing her towel to him. "You know I said tomorrow."

"I wanna go today. Pleeease."

"They invited us to come out tomorrow, Son," said his father. "You'll just have to wait."

"Aww..."

To nip the whining in the bud, Jax fetched the black and gold Nerf football from the cedar table. "Go long," he said, cocking his arm to one side. That's all it took to appease the young athlete. Nathan took off toward the pool, looking back only after jumping off the end of the diving board. The ball was already in the air, sailing five feet over his head. It landed way out in the middle of the pool, almost hitting Nicole, who was lounging victoriously on the inflated slice of pepperoni pizza.

"C'mon, Dad!" yelled the disgruntled youth, backstroking toward the bobbing ball. "You did that on purpose."

"It's hard to throw while sitting under an umbrella," Jax called back. "But stay out there a little longer with your sister, please. Your mother and I are talking."

The interruption over, neither said anything or looked at each other. Jax waited, knowing Suzy had more to get off her chest.

"For the first twenty years of my life," she finally said softly, lying back on her lounge chair, "we had to hide from the Reggs. They're gone now, and I still have to hide. And not just my face, but my identity. I wish...I don't know...I just wish."

Jax could tell those big eyes behind those big sunglasses were swelling up with big tears.

"I know," he sympathized, reaching for his glass of OJ. "This charade really blows. But you know it's not just about us and the town folks. The Desert wants us to stay low, too, at least for a little while longer." Jax took a drink of orange juice and added with a snicker, "You gotta admit, hon, they *are* right: the world isn't quite ready to learn that a good portion of its population is descended from Martians."

Suzy didn't want to laugh, but she couldn't help it.

Once again from the wings, Loretta announced she was en-route. She counted to three, and then appeared, this time with nothing in her hands. As she suspected, her employers' smart phones were lying there on the table face up and offline. Neither of them had heard the news, or their noses would be buried in the high-tech devises.

"Oh, my, she gasped. "Haven't you folks heard?"

"Heard what?" asked Jax.

"'Bout what happened to Washington? It be all over da news."

Chapter 3

President Arthur William Henning had a mild headache behind his right eye, along with a piece of sand under the lid of the left one. With his breakfast strudel in one hand, he was trying to rub the eye with his other hand, when some white icing dripped off the strudel onto his lap. His expletive succeeded only in activating his stomach acid and the Oval Office's sound-sensitive recorder that automatically kicked on by any noise over fifteen decibels.

It was not a good beginning to his day.

But then, when was his last *good* day? Last January 20, when he took office? Even that was marred by the radical left busting car windshields and burning his effigy just outside the police-lined perimeter. Maybe it was when his daughter graduated from the eighth grade with honors in May. He felt good that day. For about an hour. Then those goddamned Iranians had to go and test their second underground nuclear device. The revised treaty Trump had made them sign lasted about as long as Trump's eight-year presidency.

At least it felt good to be in his Navy-blue, monogrammed, presidential sweats and Nikes, especially after last night's stiff tuxedo and the boring state dinner with Japan's prime minister. Despite a most excellent foies gras and veal parmesan, the president and first lady thought the night would never end. Judging from the pregnant silences during desert in the state dining room and then brandy on the terrace, Kan Kishi and his wife undoubtedly felt the same.

Using his laptop to scroll through Google news on the web, Henning was not surprised to find most of the articles were divided between the third intercontinental ballistic missile test by the North Koreans in as many months, and the United Nations-brokered cease fire between Russia and Poland on the verge of breaking down. He was tempted to just roll up the paper-thin screen of the Surface 8 and stick the whole high-tech contraption in a drawer. But with chin in hand, the president kept reading, still amazed how the news media seemed to think they knew more about his business than he did. Maybe they did, what with all those goddamn leaks to the media.

The seven-foot television screen on the north wall of the Oval Office displayed Sally Kendrick of NBC News standing on the front steps of the Capitol, reporting live that an inside source suggested the democrats were considering starting a petition in the House to have President Henning impeached. Henning suspected as much. There had been rumblings. He probably could have defeated ISIS without sending in those hundred-thousand American troops into Somalia, their last stronghold. But, hell, nobody else in the UN or NATO had offered boots on the ground. It was always up to us, the world's police force. He had no choice.

"Is the strudel to your liking, sir?" came the voice over the intercom. "Need anything else?"

"I'm fine, Julia. Thanks."

Henning reached for his morning jolt of coffee that Julia had brought in ten minutes ago with the strudel. The *America's First Dad* mug paused at his lips for a thoughtful moment. It was a birthday gift from his kids just after being elected president. His stomach was already acid enough, and there was no denying the mild jitters showing up again in both his hands and heart. Would he live to see sixty? He returned the mug to its coaster on the mahogany desktop, and took a sip of water from the Evian bottle sitting on his desk since noon yesterday.

Needing some good news...any good news, President Henning scrolled down to the sports section of Google News, hoping the Cubs had won last night. They were in second place, four games behind the Cardinals, and needed to get some momentum going before the All-Star break, if they had any hope of winning the World Series again like in 2016. Thankfully, they had won last night, five to four over the Mets. "Alright!" he said aloud. Maybe God was back in his Heaven and the goat would stay in the barn. Things were looking up.

And then the lights went out.

The White House was no more immune to a power outage than any other electricity-fed building in America. But the odd thing with this particular failure was that the back-up generators didn't kick in right away, as they always did within a second.

They still hadn't after five seconds.

Enough mid-morning light was pouring through the Oval Office's south windows behind him for the president to find and punch the intercom button on his wireless desk phone. "What's up, Julia?" he sang, purposely hiding his annoyance. He had to be careful with her. During his first week in office he had learned that the private secretary he had inherited from the Trump administration—Julia Johnston—didn't like anyone giving her attitude. He was under no obligation to keep her on, and he thought seriously about firing her back then, despite everyone, including Donald Trump, saying she was the most efficient secretary he'd ever had. She'd been there since the Bush era. But in the following weeks and months, the petite, aging African/American turned out to be exactly as advertised. He even grew to like her. Whether the feeling was mutual, was still up for presidential debate.

When there was no answer, Henning's slender index finger hit the button again. "Julia? Mrs. Johnston? Are you there?" he said louder, as if that would help. Still nothing. He tipped his head back a few degrees to allow the reading portion of his wire-rimmed bifocals to better scrutinize the row of buttons. None was lighted, not even the little red light that indicated his phone was connected and working. Then he noticed his laptop was no longer on, either. It had a backup battery, yet it was as dead as the bronze bust of Reagan sitting beside it. Strange.

He remembered his wife saying she would be in the kitchen for most of the morning, planning the week's menu with the head chef. Marjorie Henning took it upon herself to meticulously lay out everything the family ate each day, from breakfast to evening snacks. His kids had never known a Kit-Kat bar, and he was lucky to get a piece of red meat once a week. The power was probably out all across the White House, if not D.C. itself. But cell phones operate on their own power. Calling her was worth a try.

He raised his left forearm close to his mouth. "Cadox, call Marjorie," he articulated into his wristwatch. When there was not the usual chime and verbal verification, the fifty-eight-year-

18

old leader of the chaotic, free world discovered the small round screen was dark and dead. Puzzled, he picked up the smartphone itself. It was also blank, its black, shiny surface mirroring only the silhouette of his angular head, backlit by the windows behind him.

"What the hell is going on here," he huffed out loud, tossing the useless device back onto the desk. It had been a good fifteen seconds since the blackout started and still no backup generators. The president pushed away from his desk, and walked to the east wall where the inconspicuous door-in-the-wallpaper led out to Julia's desk and the secretary pool. It was locked tight. "Of course," he scoffed at himself. "The power is off."

As a security measure against any number of scenarios, the double-steel door operated on electronic deadbolts that retracted only when qualified personnel placed their right thumb on the small scanner of the specially-programmed door handle. But with no power there could be no scan, and thus no way for the bolts to retract. He didn't know if there were a battery backup. But even if so, apparently it wasn't working either.

The Lincoln-thin Republican was about to bang foolishly on the soundproof door and yell for Julia, when a strong voice behind him bounced off the same door, "Mr. President. It's Agent Lewis from the Secret Service. Are you all right, sir?"

Startled, Arthur Henning spun around to see the broad-shouldered, dark-suited agent he knew only by his last name, walking out of the shadow of the seamless door hidden below the portrait of George Washington. Henning was well aware of the secret passage that led out of the Oval Office. The steps corkscrewed down five stories into the bomb-proof, radiation-proof, every-thing-proof bunker. From there, one adjacent tunnel led into the War Room, while another went far out past the White House grounds to an underground garage where a fleet of bullet-proof getaway vehicles waited. Presidents had been using this system at the slightest hint of an incursion ever since Eisenhower had it constructed during the cold war some seventy-five years ago. Henning himself had been quickly ushered into it more than once, the latest time being five months ago by Agent Lewis himself, when a mentally unhinged democrat jumped the south lawn gate and rushed the White House with an unlit Roman candle and a spatula.

"Yeah, I'm fine, Lewis," he reported to the good-looking, strictly-business agent as they closed ranks. He never did know his first name. "Any idea what's with the power?"

"None, sir," said Lewis, tapping his earpiece. "My communications are out as well. This is most peculiar."

They walked over to the windows behind the president's desk. "I see the traffic lights are still operating out there on the streets," said Agent Lewis, "so it must be only the White House."

Before the president could reply, from behind they heard the television on the north wall ding-dong back to life. Relieved, they both turned to see and hear the pretty blonde reporter on NBC News parroting what the crawl at the bottom was texting: *...it appears power is off at the nation's White House...*

"Not anymore," smiled a relieved POTUS, watching his laptop, smartphone, and watch light back up. Even his Georgetown-style table lamp was back spreading light on the press release he was supposed to proof before the scheduled press briefing at one this afternoon.

Predictably, the deadbolts released with a muffled click, and in through the wallpaper rushed Julia Johnston, lamenting the strange blackout. On her heels was Carson Boyle—the Chief of Staff—asking if the president was okay. Agent Lewis confirmed he was unharmed, and that all seemed to be back to normal. Satisfied, and before her boss could even order it, Julia snapped her right arm up to her mouth and spoke into the wristwatch, "Cadox, call maintenance." Two-tones and a verbal, "Calling Maintenance" confirmed her request.

Within seconds her smart phone revealed Jason was on the line, and she put it on speaker. "We have no idea what happened, Julia," said the baritone, obviously well-educated voice. "Everything went dead, including the sequence of all three backup generators. We are looking into it."

"Okay, Jason," said Julia. "Let us know what you find out." She punched off and looked at her boss with one raised eyebrow. He just shrugged and looked at the television, which was now reporting the power was back on at the White House.

No one said anything for a few moments. Then Chief of Staff Boyle tugged pensively on his earlobe and addressed the elephant in the room. "It smacks of an e-bomb," he said succinctly. "I hate to say it, but it's the only thing that makes sense."

"I have to agree," said Agent Lewis.

Without replying, President Henning walked back and sat down in the leather executive chair. He steepled his fingers to his lips. "It could be," he finally conceded, "but we need to…"

Just then both his wristwatch and smartphone chimed the arrival of a text message. He assumed it was from his wife, Marjorie, since most of the other people who had his private cell number were standing here in the Oval Office looking at him. He fetched the phone off the desk and read the words to himself. His expression remained blank, then he gave an incredulous shake of his head along with a sniff from his scrunched nose.

"What is it, Arthur, if I may ask?" said Boyle, trying to read his longtime friend's face. "Is it Marjorie? Is everything okay?"

President Henning continued studying the text, saying nothing. He then cleared his throat and said, "It's not from my wife." He shook his head again, this time incredulously. "I don't know what this is."

Alarmed, both Boyle and Agent Lewis stepped closer to the desk, Lewis leaning demonstratively forward on it with both hands. "No one outside the circle is supposed to have that number, sir," he said firmly. "Can you tell us what it says?"

Henning set his jaw, his eyes still locked on the small screen. He drew in a breath and read the message as if it were a letter of reprimand:

HELLO PRESIDENT HENNING. DID YOU ENJOY OUR DEMONSTRATION? YES IT WAS ELECTROMAGNETIC PULSE. IT KNOCKED OUT EVERYTHING USING ELECTRONS. BUT IT NOT A BOMB AND IT NOT DESTROY ANYTHING. WE CONTROLLED THE ENERGY WAVE FOR EXACTLY ONE MINUTE. THE NEXT ONE COMES IN TWO MINUTES AT 11:00. IT LAST FIVE SECONDS OVER ALL OF WASHINGTON. I CALL YOU AFTER. YOU ANSWER.

The president numbly extended the smart phone toward the Secret Service agent, who took it and leered at the text. "I'd say it's a hoax," said Lewis, his eyes darting back and forth, up and down the screen, "except it did knock out everything electronic. Plus how'd he get your private number?"

He handed it back to the president, who gave it to his Chief of Staff. Carson Boyle squinted through the grammatically-challenged text, his eyebrows taking turns going up and down like a teeter-totter. "This is crazy," he said, handing the phone back to his chief. "Could be ISIS. He doesn't seem American educated."

"Well, if he holds true to his word," said Henning, checking his watch, "we'll know more in about a minute."

Agent Lewis said, "Do you want me to call in some of my men, sir?"

The president shrugged. "I don't see any point just yet. Let's see what happens next."

The room fell silent, as the four people anxiously watched the countdown to the top of the hour on their atomically-synced timepieces. Forty seconds. Thirty. Twenty.

"Christ!" groaned Chief of Staff Boyle, getting antsier. "If our enemies have an EMP weapon that can knock out an entire city…"

"We don't know that," chided Julia.

Fifteen.

"Well, we're about to find out," said Boyle. "Ten, nine, eight...

At exactly eleven a.m. Eastern Daylight Time, the Oval Office and virtually all of Washington, D.C. shut down. Once again, the room was bathed only in ambient light. "Shit!" hissed someone.

Five seconds later, exactly as predicted, the power snapped back on. Every electrical- and battery-dependent device was functioning as if nothing had happened. The nation's capital had rejoined the land of the living, but now with a cacophony of impatient car horns, fenders bending, glass breaking, security alarms shrieking, people yelling. The news crew on NBC seemed in disarray with three or four reporters talking over each other: "*We have Brian on the…wait….what? It seems to be most or all of Washington…."*

Chief of Staff Boyle walked quickly to the south window to get some visuals. The steam from three or four crushed radiators was wafting into the air out on New York Avenue, as traffic was backed up beyond view. Police and rescue sirens were coming from all directions, near and far. But before he could comment on the chaos, something in the sky caught his attention. "Oh, my God! Look!" he exclaimed, pointing thirty degrees upward.

The other three scurried over in time to see a small, single-engine plane tumbling out of control about three miles to the south and only a thousand feet up in the clear blue sky.

"The blackout must have knocked out its engine and all its controls," said Agent Lewis, an ex-Marine pilot.

All four held their collective breath, praying the pilot could get the engine restarted in time. He couldn't. The plane disappeared behind some trees, followed by a small, orange flash and the delayed sound wave hitting the office's bulletproof windows with a muffled *pop*.

"Lord, I think that's a residential area," moaned Henning, looking away. "I hope…"

"That's not the worst of it, sir," interrupted Lewis. "Look up there."

Two fighter jets, looking more like toys, were spiraling out of control side-by-side, like freefalling black pinwheels.

"I was afraid of this," said Agent Lewis, his hands and nose pressed against the glass, his eyes riveted on the two planes, still high in the bright sky. "Those are probably F-22 Raptors, patrolling the air space above Washington. I'd guess originally around thirty-thousand feet. Let's hope they are high enough that they still have time to restart their engines."

"C'mon, Air Force!" shouted Boyle. "Fire up, goddamn it!"

As if on cue, two puffs of gray smoke suddenly spit out of one fighter's dual engines, followed by welcomed cones of fire. A second later the other F-22 restarted, as well. Both came out of their spins five thousand feet above the ground, and skyrocketed back into the heavens to the cheers from the Oval Office and a few out in the streets.

The phone on Julia Johnson's bony wrist erupted with incoming messages. She ignored them, trying to absorb all that was happening to her world right before her eyes. Chief of Staff

Boyle's wristwatch also lit up and chimed; it was his deputy secretary; it could wait. Secret Service Agent Lewis was already talking quietly into his watch, asking his supervisor if they should lock down the White House.

"D.C. is gonna want answers, Arthur," said Carson Boyle to the back of his leader, who was still gazing out the south window. "Hell, so is the country...the whole world, for that matter. What do we tell them?"

"What *can* we tell them?" snapped a flustered Henning, turning around to face his staff. "We don't really know enough ourselves. We'll have to wait until the sonofabitch calls back."

"*If* he calls back," said Julia.

"Oh, he will," said Henning. "This is no practical joke by some nerd hacker. He wouldn't go through all this trouble for a few laughs. He wants something."

The president's watch and smartphone chimed in unison. But this time it wasn't a text message. It was a call. There was no photo on the screen, just two words that had never appeared on his highly-secured, personal smartphone: UNKNOWN CALLER.

President Arthur Henning lifted his eyes to scope the faces of his Chief of Staff, the Secret Service agent, and his private secretary. All three looked pale. He hoped his face still showed some color, but he assumed it didn't. Drawing in half a lungful of air, Henning looked back down at this phone, punched *OK*, and brought the black device up to his ear. "Yes?" he said evenly.

"Hello...again...Mr. President," said a low, throaty voice, each word slow and measured, as if not completely versed in English and probably reading from notes. "We have your attention, yes?"

"What do you want?" said Henning, trying his best to sound presidential and impatient. "What you just did violated about a dozen federal laws."

"Others in room with you, yes?"

"Maybe," huffed Henning, not pleased with his question being ignored.

"Yes or no, Mr. President." The voice was firm.

"Yes. A few."

"They are trusted?"

"Yes. Very trusted."

"Good. If our talk is known to untrusted people, you have a world panic."

"Okay. What do you want?"

"Put phone on speaker, so all can hear me."

Seeing no problem with that, Henning did as demanded, placing the device face up on his desk. The other three drew in closer to better hear.

"All hear me?" the voice asked cordially.

Not sure if they should reply and possibly give away something the caller wasn't authorized to know, they just nodded.

"They can hear you fine," said the president stiffly. "Will you now please tell us the reason for this blatant and unwarranted attack on the United States government?"

"Yes. I am what you humans have called a *Regg*."

The voice said nothing more, expecting a response.

"A *Regg*?" said Henning, looking quizzically at each of the other three, whose collective expression showed they too were clueless. "I have no idea what a *Regg* is."

A pause.

"You do not know?"

"No. Why should we? Never heard the word before."

Another pause, this one a little longer.

"We believe you," the gruff voice finally said. "We thought this be true."

"What *be* true?"

"That you not know us, or our war ten years ago."

"Well, you're sure as hell right about that, my friend!" laughed the president sardonically, adding a sneer for the benefit of the other three disbelievers standing at the front of his desk. "And what exactly was this war about ten years ago, if I may ask?"

"Much happened," said the Regg. "Too much to tell. And much *we* not know. War end when Regg mothership escorted out near Jupiter and destroyed with not mercy."

President Henning looked over his wire-rims at the other three. Secret agency? Destroying a mothership out by Jupiter? Now this *was* smacking of some genius-grade hacker, living in a fantasy world with state-of-the-art computer equipment and a steady diet of Red Bull, who somehow managed to devise an electrometric pulse weapon with the capability of disabling an entire city.

"Are we really supposed to believe this?" challenged Henning, no longer afraid to demonstrate his irritation.

The voice shot right back with its own loss of patience, "Not matter what you believe, President. We control your government, your military, and your world. Disrupting your power was only a small demonstration. We can do it anywhere on Earth any time and not just for moments. We can destroy your entire power grid and devices forever. You not stop us."

"Now, just a minute, you little cocksucker..." spat Boyle at the phone. "You can't threaten..."

Henning's extended palm and the Regg's curt words cut him short. "I tired of you now. You listen. After our conversation, you call your leaders at *Ellsworth Air Force Base in South Dakota*. They will tell you about the five seconds with no power to the base and missile silos. Then you believe we control your defenses. And you."

Chief of Staff Boyle started to raise his phone to his mouth to make the call. But President Henning held up one finger, signaling to wait.

The low, dusky voice continued. "You tell only *Attorney General*, the *head of FBI*, and *Joint Chiefs of Staff*. No one else. The world must not know."

"And how do you expect us to explain the power outages?" said Henning.

"Your problem." There was a three second pause, then the Regg concluded, "As your movies say, I hang up now. I call in one hour. Have your officers here for instructions."

The smartphone showed the call had ended.

"Hello? Hello?" said President Henning. Whoever or whatever it was had indeed hung up. "Shit!" He said, reaching over to shut off his phone. Henning then motioned for Carson to make the call to Ellsworth Air Force Base.

Seeing "BREAKING NEWS" now flashing across the bottom third of the television screen, he told Julia to turn up the volume. The reporter's eyes were bouncing back and forth between her teleprompter and the piece of yellow paper being handed to her. She labored to keep the excitement out of her voice. This is what the media live for. "Reports are coming in from all over Washington of multi-vehicle pile-ups on interstates and major highways, plus people with pacemakers collapsing. One small-engine plane has crashed in a residential part of Crystal City. We have a news crew on its way... Many people report seeing two fighter jets lose power during the blackout, then recover just in time. Our calls to the White House have gone unanswered, yet we have verified that its power is back on...for the second time. As you recall, the White House had its own brief blackout only minutes before the one that hit Washington. We are still trying to contact the power companies to see if they have any explanation..."

Henning motioned for Julia to kill the audio. "At least until we learn more about this goat rodeo, I need all of you sworn to secrecy, *comprender*?"

Agent Lewis, Private Secretary Julia Johnston, and Chief of Staff Carson Boyle nodded and verbally confirmed in unison. They understood all too well the importance of keeping this from the public.

Chapter 4

The elevator came to a smooth stop, chimed once, and the doors separated. For the second time during his rapid decent, General Joshua Middleton swallowed hard to equalize the pressure in his tiny ears. With an added stretch of his neck, he stepped out to begin his workday, with the same thought he had regarding his surroundings every day for the past nineteen years: *Impressive.*

He liked this month's scent of lilacs, which were blooming in many northern regions topside. The soft, yet upbeat music being continually piped throughout the facility to help increase productivity and sanity was never the same and never anything but pleasant. The temperature and humidity were always so comfortable no one ever noticed, much less complained.

But mostly it was the walls, the floors, the doors, the desks...basically everything in the structure that had structure. That miracle material his ancestors brought with them when they crossed dimensions eighty years ago never ceased to amaze him. Beaker, a half-Mejan over in Chemistry, told him long ago this super-strong, feather-light alloy was a type of magnesium infused with ceramic silicon carbide nanoparticles. That meant nothing to Joshua, even though he was one-quarter Mejan himself. He knew only that this top-secret facility wouldn't be where it is, be what it is, or have developed one-tenth of the technology, if it weren't for the eleven souls working here with various Mejan pedigrees. And institutions like MIT and Area 51 would still be trying to develop the integrated circuit and stealth were it not for the formulas and equations frequently leaked to them from down here in *The Desert.*

The slender, two-star general in his crisp desert fatigues wasn't ten steps down the long, arcing hallway, when Colonel Tillman, wearing the same style uniform, burst out of the communications room and approached him with an outstretched, ten-inch tablet. Its muted screen showed a talking head from CNN.

"General Middleton," he said, anxiously, "there has been a total, one-minute-long blackout at the White House, followed by a five-second blackout of D.C. itself."

"What do you mean by *total*?" asked the general, taking the tablet with one hand, and lifting his signature aviator glasses with the other to read the scrawl at the bottom of the screen.

"Everything, sir. Lights, cars, watches," replied Tillman, falling in step with the general as they walked briskly down the corridor, lighted only by a soft, glowing ceiling. "If it runs on electrons circling a nucleus, it went dead."

Middleton hesitated at the door to his office just long enough for its hidden scanner to verify his identity from the top of his large-head with a reddish-gray buzz-cut to the spit-shine on his black, size-eight shoes. The pneumatic portal opened sideways with a barely-audible hiss, and both men stepped inside, the five-foot-six general handing the tablet back to his taller, human subordinate.

"TV on. CNN," Middleton said, turning to face the eighty-inch, 256K, 3D screen. The same blonde female correspondent came on, the audio loud and clear, "...and we have reports of every interstate jammed with massive pileups, we assumed caused by all vehicles losing power...plus one single-engine airplane has crashed in a residential area of Crystal City, a suburb of D. C...."

He had heard enough. "TV audio off," said Middleton, parking his rear against the front of his ash-colored desk, which looked like wood but was made of that same magnesium silicon stuff. "The entire city for five seconds..." mused the general.

"Yes, sir. Even knocked Raptors out of the sky. But they recovered before impact. That small plane was not so lucky."

"Reggs," grumbled General Middleton, clutching the ridge of his desktop. "No other explanation. Gotta be another batch of those sonsabitches."

"Yes, sir," said Tillman. "Only Reggs could have that kind of EMP. Other than us, of course."

"But even ours can't generate that kind of power, can it?" huffed Middleton.

"I don't know, sir."

Middleton walked around and sat down behind his desk. "Dulcie, call Pierce in Electronic Engineering."

"Calling Pierce in Electronic Engineering," replied the confident, feminine voice.

In two seconds Sam Pierce's face popped into the lower right-hand corner of the large television screen. He was fortyish, with a full head of wavy brown hair and matching eyes. One hundred percent human. Obviously talking to somebody on his headset, Pierce looked into the camera and held up one index finger, indicating he would be right with his superior.

"Sorry, General," he said half a minute later, peeling off the headset. "I was getting reports from our operatives at Andrews and the three major power companies. Andrews was seeing nothing on radar before it blanked out, and the outage was circular with a five-mile diameter. The White House was dead center."

"So, it had to be originating from above," groaned Middleton.

"Yep", said Pierce. "Undoubtedly using stealth, and probably high enough for no visual. I'd guess at least five miles up, depending on the size of the aircraft."

"Reggs," said Middleton again.

Pierce shrugged. "I don't know who else. But the last I knew, they were high-tailing it out of the solar system."

"Hold on a second, Sam," said Middleton. "Let me check the hanger bay." Pierce was nodding as he blanked off the screen. "Dulcie," said the general to his television screen, "call the hanger."

"Calling the hanger."

Short wait.

"Hanger. Captain Oreille here. What can I do for you, General?"

"Are all our craft present and accounted for, Bill?" said Middleton.

"Uh, yes, sir," said Bill Oreille, some surprise in his voice. He removed his Mets baseball cap and ran a hand over his cropped, brown hair. He then turned his round, one-hundred-percent human head to look over his shoulder into the dimly-lit hanger bay, filled with spacecraft as far as the light would allow.

"Specifically Little Sister and Dolly?" added the general.

"Yes, sir. Neither has moved since their scheduled weekly exercise two nights ago. What's up, General? Are we finally gonna blow the Iranians back to the stone age?"

"No, just checking, Bill. But just the same, make sure all craft, including the fighters are ready to launch at a moment's notice, okay?"

"They always are, sir."

"Dulcie, end hanger. Call Security."

Captain Bill Oreille was replaced with the image of another two-star general, Porter McManus. The insignias on his sand-colored desert fatigues said he was Army, and the big bald head and round eyes said he was one-quarter-Mejan, like Middleton. He also was busy talking into a headset.

"Way ahead of you, Joshua," he said, putting a hand over the microphone and looking briefly into the camera. He then went back to his conversation, "That's right: *especially* a Joint Chief. And let me know immediately if and when one shows."

General McManus slipped his headset down to his neck and looked back into the camera and Middleton's image on his screen. "We have eyes inside and outside the White House, Joshua," he said, tapping a pencil on his desk. "No doubt it's the hub of anything and everything. If the president circles the wagons, we'll immediately know who he calls in."

"And the minute one of them leaves...?" smiled Middleton.

"We nab him. Discreetly, of course."

"Of course."

"I'll let you know the second I know," said Porter.

"Thanks, Porter. Dulcie, end Security. Go back to Electronic Engineering."

"Back to Electronic Engineering."

Sam Pierce was back in the picture, now sitting behind his workstation.

"Sam," said the general, "what exactly are the capabilities of our EMP devices? I mean, what can we do and not do with them?"

Sam got up and leaned forward on the table. "Well, as you know, attached to a laser beam we can disrupt the circuits of any aircraft, including a Regg fighter, like we did ten years ago."

Middleton interrupted. "Yes, but could we do an entire city?"

"With a single fighter? No way. Something like that would require an enormous energy source, far more than you could pull from the craft's dark matter-antimatter reactor."

"Would Dolly's reactor be powerful enough?"

"I doubt it. She could take out a city block at most. Why? We planning on turning off the Kremlin's lights?"

"What's that range?"

"Still just a couple hundred yards. To knock out a circuit requires intense energy. And it lasts only as long as the pulse."

"But could we upgrade one of our EMPs enough to do a city?"

Sam shook his head and smiled. "Well, that's definitely above my pay grade, General. But I've got the mastermind herself right here beside me," grinned Sam. "Ask her."

The image on the general's screen widen to show the workstations of both Sam and the eighty-year-old, fifty-percent Mejan with a bulbous bald head. Her green, golf ball eyes blinked and a smile spread across her diminutive mouth.

"Hello, Joshua."

"How's it going, Darnus? Keeping busy?"

"Always something you humans are wanting."

"Well, since you're half human, does that mean you want something half the time or only half-want somethings?"

"You joke, like Sam here."

"Yes, I do. So, tell us, you Mejan beauty, what would it take for a spacecraft, say the size of a Regg daughtership, to temporarily knock out everything electronic in a city the size of Washington, D. C.?"

Darnus put an elongated, crooked finger to her lips and thought a moment. She scratched some figures on her datapad, and then without looking up said, "It would have to be an electromagnetic pulse, of course, and tied into the dark matter-antimatter power source," said Darnus. "So I suppose the reactor on one of their daughterships is large enough to handle the extra load. I could pull up the schematics, if you want to be sure."

"No, that's okay," said the general. He turned to his assistant still standing beside him and hissed, "Damn it! I was afraid of that." Then as an afterthought, he turned back to Darnus and asked, "How about *frying* the circuits…as in permanently?"

32

"Hmm. Not a piece of pie," said Darnus, knowing it was supposed to be *cake*. She just liked to tease the *Cro-Magnons*, as she called anyone with less than her 235 Mejan IQ. She did some more calculating, and then announced, "Yes. That would take much more power. Far more than a daughter could provide."

"Ha!" said Middleton. "So the Reggs can't knock a city out permanently. They can only disrupt circuits temporarily."

"Yes, and only as long as the EMP is being generated," added Darnus. "When the pulse ends, all circuitry is restored."

Chapter 5

At President Henning's request, Agent Lewis remained in the Oval Office as the sole source of security, not calling in any extra Secret Service personnel. The ex-Marine captain stood vigilantly beneath the portrait of George Washington, in case a quick exit to the bunker was required.

"It's gotta be the Russians, or the Chinese," said Chief of Staff Boyle, plopping his soft, two-hundred pounds down on one of the matching brown-suede couches facing each other. "I doubt Iran or terrorists. Maybe Korea. Since the North's recent success in hacking into our military mainframes in Seoul and capturing much of our classified technology…they could possibly pull off something like this."

"Why would they, Carson?" challenged Henning, sitting down opposite him on the other sofa. "That would be an act of war."

"And knocking out Ellsworth and the missile silos isn't?" countered Boyle.

The president's private secretary, Julia Johnston, stuck her head through the door and announced, "Mr. President, the only Joint Chief nearby is General Knox. He was in D.C. visiting his daughter at Georgetown. He'll be here any minute now. Richard Ellison, the FBI chief, is already here, coming through the gate. So is Attorney General Kelso. Do you have anything you want to give to Press Secretary Roman about the blackouts? She's been asking…more like pleading."

"No. Thanks, Julia," said Henning, checking his watch. "The Army and FBI should be enough for now. We can fill the other branches in later. Let's see how things go before we have to deal with the media."

As Julia exited the Oval Office, the president of the United States turned his attention back to the Chief of Staff, his best friend since grade school. "Let's not jump to any conclusions, Carson," he said with a twinge of humor, "at least until we hear more from our raspy-voiced *Regg*. Who knows? Maybe he *is* some alien species. Could be our first direct contact."

"But maybe not the kind of contact we would relish," said Boyle with no humor.

Henning's phone chimed and he put it to his ear. "Yes, Kurt." For the next minute the president listened intently, nodding and offering an occasional, "I see." After clicking off, he leaned back in the sofa and said, "Andrews Air Force base reports no radar or visual detection of any craft in the air above Washington at the time, other than the patrolling F22 Raptors and the private plane we saw crash. And according to the utility companies, the second outage was in a circular, five-mile diameter, with the White House as ground-zero."

"That means the source was directly above us, *here*," said Boyle, pointing upward, "with the pulse coming down like a cone. How could the object or whatever it was not show up on radar?"

"Had to have stealth," offered Lewis by the wall, "or be so high above the Earth it was out of range of Andrews' radar."

"And still have enough power to knock us out?" said an incredulous Boyle. "I hope to hell that's not true. We'd have no defense."

*****

Thirty seconds before the expected twelve-twenty phone call from the mysterious hacker, Attorney General Richard Kelso, the head of the FBI Richard Ellison, and the Army's General Charles Knox of the Joint Chiefs had read the original text, listened to the recorded phone conversation, and engaged in an abbreviated discussion of what all this might mean.

Chief of Staff Carson Boyle stood beside them at the front of the president's desk, while Henning sat in his executive swivel chair, running an apprehensive finger up and down the side of his taut face. Secret Service agent Lewis stood ready by the secret door, with Julia Johnston—the president's private secretary—by his side.

In the final ten seconds, the talk faded to muted buzzing, then dropped to complete silence.

Still on speaker, and lying face-up in the middle of his desk, the president's personal smartphone chimed and lit up right on time: UNKNOWN CALLER.

Henning tapped a button. "Yes?" he said with no enthusiasm.

"Ah, Mr. President," croaked the same, measured voice, "have the trusted others joined you?"

"A few," said Henning curtly. "What do you want?"

"Yes, to the point," said the Regg spiritedly. "Okay. You and us have a common enemy. *Mejans.* They are from another galaxy. They growing big in numbers. You will help us find them...for your good and our good."

The intentional pause demanded a reply. But President Henning wasn't sure what to say or ask. This absurdity was becoming more so by the minute. "Uh, *Mejans?*" he said, mostly playing along. "What the hell is a Mejan and how many of them are we talking about?"

"Our computers say three million now. Have blended with humans for many generations now. Hard to tell them from human. Most be harmless. No more a threat than you are."

"I think we've just been insulted," whispered Boyle into General Knox's ear.

"It older ones we want to find," continued the Regg, "ones of Mejan blood more pure. They are the threat to you and us and Earth."

"How so?" asked Henning, a little more interested.

"Very intelligent. Have superior technology. Must have secret bases. Spacecraft travel near the speed of light. They are ruthless, killing thousands of Reggs with one missile. We think they have laser weapons that can kill fighter jets. We want their technology, as much as you do."

General Knox's eyes were wide and glowing. *Speed of light aircraft? Jet-killing lasers? Bring it on!*

"And what do we do once we secure this technology?" asked a dubious president.

"United States and Reggs join together to rule Earth."

It was difficult to tell the gasps from the muffled snorts. This was becoming something between a scary piece of science fiction and a ridiculous attempt at comedy.

"And if we refuse to rule the world with you?" sang President Henning.

"We hope you do not. Our nations have much unity. Come from same galaxy. We share common enemy in Mejans. We can supply the devices to find them. You have the manpower."

"And if we refuse...?" Henning repeated, more sincerely now.

"You see what we do to your city, your military, your defenses, your life. You not refuse."

Chapter 6

Press Secretary Georgia Roman stepped to the podium, instantly stifling the clatter of two hundred news people from around the world crammed into the White House press room. She gave a quick nod of recognition to a few of the familiar faces, then dropped her eyes to give her notes a final once-over. The room fell silent.

Georgia hooked a lock of shoulder length blonde hair behind her ear and licked her lips. She was a very attractive woman, in her late-thirties. She looked like some local station's weathergirl with more beauty than brains; but that stereotype was quickly squashed during her introductory press briefing last December. The woman was sharp as a razor, a Harvard grad, and Pulitzer Prize winner in journalism. Still, it was her beauty that landed her the job as President Henning's press secretary. On advice from his public relations manager at the start of his term, Henning had learned that good-looking females—once proven to be at least as intelligent as everyone else in the room—can draw larger public audiences and thereby voters. They also command more respect and courtesy from the press corps, which can at times be brutal, if they don't like the information they are getting, or not getting. From day-one, Georgia had even the hardest of the core reporters in her pantsuit pocket.

"Good afternoon," she began without looking up, the television lights reflecting off the gloss of her pink lipstick. "I will read a short statement, after which I'll take a few questions. But I warn you all," she added, her brown eyes now peering over her turtle shell spectacles and blinking at all sections of the room one by one, "I will not be able to tell you much more than is already in the statement. And time is limited. So choose wisely."

Some of the press people fidgeted, some smirked, a few murmured. It would be a typical press room briefing except for one thing: the subject was far from typical.

"Okay, then." Georgia adjusted her glasses and started reading:

The blackouts this morning, first at the White House, and then for most of Washington D.C., were planned demonstrations of a new weapon our government has developed. It is meant as a deterrent to aggression by any country against the United States or any of our NATO allies.

The room buzzed with mixed reactions. The press secretary paused to look up. There was no hint of patience in her glare. The buzzing stopped.

As some of you witnessed firsthand, she continued, *it emits a pulse of electromagnetic energy that completely and effectively disrupts all things electronic, right down to a simple wristwatch. This disruption can be made to last for a few seconds to a few months. If necessary, its energy level can be amplified to destroy all electronics, rather than just temporarily disable them.*

Electromagnetic pulses—EMP for short—are not new. But until now, their power, range, and effectiveness have been limited. An elite group of ex-NASA physicists and technicians have been working for years to develop what we believe is destined to become the single most important weapon for peace the world has known since the beginning of the nuclear age. We decided to debut it at this time, considering the current instability of global affairs.

Let this serve as a warning to all governments and nations: this peace-keeping device can be deployed to any location around the globe in a matter of minutes to a few hours at the most. It will be used at the discretion of the Command in Chief of the United States and the Joint Chiefs of Staff.

Again, aggression by any nation or organization against peace-loving, sovereign nations or their people will not be tolerated.

Signed, Arthur William Henning, President of the United States of America.

Press Secretary Georgia Roman removed her glasses and looked up. Two hundred hands shot into the air amid a chorus of *Madam Secretary*. She pointed at the handsome man in the front row from the Washington D. C. division of The New York

Times. He was her favorite, since they had been dating on the semi-sly for over a year. "Yes, Mr. Marshall."

Standing up with half a smirk stretched across face, Jacob Marshall was having trouble finding the right words. He didn't want to offend the woman he loved, but this smacked of out and out bullshit. "Uh, are you kidding us, Georgia, er, Madam Secretary?" he said, looking right and left at his fellow journalists, as if speaking for them all. "You tested this EMP thing on Washington D.C without warning, on your own people, causing all kinds of damage and even the death of that pilot and who knows who else in hospitals and with pacemakers?"

Georgia had been told to anticipate that particular question. "We are very sorry about the death of..." she checked her notes, "Jonathan McCormack from Philadelphia, as well as anyone else. We had been very careful to test the EMP at a time of minimum air traffic and between scheduled flights of commercial airplanes. We had up-to-the-second flight plans from all planes leaving and coming from Reagan, Dulles and Marshall. That particular single-engine craft flew into the zone from the north and at such a low altitude, it wasn't detected by Andrews until it was too late. McCormack's family has received our deepest regrets, and they will be amply compensated for their loss."

Two hundred hands again in the air.

"Yes, Maggie."

"No offense, Georgia," snickered Maggie Allworth from ABC, "but this seems like a cover-up. I think most of us here in the press corps suspect this was the work of terrorists. We don't blame the White House for not wanting to admit it, but c'mon, saying we did this to ourselves is way beyond the pale."

One hundred mumbles of agreement.

"The White House agrees this could look like possible terrorism," said Georgia, equally prepared for this challenge. "But the president wishes to impress upon you that it is not. No one except the United States is capable of employing an EMP of this magnitude."

"Why Washington?" yelled three or four voices, not wanting to wait to be called upon.

"Why not?" said Georgia, as calmly as she could, considering she didn't believe much of this either. "We had to demonstrate its power and effectiveness somewhere, and what better place than our own capital…our own White House? It's like the scientist using himself to test a new drug, not wishing to risk the life of anyone else."

"Yeah, a *mad* scientist!" yelled someone. The room broke into raucous laughter.

"I don't think the press is buying it," sighed Chief of Staff Carson Boyle, sitting on the edge of the twin couch inside the Oval Office.

President Henning picked up the remote and shut off the television. He rose from his sitting position beside his best friend, and walked over to lean on the front of his desk. "We didn't expect them to wrap their arms around it and kiss its ass," he scoffed. "But we do have them thinking. After all, what other explanation could there be? It's a case of fiction being far less strange than the truth."

"Well, it *was* the plan," nodded Carson, leaning back on the sofa. "It's the best we could do, all things considered."

"And don't forget what this should do to the Russians, Chinese, Koreans and Iranians," said the president coming up behind Boyle to give his shoulder a passing squeeze. "They might not buy the story either. But one thing they know for certain is somebody has the means to knock out an entire city. And all signs are pointing to the United States. This has to be putting the fear of God into every one of them. And speaking of which, I want up-to-the-minute reports from the Polish border. I'll bet Putin stands down."

'Yes, in a strange, roundabout way," said Boyle, "the Reggs may have helped us avoid a number of paths to World War Three."

"It was probably part of their plan to begin with," said Henning. "They have as much at stake in keeping the planet in one piece as we do. Hitting Washington D. C. definitely sent a message across the globe."

Chapter 7

The black Chevy Suburban wheeled into the docking area of the FedEx distribution facility on Busse Drive in Elk Grove Village, Illinois. The driver put the SUV into reverse and backed up to the last bay, the red brake lights illuminating the number 22 stenciled on the platform beneath the door. The building was indeed massive. And it was only a stone's throw from its FedEx terminal at O'Hare.

When the vehicle came to a complete stop, the man riding shotgun checked his smartphone: 10:25 p.m. They were five minutes early. That was okay. Being late would have gotten them a severe reprimand from the chief, if not from Quantico itself.

FBI Agent Henry Pelekai killed the engine and leaned his athletic, forty-year-old Hawaiian body against the door. Feeling the sudden pressure from his holstered Glock 23 on his ribs, he used his right hand to shift it a few inches to the center of his chest. "C'mon, admit it," he said to his partner. "You want to know what's in those overnighters as much as I do."

"Go ahead," said, Cyrus Kinsey. "Open one up. I'll email you when you're pushing papers in Poughkeepsie."

Pelekai powered down his window and took a long suck on his e-cigarette. "Just the same," he said, blowing a stream of cherry-flavored vapor out the window. "This is about the strangest assignment we've ever been on."

"Strangest?" mocked Kinsey, the equally-fit Caucasian with the dimpled, Superman chin and perfectly-pruned haircut. He couldn't be more FBI. "What's so strange about driving out in the boonies after dark to an abandoned farmhouse to pick up a load of FedEx overnighters in five tubs sealed with white plastic wrap? *Strange*? How about demeaning? We're GS-15s, for god sake, doing grunt work."

Kinsey powered down his window, too. With the air conditioning now off, the humid summer night air was getting too close. And the smell of that candy store smoke from Pelekai's vaping wasn't helping any. "Maybe," said Kinsey, grabbing his Kevlar vest from the backseat and slipping it on. "But the chief did say it was important enough to put his *most trusted men* on it. I don't know if he was just blowing smoke up our asses, or if these packages are really that important."

"With orders to wear our vests and shoot anyone who even looks at us cockeyed," quipped Pelekai, "I'd guess *important*."

The sound of the dock door rolling up at exactly 10:30 p.m. got both agents' attention. With fingers stroking their holstered weapons, they exited the vehicle and approached the two men standing above them on the cement ledge. One wore standard-issue FedEx shorts and shirt in dark-blue with the purple stripe running down each arm. The white name tag said *Delaney* with *Night Manager* right below it. The other man's Boy Scout persona with neatly pressed St. John's Bay pants and white shirt confirmed what Kinsey and Pelekai had already been told: he was from the office of the Attorney General, probably an upper-echelon deputy. Somebody was taking no chances with this shipment.

Kinsey flicked on his Maglite and shined the beam on the two faces. "Names, please."

"Delaney," said the FedEx manager.

"Manning," said the man from the justice department. "And yours?"

"Kinsey."

"Pelekai."

Everyone satisfied and protocol honored, Kinsey punched the fob and the rear hatch of the 2024 Suburban swung up. One-by-one the five bins packed with a total of fifty *FedEx First Overnight* envelopes were hoisted up by the two strong FBI agents to the strong FedEx manager, and placed on a flatbed cart. Once loaded, the cart and the two polar opposites disappeared through a wide doorway with thick, hanging plastic strips, as the dock door rolled back down.

Their assignment completely, Kinsey and Pelekai called it in, and then headed for a drink at a nearby Radisson's lounge.

Inside the massive distribution center the night manager wheeled the cart up to one of the many conveyer belts, and—as requested by Manning—peeled the white plastic wrap from all five mail tubs. Also as requested, he began handing the envelopes to Deputy Manning one-by-one, never looking at the address labels. Without reading them himself, Manning verified each FedEx envelope was properly sealed, then he laid each one on the conveyer belt to watch them march like good little soldiers to be swallowed by the sorting machine.

"What's in these things?" yelled Delaney above the incessant noise. He knew he shouldn't ask, but it was curious that each nine-by-twelve envelop was basically flat, except for a single bulge in the center, apparently cushioned by a bubble-wrap lining.

Without turning away from his task, Deputy Manning yelled back, "Hockey pucks."

No other question was asked. Besides, no one in the building knew what was in the packages, not even Deputy Manning. He was ordered by Attorney General Richard Kelso himself to jet immediately to Chicago to supervise the mailing of the packages. He wasn't even told where they were going, and he was to make sure no one at FedEx looked at the labels, including himself. Only the sorting machine knew their destinations, as it scanned each name and address, directing them down the proper conveyances, on their way out to the chiefs of police of every major college town in the Midwest.

Chapter 8

The size-five, seven-eighths-human stopped to stare at the mannequin in the store window at Kohl's department store. The dummy was draped in a strapless, summer dress of paisley pink, not unlike the light-green one Suzy was wearing at the moment. But what she noticed most were the small, yellow-rimmed Fresco sunglasses resting on the tip of the mannequin's nose, its painted blue eyes looking out over the top as if to say, "Don't you wish you didn't have to hide your bulging eyes behind those oversized, round sunglasses?"

Almost as depressing was the tan, buckled visor, enhancing the dummy's normal forehead, also as if teasing Suzy. She self-consciously ran her fingers along the white edge of her blue, broad-brimmed hat, catching her own reflection in the store window. That Craft and Burrow floppy hat she had chosen for today's shopping trip now seemed more like a humongous, man-eating flower from the Amazon rainforest, just starting to devour her from the top down.

The Brookfield daughter stepped back to take in her entire hat-to-shoes image in the store window. It didn't seem fair. Here she was, far more attractive than that pseudo human, whose plastic body had been molded to some artist's concept of female perfection. Yet Suzy was the one who had to hide from the public, while the soulless facsimile flaunted its features like it owned the world.

Suzy unconsciously rubbed the empty ring finger of her left hand. When not in public or on their biannual trips out of the country, it showcased the beautiful five-carat-round diamond Jax gave her when he proposed ten years ago in 2015, alongside the ruby-encrusted gold wedding ring that was slipped on during the quiet ceremony at The Farm a few weeks later. But anytime she left The Mansion, both rings had to stay home in her jewelry box. How could she explain them if she were ever searched? Jax didn't wear his wedding ring away from home either.

Still, Suzy understood the scope of things. If people knew she was married to the richest man in town, or even if they suspected she was his steady girlfriend, they would pry into Jax's private affairs more than they already did. Sooner or later one of the thousands of security cameras all over town, or one of fifty thousand smartphones, or one of those pesky drones trying to violate their airspace, would snap a photo of Suzette Marie Brookfield-Jackson in an unguarded moment and discover her abnormalities. The rumors would fly. Nosy reporters, alien-hunters, and conspiracy theorists would track every move they made. The Mansion would come under siege. Life would be hell.

Eventually, The Farm could come under investigation, too. The Brookfield farm. Her family's farm. That would be disastrous, especially if things got harrier with the Russians or the Chinese or the Koreans or the Iranians. The Desert could call the Brookfields and the Jacksons into action at a moment's notice. It would be almost impossible to fly the spacecraft in and out of the ponds, or have supplies and upgraded equipment brought in on quiet wings under darkness.

And that would be only the beginning. On a social scale, once the world learned there were some three million alien cross breeds walking among them, racial bias would run rampant. Considered freaks, they would be shunned, despised, hated for looking different. Even only one-sixteenth Mejans like Nathan and Nicole would be suspect enough to get laughed at and bullied at school. Her fellow Mejans would start banding together to demand equal rights, pay, and housing. She could see them being reduced to jobless protesters, picketing city hall with signs saying *Mejan Lives Matter*.

Suzy knew secrecy had to be maintained at all costs. And so much of it began and ended with her. She should consider herself lucky to be allowed to go out among the masses at all, as she did today.

In a gesture of defiance, Suzy walked into Kohl's and grabbed the first visor she found in the "Summer Fun" section. It didn't matter that she never could or would wear it in public. It felt good just to buy it.

"Will that be all?" asked the pleasant, middle-aged female in the blue frock with the *Millie* name tag.

"Yes," said Suzy. "We're all going to the beach tomorrow, and the family dog chewed up my other visor."

"Sounds like my yorkie," groaned the clerk in empathy. "He got my husband's wingtip last week. The dog is lucky to still be alive. Do you have a Kohl's card?"

Suzy politely said she did not, nor did she wish one. She was directed to place her right thumb on the small round sensor and speak her name in a steady, conversational tone. "Susan Hines," she said, leaning in a few inches toward the tiny hole above the thumb sensor.

"Thank you, Mrs. Hines," chimed the clerk, handing her the paper receipt. "Have fun at the beach."

Probably not the best of ideas, but Suzy treated herself to an iced tea at the food court. It was another normal thing normal people do on a normal day, she told herself, even if most women don't wear huge floppy hats and oversized sunglasses inside a mall. It always felt good to be out among other people, even if she might be drawing attention to herself, like some celebrity trying not to be recognized. But Iowa City is a university town. Many people dress funny. So, what's the risk?

Tiring of people-watching, and the iced tea drained to the ice cubes, she reached down into her shopping bag and pulled out the two paper receipts for the wine and the pink visor she had just purchased, curious about the costs she had never checked. But her eye was caught first by the name on both receipts: *Susan Hines*.

"I can't show my face around here," she mouthed to herself. "I can't show my rings. I can't use my husband's name. I can't even use my own name."

All her identifications said she was Susan Hines, but she wasn't. They said she resided at 306 North Clinton Street in Iowa City, but she didn't. Deborah Collingsworth lives there, one of the clan, one generation less Mejan than Suzy. If anyone asks, she is to say *Susan* is not home at the moment, and that

Deborah is Susan's tenant, occupying the downstairs level. All neat and tidy.

Still, Suzy knew she should be grateful. All the subterfuge was her ticket to some semblance of that average life she wanted, as limited as it may be. It's how she and the kids—sans hubby, of course—could dare to walk down the streets of Iowa City to go shopping, or get an ice cream…or have any kind of freedom. Her mother, Mary Brookfield, was not so lucky. She could never leave The Farm in daylight hours; and even at night she had to avoid people. Her Mejan features were far more prominent than Suzy's, virtually impossible to hide.

Mejan features. Suzy's Mejan features. Jax used to say they were sexy, like Japanese anime characters or Margaret Keane big-eyed waifs. He doesn't say that anymore. He even seems hesitant to look at her eyes, as if they've become repulsive. Maybe it's just the old-married-couple syndrome. They are so used to each other there is no passion anymore. Familiarity breeds contempt and all that stuff.

Suzy's train of thought was interrupted by a sequence of disturbing sounds she hadn't heard for a long time. Her sophisticated, highly-specialized smartphone in her purse was beeping softly in intervals of three short bursts. Simultaneously, the smart-watch on her wrist was matching the same code with flashes and silent vibrations. It took only a blink to recall what the ominous signal was telling her: *she was being scanned by heat-seeking infrared!* But how could that be? The Reggs and their insufferable scanners that could detect the cooler body temperature and oversized head of a Mejan were long gone. She and Jax had witnessed their departure first-hand from Little Sister, as it escorted the Regg mothership out of the solar system, with their promise to never return. Had they broken the agreement and come back? This made no sense.

The one-eight-Mejan with a normal body temperature of 97.5 looked left and right down the mall's long hallways, praying not to see a wolf-faced Regg running towards her with a spray bottle of blue liquid. The memories made her shudder. But there was only the usual mid-afternoon, mild activity: some women with shopping bags, teens rotating in and out of the food court, people standing around the Cineplex, checking the movie times. Two young men in matching dark-blue tracksuits stood by a bench, arguing over something and glancing her way occasionally. They certainly weren't Reggs. Neither was that uniformed police officer down there by Macy's. Maybe some kid was playing with an infrared toy in an electronics store. Besides, the signal had already stopped.

When the cop started walking purposefully her way, looking straight at her, Suzy felt even more uneasy. None of this added up to certain danger, yet she had the strongest urge to leave. Picking up her shopping bag and purse, she walked briskly in the opposite direction from the two men and the approaching cop. She turned left by Baskin Robbins and exited the mall through the automatic doors.

Halfway to her car, Suzy glanced back over her shoulder to see if anyone was following. Nothing. She stopped on the sun-baked asphalt, looking all around the parking lot for anything unusual. Again, nothing. Relieved and feeling a little foolish, she continued on to her white Lexus sedan. That's when her smartphone beeped its warning once again.

Frightened and unsure if she should even go to her car, Alan and Mary Brookfield's daughter froze between a Buick sedan and a hydrogen fuel cell Honda, still two rows from her car. The decision of what to do was made for her, when an electric, black and gold Iowa City Police prowler quietly rolled up, cutting her off. A lone officer scrambled out of the vehicle and approached her cautiously. At the same time, the one she had seen inside came out of the mall door and speed-walked to catch up.

"Excuse me, ma'am," said the one from the mall, taller of the two, a little out of breath, "may we have a word with you?" His tone was strangely nervous and borderline apologetic.

"What's this about?" protested Suzy, looking them both up and down. With their badges, insignias, and Motorola microphones clipped above the first button of their dark-blue uniforms, they seemed to be authentic PD.

"Uh, we got a call from mall security," said the one named Gonzales, just as unsure of himself. "May we see what you have in your shopping bag?"

"I have two bottles of wine and a visor," she said indignantly. "What? Do you think I shoplifted them?"

The cops stepped closer. Suzy could tell both men found her attractive, and probably were undressing her in their minds. Despite the harassment, she enjoyed the flattery.

Gonzales swallowed. "May we see some identification, ma'am?"

"Don't you mean the receipts," said Suzy, reaching into the sack.

"Just an ID, ma'am. Please." The pocked face Gonzales was beginning to sweat. But then it was a hot and humid Midwestern summer day and the black asphalt was looking more like fresh tar.

With a huff, Suzy set the shopping bag down and rummaged through her purse for her wallet. She pulled out her driver's license and handed it to the taller one named Willis, the one who sounded the most apologetic.

He read aloud: "Susan Hines. 306 North Clinton Street here in Iowa City. Birth year 1995."

"That's right. So?"

The cop tested the card's flexibility a couple times and held it up to the sun. "Seems fake," he announced.

Suzy knew that was bullshit. It *was* fake, but The Desert makes documents more authentic than anything the government could. This was no exception. "I assure you it is real," she said decisively.

Both men took yet another half-step closer, coming to within an arm's length. "Please remove your hat and sunglasses, ma'am," said Willis.

"What?!" huffed Suzy. "I will not! What is this all about, anyway? Who are you people?"

"Please, ma'am. If you don't do as we ask, we will have to remove them for you."

Suzy looked for a way out of this. She figured she could break free and run between them, but the question was how far she could get in pumps before they caught her. Besides, where could she go?

She had a better idea. Actually the only thing she could do under the circumstances. "Okay," she said. "Give me back my driver's license, and I'll do as you ask."

The cops looked at each other. Gonzales nodded. Willis handed the license back to her. Suzy returned it to its slot in the wallet, and then shoved the wallet into her purse. With her hand still inside, she quickly felt for her smartphone. She punched the button in the uppermost left-hand corner twice. Audio and video were activated, and the broadcast signal was being sent on an uber-secure frequency to every other smartphone in her family, as well as the main receivers in the communication rooms of The Desert, The Farm, and The Mansion. Everything from this moment on was being seen and heard by those who truly cared about her.

"We're waiting, ma'am," said Gonzales.

Seeing nothing else she could do, Suzy bent her head down and slowly slipped off the over-sized, black Tiffany sunglasses. Squinting as much as she could, pretending the bright glare was too much to bear, she raised her head, keeping her profile to the officers.

"Please, look at me," said Willis.

Suzy slowly acquiesced, while still squinting.

"We need you to open your eyes," said Willis, trying to sound sterner. The woman was obviously planning to defy them to the end.

This was it. The last time Suzy had to timidly open her big, copper-brown eyes for inspection was in front of Jax ten years ago…inside her van…when he was giving her fishing lessons, among other things. She really liked Jax then, and she wanted to lay everything on the table to see if the relationship had a chance. His reaction back then indicated her features were not all that exceptional, and he even found her large round orbs quite sexy. But Jax was so into her at that point he would have said the same thing about a humpback or a hairy, black mole on the end of her nose.

Remaining sideways to them and making sure the broad-rimmed floppy hat still threw a shadow on her face, Suzy opened her eyes to about half-mast.

Rather than order her again to turn in their direction, the taller cop sidestepped to the front of the reluctant woman and bent down to see for himself, removing his own amber shooting glasses. With nothing else to do, Suzy looked him square in his probing hazel eyes and blinked hard twice. "There. Are you happy?"

The cop didn't exactly gasp, but some air did leave his mouth in a short puff. He snapped back up straight, and with big eyes of his own, nodded to his partner. Gonzales's lips formed the interrogative, "Are you sure?"

The cops were now more on edge than ever. Neither one wanted to ask the woman to remove her floppy hat. But yesterday's directive during the strange briefing at headquarters stated they also had to physically check any suspect the infrared device indicated had an abnormally large head.

"Would you mind removing your hat," the rounder Gonzales finally said, feeling it was his turn to be offensive to the darling, petite young lady, who as far as they knew, had done nothing wrong. But for some unexplained reason, each partner team of the Iowa City police force was ordered to take a turn at scanning populated areas with this strange device given to the department by some obscure source. The size and shape of an old-fashioned stopwatch, if its small, green screen started flashing red, they were to follow the yellow arrow to the target. Once confronted, they were to question him or her, paying particular attention to the size of their eyes and head. If both were verified as abnormally large, the cops were to report their findings to HQ immediately. At that time they would receive instructions on how to proceed.

"Yes, I do mind removing my hat," hissed Suzy, liking this less and less. This was obviously more than a simple shoplifting shakedown. "It's hot out here. I have things to do."

"I'm afraid we must insist," said Gonzales, reaching out and whisking the floppy covering off of her head before she could block him.

"Hey!" she protested, as her brunette bob flapped and dispersed by the motion, revealing what the hat had been hiding. Both cops took half a step back, partly to get a better look, and partly to put some distance between them and the female who was looking more alien by the minute.

In a surprise move only to Suzy, Gonzales followed orders by removing his service hat and trying to put it on Suzy. She recoiled at first, pulling her head out of his reach. But realizing resistance was futile, she stood stiffly to submit to yet another indignation by the two blue bullies. As suspected, the officer's cap—size seven and one-eighth, considered large—couldn't get past the rim of her head.

Gonzales returned the hat to his own head and said to his partner, "Better…call it in."

Jerome Willis blinked away his stare and cautiously reached for his Motorola, as if any second killer rays might come shooting out from those massive orbs. "HQ, this is Bravo Five. We have a…" he turned to Gonzales and asked, "What is it again?"

"Uh…" Gonzales pulled out his writing pad and flipped to the last page. "it's a *ten-fifteen A*."

"Uh, yes, HQ," said Willis, "we have a *ten-fifteen A* in custody in the west parking lot at the Century Mall. Female, Caucasian, five-four, one hundred ten pounds, print summer dress of green, white pumps. Fits the description."

"Ten-nine, Bravo Five," squawked the dispatcher, the code for *say again*. "You have a ten-fifteen *A*?!"

"Ten-four," said Willis. "A confirmed ten-fifteen A."

There was a long pause, before the dispatcher continued, "Bravo Five, secure the suspect and all belongings. Return directly to the station. Stop for nothing. Come in the back. Repeat: come in the back. The chief will meet you there."

"What exactly is going on here?" groused Suzy, snatching her hat from Gonzales's hand, and putting it back on her head along with her sunglasses. "I haven't done anything wrong."

"Sorry, ma'am," said Willis, twisting both her hands behind her back and fastening her tiny wrists with a plastic tie strip. "We're just following orders."

The cops led her to the prowler and placed her in the backseat. She was allowed to keep her hat and sunglasses on, but the shopping bag and purse were kept up front, out of reach. Suzy knew that while the visual portion of her smartphone would be broadcasting only the inside of her purse, everything being said would be received by her family and friends. So, she cleverly tried to get as much information as possible on the air.

"Listen, Officers Willis and Gonzales," she said loudly, leaning forward to talk through the steel mesh barrier. "You're two of Iowa City's finest. Surely you have some idea why I'm being taken away from the Century Mall and driven to the police station." When neither cop said anything, Suzy insisted, "Well?"

"As we said, ma'am," said Willis from the shotgun seat, cranking his head a quarter turn, "we're just following orders."

"And those orders were what?" challenged Suzy. "To apprehend anybody who looks a little different from you? You certainly seemed very interested in my large eyes and head. You think I'm from outer space, or something?"

"Not at all, ma'am," said Willis, facing forward, so she couldn't see his doubt.

"You scanned me with some kind of instrument, didn't you?"

"Why would you think that?" said Gonzales, turning onto Riverside Drive.

"Logic," said Suzy. "It had to be something. Conscientious police officers like yourselves wouldn't just walk up and arrest a girl for wearing a big hat and sunglasses. My guess it was infrared."

No answer.

"It was, wasn't it?" prodded Suzy with a knowing smile.

"What makes you so smart," asked Gonzales, looking in his rear-view mirror, impressed. "You some kind of techie or something?"

"I watch television."

No answer.

"C'mon, what's with that infrared?" continued Suzy, with a little ribbing. "You perverts get a kick out of seeing a woman's body heat under her clothing?"

That brought a chuckle from Gonzales. But he said nothing.

By the time they reached the station, Suzy had tried everything she could think of to uncover where the officers had obtained the infrared scanners, but they wouldn't bite. It didn't matter. Along with the homing device implanted behind her left ear, Suzy felt she had sent enough information back home for Jax, her dad, or even The Desert to take the proper action...which she assumed first and foremost would include her rescue. This whole ordeal was smacking too much of her and Jax's abduction by the Reggs a decade ago.

The police chief already had the back door open when the prowler pulled up behind the station. He and a sergeant promptly took custody of Suzy and her purse and shopping bag, and whisked her inside, instructing Willis and Gonzales to go back on patrol with the scanner.

As the two officers returned to their car, Jerome Willis whistled and said, "Holy moly, Louie! Can you believe this? Do you think we actually just bagged a bona fide *alien*?"

"I don't know," replied Gonzales, taking his turn at shotgun. "But if their women are half as cute as that one, book me on the next space shuttle to Andromeda."

Chapter 9

Suzy found herself sitting all alone on the anchored steel chair in the sixteen-by-ten interrogation room, staring at her dark reflection in the two-way mirror. The other three walls were cinder blocks in battleship gray, while overhead was one humming florescent fixture. It was good to be out of the summer heat, but this room was cold. She wished she had a sweater to put over her bare shoulders and thin summer dress. She was glad they let her keep on the floppy hat and sunglasses.

She was also thankful the chief had at least removed the plastic tie restraint and placed a Dixie cup of water on the shiny metal table in front of her. She knew if this were an ordinary arrest, she would have been booked at the front desk first, and then placed in a holding cell. But this was hardly normal. And Suzette Marie Brookfield-Jackson didn't like the looks or smell of this pretense at all. Nor did she like the sound and feel when the room began vibrating with the *thump-thump-thump* of what suggested a helicopter was landing very nearby.

In less than a minute the door of the interrogation room opened and two men in gray flight suits and helmets with dark face-shields entered. They wasted no time removing Suzy's floppy hat and sunglasses, and slipping a black cloth bag over her head. They then handcuffed her to the front of a leather belt being buckled around her waist in back. With one man on each cocked arm, they hustled her out of the police station's back door and toward the waiting chopper, one man pushing her head down to avoid the whirling blades. Her strapless dress, however, was not so lucky, the updraft causing it to blow up around her waist. If it hadn't been for the leather strap to which she was harnessed, the flimsy dress would have gone up over her head. It was embarrassing enough as it was.

The woeful wife of Jax Jackson was lifted into the chopper and strapped in with a lap and shoulder harness. Large headphones were placed over the black hood in the general location of her ears. For the entire trip, she would hear little and see even less.

From the occasional brushing of elbows, she knew someone was sitting on her left. Stretching her legs brought her feet in contact with the back of the front seat. At least a four-seater, she surmised. If memory served her correctly, its top speed was about one hundred and fifty miles per hour. She needed to keep some sense of time, so she could calculate the total distance of the flight. Her keen sense of direction said they were heading east, maybe a little northeast.

Suzy was frightened, but mostly dumbfounded. This was no doubt about her Mejan features. But who was so concerned and why? Had the United States government somehow uncovered The Desert's secret base? Had they finally learned about the Mejan/human alliance that had been in effect since the Roswell incident in 1947? Were they rounding up everybody with Mejan blood? For what purpose? Was this in any way connected to the blackout in Washington two days ago?

She assumed she was being spirited away to some secret location where she would be poked, probed and studied. Of course, they would interrogate her. Would General Middleton and the rest of the team at The Desert be upset if she divulged what she knew about them, their advanced technology, the past Regg war, and a few dozen other secrets? Did the U. S. government now have possession of the infallible truth serums the Reggs had used on her and Jax, and they in turn had used on the Reggs? If so, she wouldn't be able to resist answering truthfully any question asked of her, regardless of how personal or revealing it may be. They couldn't blame her for that.

Suzy might have been more worried, if it weren't for the little homing chip she and all members of the team had implanted under the scalp behind the left ear. Jax had one. So did Dad and Mom, her brothers David and Mike and their wives. And of course, now her two children. One of the better inventions from the old Mejans, the tiny implant, no bigger than a pinhead, sent out a homing signal that could be picked up as much as five hundred miles away, as long as the person wasn't in an enclosure of metal or concrete. Even now, inside a helicopter a thousand feet in the air and miles from home, they might have a fix on her. It was only a matter of time before she'd be found and rescued.

*****

Suzy felt her forward momentum begin to slow, and the sinking feeling in her stomach as they lost altitude. The sudden jolt confirmed they were back on terra firma. She estimated the flight had taken about forty minutes, so they were no more than one hundred miles east of Iowa City.

A pair of hands deftly unbuckled her safety belts, as the door on the pilot's side slid open, followed a few seconds later by her own door. She was hit by the same summer heat and humidity she had just left in Iowa City. There was the familiar odor of corn growing in the field, mixed with the helicopter's diesel fuel exhaust.

No one spoke. Two strong hands helped her out of the chopper, and held her head down again as she was hurried away from the spinning blades. Her sundress blew up to her waist again, with nothing she could do about it. Embarrassment was becoming routine.

The downdraft also blew up the smell of grass, which her feet confirmed was thick and soft. She guessed Kentucky blue grass, like they had at her folks' farm. Suddenly, the strong hands forced her to stop. Someone knocked on wood. A door on rollers opened, but not by much. From the crinkling sound of stiff paper, she guessed her shopping bag was being handed off to someone. She hoped her purse with the active smartphone was in it. She was then turned sideways and gently pushed through the small opening. The door rolled shut quickly, apparently leaving her escort on the outside.

Standing alone for the briefest of moments, Suzy smelled the unmistakable truth of where she was. A farm girl born and raised, she knew every odor of every facet of such a building: pigs, cows, horses, sheep, hay, straw, alfalfa, oats, fresh wood, old wood, you name it. This structure had some of those, especially old wood. But none of it was fresh. This barn hadn't been used for anything more than storing hay bales for years. The sensation of dirt and straw scrunching beneath her feet suggested it hadn't been cleaned for that long either. What in the world were they doing in an old barn?

She heard the chopper leave. A hairy hand brushed against hers, as it grabbed the short chain between her handcuffs and pulled her forward. She stumbled for a couple steps across the barn floor, before being guided up an incline with some give to it, like hard plastic. A new smell hit her nostrils through the cloth, one completely different from the barn's, yet it had a twinge of familiarity to it. The ramp turned into a level floor, as she was pulled forward a couple more steps. A door closed behind her with a pneumatic swoosh. Simultaneously the air pressure changed. Suzy sensed she was in a small chamber.

Her headphones were removed and carelessly tossed to the floor with a clunk. Then came the metal handcuffs, being left to dangle by the chain at her stomach. Suzy was spun not-so-gently halfway around, so the buckle at the back could be undone and the wide belt removed. That felt good, even though the sweat it had produced left her sundress stuck to her waist.

Finally, off came the black hood. The sudden brightness caused her large black pupils to contract, as she squinted at the first look of her surroundings. She assumed she was facing the pneumatic door she had just come through. It was a silvery-white with rounded corners like the door of a ship's bulkhead, but ran from floor to seven-foot ceiling. And instead of a wheel-locking device, there was just a lighted keypad on the wall, with three rows of three buttons each. On each button were hiero-glyphic-type markings. She never did know what they meant, but she easily remembered who used them.

Reggs!

Every hair on her body stood stiff. Her skin felt clammy from the inside. Without turning around, her head pivoted slowly left and right to take in as much of her surroundings as she dared. The walls were also a silvery-white and just as nondescript as the door. There was no doubt, *she was in a Regg spacecraft*. The combination of the architecture and that godawful smell of old meat methane flashed back memories of the hours she and Jax had spent inside that Regg daughtership at the bottom of the Coralville Reservoir. At the time it wasn't so traumatic for her, because from the onset she was under the influence of those funky, feel-good, truth-spilling drugs. But the nightmares she had for months afterwards made the experience far more real and far less pleasant.

The last thing Suzy wanted to do right now was look behind her. But curiosity trumped fear: she had to verify who her captors were. Besides, there was always the slim chance they weren't who she thought they were. It still could be the CIA or NSA with a flatulence problem trying to learn more about her Mejan heritage...about The Desert...about her ties to them. But that odor the Reggs cast off was unmistakable. No human discharge had ever smelled like that.

Suzy held her breath and slowly turned around.

Even though she knew what she would see, the scream caught in her throat, coming out as a horse gasp. She was face-to-hairy-necks with two six-foot Reggs, those narrow-set, yellow, wolfen eyes staring down at her with a curiosity of their own. They had never seen a Mejan before, only heard about them through the scattered, sketchy broadcasts intercepted ten years ago during their frequent trips to Earth for supplies. Now here was one of them in the tanned flesh: a true, big-eyed, big-headed Mejan. The enemy.

Survival instincts snapped in Suzy's brain. She automatically crouched to defend herself from what might happen next, her fists out in the defensive position. But the two Reggs were bigger and cat-quick, each grabbing one of her wrists and pulling her hands over her head. Before she could scream in their faces, each wrist was secured by a leather strap, which was connected to another thick piece of leather threaded through an eye-bolt in the low ceiling of the craft. When they let go, Suzy was dangling like a piece of meat. At least her pumps were still touching the floor.

In light-green jumpsuits and orange boots, both of the thin Reggs took steps back to study their captive. Suzy was too frightened to yell obscenities at them, or demand her immediate release, or even cry. She just stared at the two sets of yellow eyes with the vertical, black pupils recessed deep into the mass of hair. But there was something different about these two Reggs. That hair was of a lighter gray than any of the others from yesteryear. And their snouts were about an inch shorter.

They were probably from the same planet, just different countries and therefore races.

One of the subjects of her worst nightmare—chapter two—finally spoke, growling Reggese to the other. It nodded, and then stepped forward to Suzy, bending down to grab the hem of her green-print, summer dress. With one downward jerk, the Regg unceremoniously pulled the strapless dress clean off Suzy down to the floor. He, she, or it then just as methodically pulled down her white panties and took off her shoes. It took him a moment to figure out the clasp at the front of her bra, and it soon joined the rest of the quaking woman's clothing on the metal floor.

The denuder joined the other to study the now-naked Mejan with great interest, making comments in their native language. The occasional toothy smile and snort were particularly degrading. Suzy assumed these werewolves found her body just as revolting as she found theirs.

Then things got considerably worse. A small table hinged to the wall was unlatched and swung down to reveal a variety of ominous-looking instruments, including surgical gloves, which both Reggs pulled on. One Regg held her head firmly while the other wrapped a pliable measuring tape around it to determine its circumference. That wasn't so bad. What was bad, however, was when he then pressed a set of calipers deep into one eye socket to measure the diameter of her ocular orb. The pain and terror were almost as gut-wrenching as the stench of his breath. Suzy did the only thing she could: she screamed right in the Regg's face.

Her right eye throbbing, the hapless captive wondered where the hell were the drugs they had used on her last time. Were these assholes simply sadistic or did they forget to bring the sprays? It didn't make sense. Maybe their chemists had never developed them.

The poor excuse for one of God's creatures then put the calipers down on the table and picked up a thermometer with a digital readout, part of the booty lifted from a Walgreen's warehouse just a month ago in anticipation of just such a kidnapping. Suzy knew exactly what was coming. If she had any dignity left, its remnants were about to wisp away into the ether.

She was spun around to be facing away from him. With all the delicacy of a lumberjack wedging a tree, the heartless canine inserted the thermometer where objects are supposed to exit only. In five seconds that seemed like ten minutes it beeped three times, signaling it was done. Suzy knew it would read almost one degree cooler than most human's rectal temperature, the final proof of her Mejan lineage.

Back at the table, the Regg picked up a device similar to her smartphone and spoke Reggese into it, presumably to document the results and send them off to a higher echelon.

The tests seemed to be over. Throughout it all, Suzy kept praying and focusing on one question: where in God's name was the cavalry?

When it came time to go through her shopping bag and purse, the only things of interest were the wine and her smartphone. Still hung uncomfortably from the ceiling, her arms drained of blood and falling asleep, Suzy had to watch as her abductors sat cross-legged on the floor of the small spacecraft, passing back and forth one of the two bottles of merlot. When it was gone, neither one seemed even the slightest bit inebriated. They just kept watching Suzy, all four yellow eyes locked on their trussed-up prize. They had seen plenty of naked human females on the DVDs stolen from the Walmart distribution center in Apple Valley, California, but never one in the flesh.

One even took a moment to get off his bony, tailless ass and come over to squeeze Suzy's breasts. Regg females had them, too, but much smaller and barely visible under all that hair, even if they were lactating. When the alien perv rubbed her crotch and kneaded her behind, Suzy seriously considered kicking it in the gonads, if it had any. But she knew that would result in something she would appreciate even less.

The two Reggs seemed to be waiting for something, maybe orders from headquarters, Suzy reasoned. Surely they want to get me to a daughtership, one with better lab and incarceration facilities. I hope *they* have the drugs. They sure as hell aren't gonna let me go. Ah, that's it! I'll bet they are waiting for dark, so this ship won't be seen flying out of the barn, or the daughtership coming in to take me. That's what we do at The Farm. Yeah, that's when the cavalry will be here to save me.

Suzy's analytical mind started doing the math. Let's see…the cops got me to the stationhouse around three o'clock; I was in the interrogation room for about twenty minutes; the flight here took forty minutes; they've been working me over for about twenty; it's taken them another fifteen to kill that bottle of wine; so, it must be about four-forty-five right now. It's June tenth. Sunset in Iowa City is around eight-forty. But we're closer to the Quad Cities, so subtract five minutes. It won't get completely dark until nine-thirty, unless it's overcast. And it wasn't. That's around five hours from now before these assholes can leave this barn without fear of being seen. I'll bet The Desert brains are thinking the same way. They don't want to be seen flying one of our spacecraft in here either. On the other hand, I know everyone wants to get me out of here as soon as possible. So rather than wait to fly in, maybe they are already on their way with a car or truck. That would take less than an hour down Interstate 80 from Iowa City. They could be here any minute. But I doubt that…too risky in daylight…if pushed, these Reggs could ram this ship right through the barn's ceiling and take off with no way to follow them. C'mon, girl. Whether they rescue you sooner or later, you need to hang on.

Eventually, the Regg with the extra hash marks on the shoulder flaps of his light-green jumpsuit motioned for the other to hand him Suzy's smartphone. He played with it for a short minute, pushing buttons and even shaking it a couple times, but it wouldn't turn on. He had no idea it was sending out a signal anyway, as was Suzy's GPS implant under her scalp. Even if the signal couldn't penetrate the police station's interrogation room, or the chopper, or this Regg craft, it would have gone out at the times in between, including and especially when she was being led from the chopper to this Regg spacecraft in the barn. They definitely would know exactly where she was.

Obviously frustrated, the higher-ranked of the two Reggs got his lanky form up from the floor and approached his captive. He pointed to the black mobile device and for the first time spoke in English, "Make work."

Suzy wasn't all that surprised. Virtually every Regg she and Jax had encountered during their past abduction and interrogation had at least a working English vocabulary. They found out from their captured Reggs that it was mandatory for all the Reggs with the aptitude and higher IQs to learn the various languages of the Earth inhabitants they were soon to conquer and enslave.

Suzy just glared at him defiantly.

"Make work," he repeated, poking her bare stomach with the smartphone.

"It's probably broken," said Suzy flatly.

"You lie."

"The cops dropped it when they searched me."

The Regg studied the casing. "You lie."

"If you don't believe me, the *on* button is on the top there," she said, nodding. "Press and hold it for two seconds. You'll see it's broken."

The Regg didn't even try that button. Suzy assumed it didn't fully understand her instructions. Besides, it didn't dare risk pushing the wrong buttons and have the device self-destruct. That would really piss off HQ. So, it did the only thing it could think of in its frustration. It slapped her across the face.

The slap took away her breath, but Suzy shook off the pain, determined not to cry. "Anytime now, family," she thought through gritted teeth. "Anytime."

Chapter 10

Jax Jackson jumped off the treadmill to better read his smart-watch. It had just started buzzing and flashing in a prescribed sequence, signaling that an audio-visual broadcast from Suzy was coming in. He assumed she had found something of in-tertest on her shopping trip, and wanted to run it by him. Prob-ably the brand and year of the wine for taking to her parents' farm tonight for dinner.

Wiping his face and hands on a towel, he plucked his acces-sory smartphone off the green felt of the nearby pool table and pushed the speaker button three times. The four-inch screen showed only a fuzzy dark-gray, but the audio was fairly clear.

"Please look at me," said a man's voice. There was a pause, before he added with more authority, "We need you to open your eyes."

"What the hell?" mumbled Jax, quickly tapping two buttons on his smartphone to turn on the eighty-inch television against the north wall of his rec room. The screen was still dark-gray, but the audio was a little better, now in total Dolby X9 Surround Sound.

"There. Are you happy, officer?" It was definitely Suzy's voice.

Jax heard some rustling sounds, before another man finally said, "Would you mind removing your hat?"

Jax was getting worried. "What the hell is going on here?" he said out loud. It sounded like some cops were shaking down his wife. But for what reason? Asking her to take off her hat didn't sound good at all.

"Yes, I do mind removing my hat," spat Suzy.

"I'm afraid we must insist," said the same voice. There was a scuffling sound for a few seconds, a pause, then a defensive "Hey!" from Suzy.

For the next few minutes Jax stood transfixed in front of his television screen, listening to the ongoing broadcast, his legs shaking. He heard a cop calling in to headquarters, Suzy protesting, and then being put in the patrol car. That's when the audio became almost crystal clear.

"Listen, Officers Willis and Gonzales," said Suzy purposefully loud. "You're two of Iowa City's finest. Surely you have some idea why I'm being taken away from the Century Mall and driven to the police station." Pause. "Well?"

"Atta girl," said Jax, pumping his fist, fighting back tears. "Fill us in."

The dialog continued, with Suzy suggesting the officers had scanned her with a thermal imaging device of some kind. But the cops stayed tight-lipped.

"C'mon, what's with that infrared?" pushed Suzy wirily. "You perverts get a kick out of seeing women's body heat under their clothing?"

That was the last of the broadcast. But it was more than enough information. Suzy had done her job in spades. Unfortunately, the infrared element was reminiscent of terrifying times of days past. And even worse, Suzy's Mejan features had been uncovered.

Throwing the towel around his neck and running up the white carpeted stairs to the main floor of the multi-million-dollar estate he inherited when his folks were killed in a car accident fifteen years ago, Jax raced across the marble floor of the foyer and straight into his den. Slamming the heavy wooden door behind him, he punched up the smaller television screen beside his workstation. His mother-in-law, Mary Brookfield, came on, looking worried.

"Did you get all that?" blurted Jax.

"I did," said Suzy's big-eyed, big-headed, one-quarter-Mejan mother. "I'm worried, Jax. Really worried. There's something going on here. Alan is on his way in from the field. We need to call The Desert."

"I agree," said Jax. "Go ahead. Link me in."

Jax's screen immediately split, with Mary on the left and a blank on the right. Five seconds later that side filled in with the familiar craggy face and narrow chin of Joshua Middleton, a two-star general in the United States Air Force. His reddish buzz-cut had added a few gray strands of fifty-five-year-old hair on the sides. But he still wore those signature aviator glasses, hiding his abnormally large eyes. He was just as much Mejan as Mary Brookfield.

"We fully expected to hear from you," said the general, looking down at a second monitor. "Suzy darling seems to be in a pickle, huh? We got her GPS entering the Iowa City police station's back door four minutes ago. Then we lost both signals. The place has a steel roof. We are right now repositioning our Sentry 3 satellite so we can keep optics on the immediate area."

"I could go get her," said Jax, the trepidation in his voice coming from concern for both his wife and himself. Jax never did care much for confrontation. But Suzy was in trouble, he was her husband, and he was expected to do something. "I'm only five minutes from the police station."

"Let's hold off until we can get more intel," said the general. "Since they took her in the back door, they aren't treating her as a normal perp. If you went in there asking to see her or why they are holding her, they'd probably say they have no idea what you're talking about. And if they did, they'd certainly wonder how you knew she was there."

"But we can't just leave her there," whined Mary. "God knows what they might do to her. It's seems pretty obvious they are interested mainly in her genealogy."

"And what about the infrared scanning," added Jax, forgetting he was standing there in front of The Farm and The Desert, shiny-wet from his once-a-week workout, wearing only basketball shorts, running shoes, and the towel around his neck. "Jesus! This smacks of Reggs."

The ensuing silence spoke volumes. Then the general slowly lifted his head and appeared to look hard at Jax and Mary, his forehead knitted. "I'm sorry to tell you folks this…but it seems that these might very well be some Reggs…or some species very close to Reggs."

Mary Brookfield burst into tears just as Alan—her husband, Suzy's father—came into frame and folded his arms around her. "How long have you known this, Joshua?" retorted Alan, making no attempt to hide his anger. "And when exactly did you plan on telling us?"

"We didn't know ourselves until a few minutes ago," replied General Joshua Middleton. "Apparently the Reggs' first contact was with the White House after those blackouts. It took us a while to learn that only the AG, the Joint Chiefs, and the head of the FBI were then brought into the loop. Then it was a matter of getting one of them—in this case General Knox with the Army, who was the most accessible—to sit down and fill us in."

"Yeah, I'll bet," laughed Alan sinisterly. "More like he was thrown into the back of a black Suburban and sprayed with truth serum."

The general flashed a quick smile, "Something like that." His face then turned stern again. "Anyway, we had just gotten that report, when Suzy's feed started coming in."

"So, what does the report say?" pleaded Jax. "Did Kahn renege on our deal, and come back anyway?"

The general wasn't sure how to answer Jax's question. As far as Jax knew, and Suzy knew, and everyone except a select few personnel knew, the Reggs' supreme leader, self-named Kahn, and his entire Regg nation had been escorted out into the solar system and released, the Reggs promising to never come back to Earth. But the truth was, under the influence of the powerful truth chemical, Kahn had confessed they would indeed be back, probably within a few weeks. That left no choice in the matter. The Regg mothership—the size of a small island and loaded with daughterships, squadrons of fighters, and over a thousand souls —was blasted into space dust by a 50-kiloton nuclear missile, launched from its escort, The Desert's top-secret spacecraft, code name *Little Sister*. A doctored video was shown to Jax, Suzy, et al to spare them the reality of the unavoidable, yet soul-ripping genocide.

So, while the general knew it couldn't possibly be the original Reggs, he couldn't tell these people how he knew. On the other hand, he didn't know for sure who these new marauders were either. He decided to leave the answer open to debate. "They either reneged," offered the general, "or these aren't the same Reggs, or even the same species."

"What makes you say that?" asked Mary.

"According to our most-cooperative General Knox," continued Middleton, "they haven't shown their faces, so we have no idea what they look like. They obviously know about us Mejans, but they act like they know less than they should. And this time, they're coming at us with a completely different strategy."

"Which is?" asked Alan.

"Well, as you might have guessed, the Washington D.C. blackout was their doing. If it is the same bunch of Reggs, it would seem they have spent the last ten years upgrading their EMP devices to the point of rendering entire cities helpless. They are using that threat to coerce the military and law enforcement into helping them to locate and capture as many people with Mejan blood as possible."

"To what end?" asked Alan, not sure anyone wanted or needed to hear the answer.

"The aliens have not made that clear. We can only assume they want to round up as many of us as possible, so they have a better chance of colonizing the planet under their terms...like before. And job-one is probably to locate our secret base and major outlets, like you Iowans, and take us out. We are their main threat."

"But if they are the original Reggs," said Alan, "they already know much of it. They know where our farm is and where your desert base is, since they tried blowing it up back then."

"That's what seems odd," said the general, not bothering to inform The Farm that The Desert had since moved. The less they knew, the better. "So far they've acted like they don't know any of this. Otherwise, why would they strong-arm cops and selected military across the U. S. to help locate us? They could have attacked you folks again at your farm and grabbed one of you. Instead, the Iowa City cops seem to have lucked into scanning Suzy at the mall. We haven't heard of any others being abducted, but we're sure there are, or soon will be."

"So, all the more reason to get going and free my daughter" insisted Alan. "Lord knows what they are going to do to her. At the very least they'll interrogate her. And they'll use the truth drug, so she'll tell them everything. That puts your ass in jeopardy as much as ours, General. We need to move fast."

Holding up a finger, Middleton said he'd be right back, and slid off screen. Jax took the opportunity to switch the three-way conference over to his smartphone, so he could run upstairs and get some clothes on. He also needed to tell Loretta and Odett to watch the kids, as he would be busy and incommunicado for the foreseeable future.

Jax had managed to throw on a white polo shirt and tan Haggar slacks, when the general was back onscreen. "I've been consulting with my team," said General Middleton, "and we all feel the best course of action is to wait."

"Wait?!" howled Mary. "For what?"

"Listen," said the general. "Calm down. Getting Suzy back home safe and without her giving the enemy any damaging info is our top priority. As long as she's at the Iowa City Police Station, we're quite certain she's safe. They are probably holding her until she can be transported to where some Reggs can study, er...question her. Once she comes out of the stationhouse, we can track her both electronically and optically. Sentry 3 is now in position, and one of our craft is on its way to hang above Iowa."

"Little Sister?" interjected Jax, remembering his time with Suzy onboard the magnificent ship, as it escorted the Reggs out toward Jupiter. Little Sister had a chokehold on the Reggs once; she could certainly do it again.

"No," smiled Middleton. "We won't need anything that extreme."

"What then?"

General Middleton let out an impatient sigh. "That's classified, Jax, and no need for you to know, anyway. Rest assured it will be enough to rescue Suzy. And more."

It took a second for the light bulb to flash on over Jax's head. "Of course!" he chimed into his smartphone, being held out at arm's length as he came down the stairs to the main floor. "We'll turn the tables on those hairy mothers and capture *them*!"

"That is the plan," grinned the general. "Something you know quite well, huh, super-star?"

While proud that for once in his life he had overcome his innate fear of confrontation to overtake the Reggs and their spacecraft ten years back, Jax wished the general hadn't brought it up at this particular time. Believing he was some kind of brave might mean he'd be expected to perform some kind of heroic event again to rescue his wife. While he wanted her back safe and sound more than anything, he'd just as soon someone else did it this time. Jax's bravery hinged on a surge of adrenalin while being armed with a bottle of that *gray-to-obey* spray.

The general continued. "We'll follow Suzy wherever they take her. Then when the time is right, we'll bag the kidnappers and probably one of their spacecraft, too. We'll find out who they are and what they're up to."

Just then, everyone's devices lit up or buzzed or started beeping. Suzy's GPS implant had her moving out the back door of the Iowa City police station. The audio from her smartphone revealed a loud whirring noise. The Desert's private Sentry 3 satellite showed a small, hooded figure already being lifted into a waiting, four-door helicopter by a larger figure wearing a gray flight suit and helmet. The satellite's camera didn't have enough time to zoom in and obtain a visual confirmation that it was Suzy, but with the familiar flapping green sundress, Jax assured everyone there was no doubt. The escort then ran around to the other side, climbed in, and the chopper wasted no time taking off, banking to the east.

"We're losing her GPS and smartphone signals," said General Middleton. "But our eye in the sky will track her all the way. I suspect they won't go too far…probably to wherever some of those sneaky, paranoid bastards are hiding."

Chapter 11

The next forty minutes dragged on like forty hours. General Joshua Middleton leaned against the communications room table with a fresh cup of coffee to watch the live satellite feed from his secret location someplace under the ground in some unknown location. Alan and Mary Brookfield watched from The Farm's command center five miles north of Iowa City, Iowa, side-by-side in their rolling office chairs, too tense to partake of anything other than an occasional shot of Templeton Rye whisky. Patrick Jax Jackson paced the floor of his den, never once taking his eyes off the whirling blades of the chopper, as seen from high above in the troposphere through the two-hundred-power lens of Sentry 3's camera. It also had optional infrared mode, if there were cloud cover. So far there was none. The picture was incredibly sharp.

The chopper finally landed eight and a half miles north of Interstate 80 and fifteen miles west of the Mississippi River in the middle of a green sea of waist-high corn. There was nothing around for a half mile in any direction, except for an old barn with weather-worn gray shingles. The chopper set down a hundred feet from the barn's north side.

"Here we go," said the general, setting the coffee cup on his desk and picking up a remote.

This time Sentry 3 zoomed in to clearly frame a black-hooded Suzy being hustled from the chopper to the barn, presumably by the same man in the gray flight suit. With her light-green summer dress flapping in the powerful draft, it was definitely Suzy. The eye in the sky camera zoomed in even closer to reveal she was handcuffed to her waist by a leather belt. Jax wanted to put his fist through his television screen.

Because the large, hanging double-doors of the barn were closed, Suzy's escort paused in front and knocked. The doors opened just enough for the shopping bag to be passed through and set down on the floor. Suzy was next, being gently guided through sideways, a tight squeeze. Continuing to follow his strict orders, the escort didn't follow or even attempt to look inside. Instead, he quickly returned to his aircraft and clambered into the back seat Suzy had previously occupied. The chopper lifted off and out of the picture.

"Ten to one that's where the bad guys are," said General Middleton, giving the *go-ahead* motion with his hand to someone off-screen. "Probably in a small spacecraft."

"Get going!" yelled Jax, although his extra volume was unnecessary. "You can be there in an hour."

"Half that, if we take one of our fighters." That was Suzy's father, Alan, almost as adamant.

"Relax, men," cautioned Middleton with both his hands. "Let's not get ahead of ourselves. You know we can't go flying in there in broad daylight. And what are you gonna do once you get there by ground transportation?"

Alan thought fast. "I could blow the doors off their spaceship with my smartphone."

"Highly unlikely, cowboy," said the general. "You may be able to knock a man down with it, but their craft isn't going to be made of tin." Before Alan could propose what everyone knew was coming next, the general added, "And forget its laser feature. At best, in about a minute you'd burn a small hole in their ship. Then what? They'd take off for the wild blue yonder before your laser recharged. Or they'd open the door and blow you away with one of their own weapons, which at this point we know nothing about."

"Well, shit, General," hissed Jax, overdoing the bravado, now that he knew he wouldn't have to take part in the rescue. "We gotta do something. We can't just sit here. The Reggs could take off any minute with Suzy still onboard."

General Middleton moved closer to his camera, so his face and words would have more impact. "We *are* doing something, folks," he half-grinned. "The plan is already, shall we say, *in the air*. As we speak, our craft is hovering over the barn a few miles up. If the Regg craft tries to leave…well, let's just say it won't get more than a few feet outside of the barn. Besides, logic dictates they aren't going anywhere until dark. They can't risk being seen any more than we can. It's the same old clandestine protocol we've always lived under."

"But the Reggs have already made their presence known to people," said Jax.

"Only to a select few in the highest ranks of the government," said Middleton, "hardly the general populous. Did any of you catch the White House Press conference yesterday about the blackout?"

Mary raised her hand. "It was a joke," she sneered. "They aren't telling the public anything."

"Exactly," said the general. "Even Suzy's cop friends obviously had been left in the dark. They were given an infrared scanner and told to find someone with a lower body temperature and bigger head than normal and check them out, without being told why."

Spirits were beginning to lift. Hearing that the Reggs could not take Suzy any farther than the barn was calming news. But it didn't solve the issue of her being held prisoner until dark, which was still hours from now. Who knew what those soulless mongrels might do to her in the interim?

It wouldn't be so bad if they applied the same drugs on her the Reggs used ten years ago on both her and Jax...particularly the *gray to obey* spray, which instantly puts the recipients in a mellow, obedient state of mind, gladly doing anything requested by their new master. If they came at her with needles and scalpels like before—which is what had elevated Jax's adrenalin to the Tasmanian Devil level—she'd still feel pain. But without the associated fear, she wouldn't mind it so much.

Alan couldn't keep the question to himself. "General, if this is a new group of Reggs, they might not have those same drugs. And if that's true, it means this time Suzy will have to endure whatever they do to her without the benefit of that *I-don't-give-a-shit* spray."

The general ran a small, troubled hand over his balding spot. Suzy's dad had a point. And even worse, the general was the only one on this three-way video chat who knew these couldn't be the same Reggs. So, the odds were they didn't have the Terrific Trinity of drugs: the *gray-to-obey*, the *blue-be-true*, or the clear *amnesia* spray that erased all memory for the past four hours. In the previous covert war, both sides had used them all to their advantage. In fact, Jax and Suzy—among many others—had no idea the amnesia drug had been used on them by their own side, so they would have no memory of watching the Regg nation being obliterated by the nuclear missile.

"What you suggest, Alan, is possible," said the general, hoping to soften his concerns. "But let's say there are none of these drugs involved. First of all, it seems unlikely that Suzy would have to endure any physical abuse in a spacecraft small enough to fit inside a barn. It's probably just a scout ship with a small crew, whose only mission is to verify Suzy has the physical attributes of a Mejan, and then transport her to a larger craft for any further testing." He purposely left out "*and permanent incarceration.*"

From the look on his three comrades' faces, they liked this logic, but weren't completely sold.

"Furthermore," continued Middleton, "even if…and I emphasize *if* she has been traumatized in any way that would hang in her psyche for years, don't forget *we* have those drugs. One whiff of the amnesia spray, and she'll remember nothing about the last four hours, which would be about how long she will have spent in the barn by the time we rescue her after dark."

The other three were now having trouble hiding their relief. The general and his top-secret Desert, which was well-staffed with various degrees of Mejan bloodlines, always seemed to know the best course of action. But the over-protective Alan couldn't stop himself with one more challenge. After all, this was his daughter and her rescue was still hours away. Waiting was going to be agonizing for everyone.

"Of course, if we rescued Suzy *now*," Alan Brookfield said with a doleful smile, "she wouldn't have to remember even being stopped by the police."

"Nice try," sympathized the general. "But we have to wait until dark. Suzy will be fine. You folks worry about yourselves."

Jax had a question. "I assume the spacecraft you have hanging over the barn has a name."

"It does. We call her *Dolly*."

"What all can Dolly do? Is she smaller than Little Sister. Is she something new? Better?"

75

"Go get some rest, Jax," said the general, walking out of view. "All of you. We'll be in touch shortly."

Chapter 12

Jax leaned forward against the wheel of his black, 2025 Lexus SUV, just half a mile north of the old barn, impatiently waiting for the northwestern horizon's orange glow on his right to extinguish. He had always liked late-spring-early-summer, and Daylight Saving Time. But not tonight. It was taking forever to get completely dark, particularly with the cloudless sky. And the worst part was that even if the night became totally black, there was no guarantee the barn door would open and whatever was in there would come out. The fact remained that all of this had been pure speculation by his old friend General Middleton and his Mejan brain trust at The Desert. Even if it made perfect sense, and even if were from the greatest minds on the planet, it was still speculation.

Who knows? Maybe it wasn't aliens that took Suzy. Maybe it was the government or the military or some Russians doing this for their own reasons. Maybe the barn was a secret base with an underground system, like the Brookfield farm has. Maybe they had already taken his wife miles away underground, and he and the crew of the mysterious spaceship named Dolly were just hanging around with their thumbs up their collective exhaust pipes, waiting for something that was never going to happen.

"Christ!" said Jax, banging his fist on the black leather dashboard. "Get it together, Jackson! She's in there, and it's all going to work out."

His emotional outburst wasn't just from anxiety. There was a good measure of fear streaking across his mind, as well…and not necessarily for Suzy's safety. If there was one thing Patrick Jackson feared more than confrontation, it was confrontation with another bunch of Reggs. He had managed to buck it up ten years ago, when that Regg lab technician was about to stick a long needled into his wife's stomach and her resident fetus. That caused something to snap in Jax's chicken mind, and he went ballistic with a Rebel yell.

Such an encounter was highly unlikely this time. Jax's only job tonight was to position his vehicle on County Road 29 at just the correct angle to see inside the barn from the ground level, if and when the big doors reopened. It was assumed he could get a good look at the resident spacecraft, or whatever was in there. Everyone else on this mission was presently in the air, able to see little more than the top of the barn.

For the umpteenth time Jax put the night-vision binoculars to his eyes and scoped the barn doors, awash in a bright, mono-chromatic green. Still no movement. The digital readout at the bottom of his vision ticked away at *10:12:15 p.m.*, thirty seconds later than the last time he looked. "C'mon. It's dark enough," he whispered. "Prove us right. Come out. Come out, whoever you are. I want my baby back, baby back."

A watched pot never boils and a barn door never opens. So when it finally, mercifully did open five minutes later, Jax's bin-oculars were on his lap and his attention had drifted off to the conversation he and Suzy had yesterday morning at the pool. There was no way he could have gone shopping with her, like she asked. The whole town—and then the whole world—would discover the richest man in southeast Iowa was dating or married to some celebrity hiding under that floppy hat and huge sun-glasses. Their secret would be out and their ability to ever go out again together like this would be impossible. Besides, Suzy had gone out alone or with the kids hundreds of times over the years. Why did she want him to go with her today of all days? It was probably like she said: she was tired of hiding, tired not being able to do things in public with her family. Hell. He felt the same way. Goddamn small-minded humans.

Chapter 13

The simultaneous chirps of his synchronized smart devices snapped Jax's focus back to the present. Blinking, he anxiously peered down at the message on the lighted screen of his smartphone. *Activity. Wait for signal before approaching.*

The night-vision binoculars were slammed back to his eyes. Sure enough, the large, hanging doors were being pushed open by someone or thing. He zoomed in closer. The figure was bipedal, about six feet tall, wearing a jumpsuit and boots of indeterminate colors. Poking out of the jumpsuit was a bunch of hair with an elongated snout. Jax knew it well. It indeed was a Regg!

Jax gasped...from both relief and fear. He was elated that General Middleton and his Desert staff were correct in their assumptions. His darling Suzy was definitely in there and was about to be rescued and brought back to her loving husband and family. On the other hand, the unbelievable return of those hairy sonsabitches signaled clearly that Regg War Two-point-Oh was underway. And so far this one looked to be different from the first in some respects, and about the same in others.

Shaking so much, Jax had to rest the binoculars on the steering wheel. He watched as the Regg continued sliding one hanging barn door open as far as it would go, and then the other. There, nestled back in the green shadows, was the faint outline of some kind of structure, the size of a cargo ship's container, but with rounded edges and a flat bottom. It looked like the open end of a gigantic loaf of Italian bread cut in half. The Regg walked back to his craft and knocked on the hatch. It opened from the top down, the flash of its inner light almost blinding Jax. Squinting through the pain, he quickly clicked off the night-vision mode to watch in normal, ambient light. By the time his pupils had enlarged again, the Regg's lanky silhouette was walking up the ramp.

Standing to one side was another Regg, dressed exactly the same, his finger on a control panel, waiting to close the hatch. On the other side of the craft, sitting in a padded seat attached to the wall, was Suzy, handcuffed with a zip tie, and naked as a jaybird, except for the double-shoulder and waist safety harness securing her in place. They had her ready for take-off.

"I have a positive on Suzy," he gurgled into his smartphone. "She is seated…about ten feet in from the hatch. She is awake and looks ornery." Jax gave a nervous laugh of relief and added, "I pity the Reggs."

"Roger that. Great news, Jax," squawked his phone.

Suzy was, in fact, glaring defiantly at both Reggs, her big eyes pinched halfway closed, her hatless head cocked at an angle of defiance. And then, just before the door swung completely closed, Jax could swear she winked…not at the Reggs, but at him. Chills ran down Jax's arms and legs. It was just like his wife to not only expect a rescue at this time, but to have a pretty good idea how it would go down. He admired her intuitive, analytical mind. He envied her grace under fire. He hoped his kids took more after their mother.

"Good thing I brought a blanket for her," he laughed to himself, flicking away tears.

As the door sealed shut, extinguishing all light, Jax was blind again for a moment. But compared to the pounding of his heart and the three quarts of stomach acid, he hardly noticed. He switched the binoculars back to night-vision.

Like a delivery truck backing out of a warehouse bay, the loaf-shaped spacecraft silently eased out of the barn, barely a foot off the ground. Once all seventy feet of its length had cleared the door, it did a slow, ninety-degree spin to face east, positioning for take-off. But just then, as a surprise to no one involved in this episode except the Reggs inside, their ten-foot-high spacecraft suddenly dropped to the ground in a small cloud of green dust. It sat there, motionless, helpless.

Jax's devices chirped and lit up with the single word: *Go!*

Jax pulled on his night-vision goggles. With headlights still off, the SUV spun gravel and raced up County Road 29. Thirty seconds and six hundred yards later, it took a hard right onto the one-lane tractor path that dissected two cornfields. It resumed a break-neck speed toward the barn, bouncing hard over bumps and dips. Jax's head hit the ceiling four times.

"Remember, no closer than sixty feet, Jax," spouted the smartphone in his lap, "or you'll be in the cone."

"Roger that," he yelled too loudly, hitting the brakes and sliding up well short of the disabled spacecraft, semi-visible is washed-out green. It appeared to be countershaded: dark on top, a lighter color on the bottom, typical of any aircraft wishing to be as inconspicuous as possible...like their own stealth fighters.

"Stay put," said his phone. "Wait for the chopper."

Jax did as he was directed. This procedure had been covered two hours earlier during the ten-minute briefing in which he would rather have not taken part. The Desert had determined that ground transportation would be a far simpler and more clandestine method of evacuating Suzy back to Iowa City than using some form of aircraft. And who better to take her by car than her loving husband? Going along on the actual rescue mission had Jax wishing he was someplace else. But he couldn't let the others know this.

Dressed in the prearranged all-dark clothing and his night-vision goggles still in place, Jax slid out of his vehicle. That turned out to be the only way he could have known a helicopter was arriving, as it descended out of the night sky like a stealthy phantom, its blades not even rotating. It settled two hundred feet on the other side of the Regg craft without the slightest sound or disturbance of the standing corn. It didn't even disrupt the incessant trilling of a few million invisible insects in the humid, summer night air.

Jax shook his head in admiration. The Deseret never ceased to amaze him. They had incorporated the same Mejan-devised, antigravity power source in the helicopter that they had in other commonplace aircraft, like 747s and fighter jets. The clever idea was that if anyone saw it flying across the sky, they wouldn't give it a second thought, just another airplane. He recalled The Desert vertically landing that monstrous C-17 cargo plane ten years ago at the Brookfield farm after dark, without a sound and without the neighbors having a clue. Twice.

Three figures in all-black fatigues and night-vision goggles piled out of the Sikorsky UH-60 Black Hawk helicopter. They walked forward carefully, keeping an eye on their GPS readouts, calculating their distance from the incapacitated Regg space-craft. All electronics in a fifty-foot radius around the craft were being disabled by the concentrated electromagnetic pulses raining down from Dolly somewhere in the atmosphere. If the men got inside that cone, none of their equipment would work either. The Reggs' electromagnetic pulse weapon now had nothing on The Desert's newly-upgraded EMP cannon.

One soldier named Sampson was carrying an MX4 military rifle in one hand and a smartphone in the other. He circled wide to the left and took a knee sixty feet from the rear end of the ship at a slight angle. Jax knew the mobile device Sampson was pointing at the Regg's hatch was set to stun with its *USLAP* (Ultra Sonic Laser Accelerated Pulse) feature. He had the same option in his smartphone; it generated a concentrated sound wave along a laser beam that could knock a man down at two hundred yards. Of course, Jax's device was undoubtedly out of date by now. He wondered what the newer issues could do. If the Reggs didn't cooperate, he might find out.

Just the same, in his designated role as back-up, Jax took a nervous knee at the opposite corner from the soldier, aiming his smartphone at the hatch, his USLAP feature activated. No one was to die tonight. And that held especially true for Suzy, if she happened to get in the line of fire.

The second soldier—Dewitt—aligned himself to the side of the Regg craft toward the back end, stopping a good ten feet from the edge of the cone. He snapped open a tripod supporting a small laser gun that looked like a home movie camera. He made some adjustments, causing a small red dot to appear on the side of the craft. "I'm three feet in from the back, and six feet from the bottom," he called softly, just loud enough for all on the team to hear. "That should be well clear of Suzy, right, Jax?"

"Um, roger," said Jax, the only member of the team who had actually seen inside the Regg vehicle. "She's at least ten feet in. If you burn a hole through anyone, it will be a Regg. Please do."

"We need them for interrogation, Jax," laughed Dewitt.

Wasting no time, the third soldier—Nelson—took off his goggles and walked purposely into the EMP cone. Anything electronic on his person immediately went dark. But he wouldn't need it anyway, just the pressurized canister he was carrying. Once next to the ship, Nelson signaled to Dewitt, who switched on the laser gun. The same round dot on the fuselage expanded to the size of a golf ball and increased in power mega-fold. In one second, a hole was burned through the hull of the Regg's spacecraft, and Dewitt immediately flipped off the laser.

Just as fast, Nelson shoved the nozzle of the canister into the smoldering hole and opened the valve. Some thousand cubic inches of Fluothane and Neothyl filled the inner chamber, putting everyone to sleep in a matter of seconds. Nelson could hear and feel something inside fall to the floor with a thud. He pictured one of the Reggs stumbling through the pitch-blackness to try opening the rear hatch, only to see a red hole appear in the fuselage just before he passed out. Smiling at the image, Nelson shot a thumbs-up to the team and backed away from the craft to rejoin Dewitt outside of the cone.

Dewitt re-fired the laser, this time making short work of carving a new door in the side of the ship, large enough for a man to climb through. He then clicked off the laser and picked up a battery-operated spotlight and shined it into the hole. No movement, just curls of smoke wafting out of the opening.

To keep a steady stream of illumination on the target, Dewitt edged along just outside the perimeter of the EMP cone, shining the light in the hole at an ever-increasing angle. Working in tandem with him, Nelson was back at the craft wearing a gasmask, looking inside to ascertain all onboard were knocked out. From the spotlight reflecting off the inside walls to help illuminate the scene, through the smoky haze he saw both Reggs lying on the floor. Suzy was slumped over, well secured to her seat against the far wall. She appeared unharmed. Nelson gave another thumbs-up.

Sampson raised his wrist to his mouth. "Hello, Dolly," he said into the device. "All is secure down here. You can turn the lights back on and begin your descent."

"Roger. On the way."

That was another feature of The Desert that always fascinated Jax. Anytime someone transmits anything to anyone connected to this super-technological, super-secret organization, they never have to worry about eavesdroppers. All audio and video signals are not only instantly encrypted, they are re-encrypted every half second, thanks to an ingenious program his own Suzy had developed two years before he met her, when she was only eighteen. Any outsider trying to tune into the private frequency gets rewarded with mind-numbing static.

And now he was only minutes away from having his precious little computer nerd back in his arms.

Chapter 14

The EMP cone was lifted, and all electronic devices resumed complete function. A couple dome lights inside the Regg spacecraft powered back on, and Nelson climbed through the new door, still wearing his gasmask. Knowing exactly where the switch was and which buttons to push, he opened the rear hatch.

Jax ran back to his car, claiming he had to drop off his night-vision goggles and pick up the gasmask and blanket he had forgotten. But it was mainly to conjure up some courage and dislodge urine in some place other than his shorts. Being back inside a smelly Regg spacecraft was not high on his bucket list. But his wife was in there. He had to go.

Once his breathing was under control, Jax cautiously joined the others onboard the revitalized spacecraft, all three also wearing their gasmasks. Dewitt and Sampson had gone straight to the sleeping Reggs and secured their hands and feet with plastic zip ties. They were now going through the Reggs' pockets and compartments, looking for communicators and anything else of interest.

Nelson was forward in the cockpit checking out the controls. They were almost exactly the same as the Regg fighters and daughtership he had studied hands-on ten years before. Those aircraft had been captured, first by the Brookfield clan when they were attacked by a band of Reggs from both the air and land, and then later when an adrenalin-pumping Jax almost singlehandedly subdued the crew of a daughtership and flew it into the belly of Little Sister. That spelled the beginning of the end for the Reggs...at least, for that group of them. No one knew who these new ones were. But after tonight, The Desert most certainly would.

Jax went straight for his comatose wife, giving the passed-out Reggs a squeamish, wide berth. Job-one was to find her clothes, which were not in sight. Only her smartphone was lying on the floor closer to the cockpit. So, one-by-one he lifted the lids of the bins lining the floor on both sides of the craft. He found her purse in the one right next to Suzy, along with the shopping bag containing only a tan visor and a couple paper receipts. Underneath were cans of Dinty Moore beef stew, Hormel spam, and Chicken of the Sea tuna. Like their predecessors, these lazy Reggs obviously preferred pilfering Earth's grocery outlets, rather than doing their own agriculture.

He finally found her clothes tucked in with eight-packs of Bounty paper towels and White Cloud toilet paper. Why should he be surprised? There were also two wine bottles in the bin, one empty, one unopened.

During his searching, Jax occasionally made furtive glances at the other men to see if they were checking out his wife's state of undress. But they seemed to be purposely diverting their eyes, probably out of respect for both her nakedness and her eight-hour-long ordeal. Jax was grateful, yet a part of him wanted them to notice just how incredibly sexy his wife was. These guys, however, were a class act.

Jax stuffed her clothes, floppy hat, shoes, purse and smartphone in the shopping bag. Using his Swiss Army knife, he cut the plastic ties on Suzy's wrists and ankles, then unhooked her safety straps and wrapped the blanket around her. With the bulging shopping bag in one hand, he hoisted her limp one hundred and ten pounds into the cradle of his arms and carried her outside the craft straight to their SUV.

Once away from the sleeping gas, Suzy began to come around. She managed to wobble upright on her bare feet as Jax slipped the light-green summer dress on over her head, followed by the white pumps on her feet. He opened the passenger side door, and tossed the gasmask and shopping bag with all its contents into the back. With Suzy's arms loosely around his neck, Jax lifted his groggy wife onto the black leather seat. He would have buckled her in, but he knew they weren't going anywhere just yet.

"W-what's going on," she mumbled, her big eyes opening halfway.

"You're safe, sweetheart," said Jax, a lump catching in his throat, as he leaned in to kiss her cool cheek. "It's all over. I'm taking you home."

That brought a smile to her lips. Home sounded real good. Nathan and Nicole. A warm bath. Food! She was starving.

As Jax walked around and climbed in the other side, Suzy opened her eyes wider and looked around. She knew she was inside their Lexus, because she recognized the leather necklace Nicole made for her birthday, with the pretty blue, heart-shaped stone she had found at The Farm. Nicole had used her grandpa's engraving tool to carve *MOM* on it. The silver-dollar-sized stone was too big to actually wear and too precious to shove in a drawer. So, it was designated to hang over the family SUV's rearview mirror forever.

Beyond the windshield, she couldn't see much of anything. The only illumination seemed to be coming from something with its backend open, spilling soft light out onto the immediate green grass. Two men came out of the opening, stopping to remove their gasmasks and put on their night-vision goggles. As they walked off into the shadows, the hatch closed and the terrain went dark.

"Oh, good Lord!" she gasped, the day's events flooding back to her memory. "I was in that godawful hell-hole!" She turned to look bug-eyed at her husband, grinning at her from behind the wheel. "*You* came for me, Jax?"

Jax reached over and squeezed her hand. "I didn't do much," he smiled. "It was mostly the general, The Desert, and those guys out there. I just tagged along. But there was no way I was staying home."

Suzy climbed over the SUV's console and landed in her husband's lap. The kiss was wet and intensive. For the second time since knowing him, her man had shown courage, coming to her rescue. When Suzy first met Jax over ten years ago, he was not a brave man by nature. He had folded under the slightest pressure all through his life, and especially the night the Reggs assaulted The Farm. Being an outdoorsman and a good shot, Jax was supposed to take out any Regg trying to enter the main residence. But when the time came, he melted into a ball of self-preserving goo, and Suzy had to unlock the M-16 from his quivering hands and do the job for him.

Her husband unexpectedly redeemed himself a few weeks later when he and Suzy were captured by the Reggs and taken aboard one of their daughterships for interrogation and examination. Seeing that lab technician about to stick a foot-long needle into his wife's stomach and unborn child (Nicole), Jax snapped. Disregarding his own safety, he took on four Reggs like Vin Diesel on uppers, knocking out two, shackling one, and taking the last one as a hostage to help Jax capture that craft, which eventually led to the end of that particular clan of Reggs.

Now here was her husband, displaying bravery again, taking part in saving her from the Reggs for the second time. She wanted to crawl inside him.

The emotional interlude was abruptly interrupted by a voice on Jax's smartphone, "Ready to violate you, Dolly. Open wide and enjoy it."

"Huh?" grunted Suzy, releasing her hold on Jax's neck. "They're calling me *Dolly*?"

"Not you," laughed Jax, turning her around on his lap to face out front. "We might want to watch this."

"Watch what?" said Suzy, sliding back into the passenger seat. She peered through the windshield into what to Jax was nothing but blackness. Yet her large pupils let in enough starlight to see the specter of both the Regg spacecraft and the old barn.

Jax stretched to grab the night-vision goggles from the backseat. "Here, put this on."

Suzy slipped it on over her head, while Jax fetched the binoculars with the same thermal-imaging function off the dash and put them to his eyes.

"Roger," said the smartphone. "Dolly is willing. Please be gentle."

With the scene now bright in washed-out green, the Jacksons watched as the Regg spaceship lifted smoothly and silently off the ground, going straight up as if on a skyhook.

"What the hell...?" breathed Suzy. "Are we letting the Reggs go?"

"Hardly," snorted Jax. "That's one of us—Nelson—flying their ship...right up into Dolly."

"And what exactly is this Dolly?"

"There she is...look. Up higher."

Craning their necks, they saw a large void in an otherwise star-speckled sky. Widening their field of vision, they could make out Dolly's oval outline and some of her contours. It was difficult to determine her size with nothing behind her for perspective, but Jax guessed Dolly was maybe half a mile across.

As the Regg craft continued drifting upward at a steady, careful pace, a bright hole in the bottom of Dolly began to slide open, causing Suzy and Jax to quickly look away to avoid scorched retinas, especially Suzy's. She took off her goggles and Jax lowered his binoculars, so each could view the hole with normal optics, now realizing it wasn't very bright at all. It was more like a soft blue hue glowing from the ceiling of Dolly's bomb bay. Only someone directly underneath would even see it. There was no ring of green LED lights ringing the square portal like the time Jax had to fly the Regg's daughtership up into Little Sister.

Nelson maneuvered the Regg craft expertly into the aperture, and the doors closed tight. Jax raised his binoculars again. Suzy didn't have to put the night-vision apparatus back on; she could see Dolly hanging in the air well enough to know the ship hadn't left yet, presumably needing a few moments to batten down the captured Regg ship for what was going to be a fast trip back to The Desert…wherever that was.

"Glad to have you back safe and sound, Suzy," said the voice through the speaker of Jax's smartphone. "Good job, Jax."

"Thanks, guys!" said Jax.

"Yeah, thanks a million you guys," chimed Suzy. "I owe you one."

"Go get some rest. You'll be hearing from General Middleton soon. Before this night is over, our hairy friends here will be blabbing away, telling us everything we want to know."

"Yeah, thanks to good ol' *blue-be-true*," chuckled Jax. "These Reggs might be vicious, relentless, and ugly, but they sure knew their chemistry."

"Oh, all three mixtures are even better than before," squawked the voice. "Once our Mejan chemists got their hands on those drugs, they not only duplicated them, they improved them."

"Well, how about sending me a batch?" said Suzy, only half joking. "I could use the *gray-to-obey* one on my hubby now and then."

"Will do," laughed the voice. "Y'all take care now."

89

Jax and Suzy watched the void in the stars get smaller and smaller until it disappeared altogether. Remembering the Black Hawk helicopter, Jax scoped over to where it had set down earlier. It too was gone. Without a whisper.

"Speaking of drugs," said Jax, sticking the binoculars in the glove compartment, "they didn't use any on you, did they?"

"No, they didn't," sighed Suzy. "And I was surprised. I was actually hoping they would so I wouldn't be scared, like the last time."

Suzy went on to describe how she was tied to the ceiling while the one Regg measured her head and then eyeball. Jax winched, checking out the red marks around her eye. She left out the part about the thermometer. But they never did any of the other invasive procedures of ten years ago. They mostly just sat on the floor, waiting, drinking the merlot, and staring at her, obviously finding her naked, hairless body curious, if not repugnant.

"I got the feeling these are not the same Reggs," she concluded. "Similar physical features, yet shorter snouts. And the way they looked at me, like they had never seen a human up close before."

"And they didn't use any kind of truth spray on you," nodded Jax, to repeat Suzy's revelation.

"Exactly. "I would have told them anything they wanted to know. So, they either didn't have any with them, which is doubtful, or this is a new bunch of Reggs and they know nothing about these chemicals."

The Jacksons sat silently for a few moments, chewing on the concepts.

"Well, screw 'em," Jax said definitively, clicking his seat belt shut and starting the engine. "Ready to head home?"

Suzy flicked her finger on the silver buckle of the shoulder strap, still hanging loosely by the side panel of the door. "Tell me I don't have to put this thing on," she groaned.

Jax looked over at her. He saw her point. After what…eight hours of being bound up in everything from plastic ties to a shoulder harness, that poor woman deserved her unrestrained freedom…automobile safety procedures be damned. "Of course not, Suzy Q," he smiled sympathetically. "I'll drive carefully."

"Thanks!" she said, sliding over the console again to sit crossways on his lap and render a grateful peck on his lips. "And exactly how far away are we from home, anyway? I guessed about forty minutes by my helicopter ride. And we're mostly due east of Iowa City. Right?"

Jax was amazed. "Very good, honey. You're spot on."

"So, I'll bet we're not far from I-80, are we?"

"Nope. Just eight miles north."

"So, with cruise control and tinted windows," she said seductively, reposition herself to now straddle her man, "we could take the interstate home in the slow lane, huh?"

Chapter 15

"Make yourselves comfortable, people" said the talking-head, belonging to General Joshua Middleton, dressed in his usual sand-colored desert fatigues with two black stars on each lapel, teleconferencing from his secret base in some nebulous location. "I have tales to tell."

The underground communications room at the Brookfield Farm buzzed with anticipation, as everyone took a seat or grabbed a last-minute refill of something. They had been expecting a report from the general sometime today, and his preliminary signal six hours ago gave The Farm time to round up everyone for the two p.m. video chat.

Present were Suzy's parents—Alan and Mary Brookfield—plus Jax, Suzy, and her two younger brothers—David and Mike. The latter's wives were absent, having volunteered to babysit the six children. It was not much of a chore, actually, since the kids loved coming to the farm, what with its new water park and playground equipment that would rival the fanciest resort in Florida. There were also a regulation Little League baseball diamond with actual dugouts, basketball and tennis courts, and of course all those farm animals to throw sticks at and the haymow to play hide-and-seek in. But today's rain forced the kids indoors, so they had to settle for the downstairs recreation room, what with its five state-of-the-art 3D televisions with the latest Dolby X9 Surround Sound, all the latest X-Box 2025 games, five pinball machines, four arcade games, three bowling lanes, two wet bars, and one well-stocked pantry with enough food and drink to challenge 7-Eleven.

Yes, the children were happily occupied, while the adults were down one more level, hiding in the secret communications center to conduct their secret business. The kids couldn't have cared less. And based on what the adults were about to learn, the youngsters would remain in ignorant bliss, at least until they were old enough to learn the truth about the world, The Farm,

The Mansion, The Desert, and their Mejan ancestry. They would also be told about the evil aliens known as *Reggs*. But hopefully that subject would be taught as history, rather than as current events.

"It will come as no surprise to any of you," the general began all business-like, "that our two captives have been most cooperative."

The group twittered, picturing the hairy hostages being sprayed in their dogfaces with the upgraded versions of the *gray-to-obey* chemical, followed immediately by the infallible truth-inducing *blue-be-true*. The Reggs would be falling all over themselves to please their new masters with their most intimate and carefully guarded secrets. Alan, Jax and Suzy knew the effects well, all three having been subjected to the sprays after being kidnapped by the Reggs years ago. Suzy's grandmother, Helen, had been taken hostage along with Alan, the Reggs being most interested in her fifty-percent Mejan pedigree.

Sadly, grandma died five years ago at the age of seventy. She never could completely adapt to Earth's air with its higher-oxygen and lower nitrogen content than her home planet of Meja. So, she often had to wear a gasmask providing extra nitrogen. She was happy to move on.

"And as we expected," continued the general, "this is a whole new pack of those sneaky, paranoid sonsabitches. Their mothership—virtually the same as the other one—was hiding on the moon, deep in the Crisium Basin, which is just inside the western horizon of the so-called *dark side*. So our satellites and telescopes never did notice it."

The general looked down at his datapad and began reading off a checklist of items. "From what our two songbirds know of their own history, it seems they left their depleted home planet at the same time as the other Reggs, but went into different solar systems in search of another world to pillage. When they didn't find one, they came to ours in 1940, arriving fifteen years after the first Reggs got here in 1925, which as you all know was five years before our Mejan ancestors transported in from their home dimension.

"Discovering they were too late, they decided to just hang out on the moon in their island-sized mothership and see how their

93

countrymen handled conquering the earth. They thought that even if the first group was successful, they—the latecomers— could either move in to share the spoils or eliminate the competition altogether. No love lost between Reggs nations. So, they bided their time, upgrading their various spacecraft and weaponry, especially the EMP devices they earlier used on Washington D. C."

When the general paused to take a slug of coffee, Mary used the opportunity to ask, "If I may, General, how were they able to observe any of the goings-on between us and the first Reggs?"

"Like their fellow moochers," said General Middleton, "they make frequent, surreptitious trips to Earth to raid our warehouses. It was during those earlier trips they could eavesdrop on communications between the other Reggs...same frequency and all. Of course, they could never intercept our transmissions, thanks to Suzy's super-duper encryption program that still keeps our frequency impenetrable to this day."

The mild applause by everyone might have been more robust and Suzy's blush a brighter pink were it not for the fact she had written that code over twelve years ago as a teenager, and it was pretty much considered old hat now. Suzy's thoughts at the moment were more along the lines of, *Yeah, but what have I done for you lately, besides getting myself captured for the second time by the enemy?*

The general looked back down at his datapad, and continued. "So, they had a general idea of what their cousins were up to, which, as we all remember, was to kill off most of Earth's population with various pathogenetic pandemics, and then make slaves of the remaining few so they had somebody to grow food and raise livestock to feed them and wait on them hand and foot. These Reggs also have a telescope more powerful than our own Hubble or James Webb Space Telescope, so on clear days they were able to observe a few goings-on."

"Like us escorting their cousins' hairy asses out of the solar system?" asked a cheeky Jax. That brought a round of cheers from the group.

The general was on the spot again. He was the only one in this conference who knew the truth, that the Reggs had been destroyed, not simply driven away. "Uh, yes," he said carefully, "they did watch from the moon. And being certain their fellow Reggs wouldn't return, they saw the door to Earth was wide open. And in they came."

"That spacecraft Suzy was in..." said Jax, "its front end looked like one of their fighters but with a bigger back half."

"Quite true," said Middleton. "Again like their predecessors, a top priority was to kidnap people with Mejan blood. So, they modified a fighter with a larger cargo hold to support up to three hostages, along with the crew of two in the standard cockpit. It has just enough onboard instrumentation to take the hostage's body temperature, head and eyeball size. If verified to be Mejan, the two Reggs were to fly him or her back to the daughtership for a more complete examination and interrogation."

"And if they weren't Mejans?" asked David, the older of Suzy's two brothers.

"You can guess," said the general with a sneer. "This group is as barbaric as the first one. Either way, the hostage would never be seen again."

Suzy's face lost some color. Jax rolled his chair over to behind her. He wrapped his arms around his wife and tenderly kissed the back of her neck. He wished they could have administered the amnesia spray to her as soon as she was rescued last night. But the general and his staff felt it was important Suzy remember everything that happened to her during those eight hours. They needed as many details as possible. Suzy agreed without hesitation. She was one strong woman.

General Middleton looked anxious, shifting his weight from foot to foot, waiting for Jax to finish his empathetic caress of Suzy. He couldn't blame Jax for doing it, or Suzy for needing it. But time was not standing still.

Chapter 16

"If we can continue," said the general. "We still have a lot to cover." All eyes left Jax and Suzy and centered back on Middleton. "So, judging from their use of EMPs instead of diseases, this group is coming at us with a different strategy. But we're not completely clear on their end game. Our two Regg captives—who, by the way, we have named Hose-A and Hose-B—don't know much themselves. Their assignment was to be ready if a prospective target in their designated region of the Midwest was located. As it happened, unfortunately, that was you, Suzy." The general bowed sympathetically. Suzy nodded back with no expression. Jax kissed her neck again.

"From the information Joint Chief General Knox so willingly provided us," continued Joshua Middleton, "the Reggs are saying we are the bad guys, aliens who have infiltrated the planet and its people, with designs on eventually taking over. Whether anyone believes them, doesn't matter. Under the threat of more total blackouts of our major cities, the White House has no choice but to help the Reggs find Mejans.

"From Hose-A and Hose-B we've learned they know we have spacecraft at least equal to theirs, although they never got a good look at any of them. Too far away. Traveling too fast. They did follow one of our craft through a telescope, which was Little Sister, as she escorted the other mothership out of the solar system at sub-light speeds. But all they got was a faraway glimpse of her cute butt.

"They suspect we have secret locations around the globe. The Hose boys didn't know if the plan is to find and destroy us, but it seems the logical thing to do. With us out of their way, they have an easy path to ruling the earth."

"But they have no idea where your base is, do they?" asked Jax. "Hell, we don't even know where you are, General. We never have."

"That's why you never will, nor will anyone who doesn't work here." The general looked directly at Suzy on his monitor. "Suzy darling…imagine if you knew our location and the Reggs had been able to get the truth out of you." Suzy pursed her lips and nodded. A few others in the Brookfield communication room cleared their throats.

General Middleton's face moved closer on the screen. "Listen, folks," he said quieter, as if about to offer a stock tip. "It's time you knew we at The Desert are far more than a covert operation developing state of the art technology, weaponry, and aircraft. We are the planet's protector, *literally*. And I don't mean just from aliens, but from ourselves, as well. No government, including our own, knows there will never be nuclear destruction, thanks to us. I'm not at liberty to divulge any particulars, but suffice it to say any intercontinental ballistic missile launched from any country will not fulfill its mission. The missile will be diverted away from Earth and destroyed with its nuclear payload completely neutralized. That has been *our* primary mission since the end of World War Two. The tensions around the globe between major powers are reaching the breaking point on many fronts. Hell, you know that before Washington's blackout, Putin was about to order his tanks across Poland's boarder. North Korea was about to a test an underground hydrogen bomb for the third time in five years.

"The bottom line, people, is our base and outlets like yours must be protected at all costs. The first Reggs tricked us into revealing our location here at The Desert, and they did some damage. We aren't sure, but we suspect this new batch is not aware of that attack or where we were. But it doesn't matter, because we aren't there anymore."

"What a surprise," said Jax sarcastically.

Alan rose from his chair beside his wife and loaded up the question that had been hanging unasked since the beginning of the conference, "General, what about the spaceship you suspected the Reggs were going to take my daughter to? Surely the Hose boys knew where it was and told you."

Middleton adjusted his aviators and sighed, "They did and they did. Unfortunately, by the time Dolly got there, that ship had sailed."

Three groans. One vulgarity.

The general continued: "When the scout ship with Suzy didn't show up or report in at the time they were expected, the waiting Reggs undoubtedly knew something was wrong and beat feet for parts unknown."

"So, now what?" asked Jax. "We really needed that daughter to lead us to the mother."

General Middleton looked to his right and motioned to someone. "Now that we know the Reggs' M-O for abducting Mejans," he said, putting his hand on the shoulder of the young man coming into frame, "we go to plan-B."

About thirty, five-foot-nine and slender, the handsome man with large blue eyes and shaggy chestnut hair hanging straight down around his shoulders was clearly of Mejan descent, probably the same percentage as Suzy. The black, double bars sewn onto the collar of his desert fatigues said he was a captain in the U. S. Air Force. The name tag said SMITH.

"I'd like you all to meet Captain Gregory Smith," said the general.

Everyone at Brookfield rose to their feet to welcome the young officer with an assortment of social niceties.

"We're sending him out there to Iowa for a while," said the general. "If it's convenient, I trust you can find a room for him at one of your domiciles."

"Oh, no problem," chimed Alan. "Glad to have you, Captain Smith."

"Yes, of course," added Mary. "All our guest houses are occupied with farm hands and their families. But we have an extra bedroom here at the house."

"He could stay at our house in Iowa City," blurted Suzy. "We have lots of extra rooms. Don't we Jax?"

Chapter 17

Reclining far back in his office chair, Jacob Marshall mindlessly looked for an answer in the patterns of the squiggly holes of the ceiling's acoustical panels. He was on the third floor of the New York Times Washington D. C. bureau, trying to decide if it was worth another attempt to get through to Press Secretary Georgia Roman at the White House.

Since those back-to-back blackouts two days ago, there had been yet another one, this time a news blackout. Georgia wasn't returning his calls, even when his latest voice messages said they wouldn't talk shop, just enjoy each other's warm bodies tonight under the covers. Still nothing. Jacob was growing horns in two places: his libido and his need to get to the truth.

Why would the president make her dump such a load of farm-yard manure on the Washington press corps? *Exhibiting a new electromagnetic pulse weapon in order to deter the Russians and everyone else from any kind of aggression.* Yeah, right! The last place a clear-thinking leader of the free world would demonstrate something like that is Washington D.C. He'd hit Moscow or Tehran or Pyongyang. That would really drive the point home. That press conference needed to be filed away some-where between *Fabrication* and *Fallacy.*

Jacob had decided to rule out Pepco or any power utility; they could throw a few switches and knock out all of the city's elec-trical grid, but not everybody's smartphones, including his own. It probably *was* an EMP device, as they were told. But not from our arsenal. He'd say the Russians, except Putin had suddenly pulled his tanks off the Polish border, as if he had taken President Henning's threat seriously. Why would he do that if Russia was the one with the EMP?

The reporter's chiming smartphone on his desktop and the buzzing on his wrist broke his musings. He pushed back the sleeve of his white dress shirt to read the screen: MICHELLE STAMM. He didn't know her. Could be important. He punched OK. "This is Jacob Marshall. What can I do for you?"

There was a moment of silence before a woman cleared her throat and asked, "Is this really the famous Jacob Marshall I see on talk shows and watched at the White House press conference two days ago?"

"Could be," said the hefty, six-one political reporter. "I was there."

"Oh, good." The woman sounded relieved. "I liked the way you challenged the White House's explanation for the blackout. It sounded pretty fishy to me, too."

Jacob waited for something more. When it didn't come, he said, "Is there something I can do for you ma'am?"

"Oh, yes, I'm sorry," she said. "I, ah, my name is Michelle Stamm. I live in Lincoln, Nebraska, not too far from the Corn-husker campus. I saw something strange yesterday, and, well, I feel I needed to tell someone I could trust."

"And you trust *me*?" Jacob loosened his navy-blue tie and smiled.

"Yes. You have impressive credentials and an honest face. I see you on the political talk shows all the time. I read your book, *I C D. C.* All things considered, you're a good reporter."

"Well, thank you, ma'am. I try."

There was another brief pause.

"You still there, Michelle?

"Oh, yes. Sorry. Still here."

"You said you saw something. What did you see?" Jacob was mildly interested, but he had things to do. And now his secretary was motioning for him from the other side of the glass wall.

"Well, I think I saw an alien."

The New York Times reporter pulled the phone away from his mouth so she wouldn't hear his groan. Another crackpot. "An alien, huh? You sure?" He gave his secretary the eye-roll. She smiled knowingly, and walked away.

"I'm pretty sure. He had huge eyes and a head like a water-melon."

Jacob was running out of patience along with his curiosity. "You should call the Enquirer, Michelle. I'm not..."

"No," protested the middle-age woman. "This isn't that kind of thing. This was real. This was not human. At least, his head was not completely human. And it looked like he was being abducted right off the street for no reason."

"Then you should call the Lincoln police."

"That's part of the problem," said Michelle Stamm. "It *was* the police that took him.

"Huh?"

"Yes. The police. It was night. I was walking home from a movie. I had just passed by this man, who I assumed was a student, except he was wearing sunglasses at night and a hoody. Just then this squad car pulls up beside him, and two cops jump out and start talking to him, shining a flashlight in his face. He didn't seem to be doing anything illegal, just walking down the sidewalk. Suddenly they start roughing up the poor man, pulling off his hoody and sunglasses. They hit his face with the flashlight again. That's when I saw the big eyes and head. They quickly shoved him into the squad car. They just sat there for about a minute before finally driving away. Weird, huh?"

Jacob Marshall went into standard placation mode. "Yes, that is rather strange, but there's really nothing I can do. I cover politics. You need a paranormal investigator. I can get you a name, if you'd like."

"No. No," said Michelle adamantly. "As I said. This needs to be investigated by a real reporter. And you're the only one in the media I feel I can trust, even though you are a liberal. I want my name left out of it. I teach third grade."

"Okay," sighed Jacob. "I've got your name and number, Ms. Stamm. I'll poke around, and if I find anything, I'll get back to you. Okay?"

"Oh, thank you!" she gushed. "I knew I could count on you. The media these days is so corrupt…"

"Okay. Thanks for calling. My secretary is getting impatient with me. Gotta go. Good-bye."

*****

Thirty minutes after that strange phone call, Jacob Marshall stood at the window of his office, looking out across Seventeenth Street, just one block north of the White House lawn. The whole fiasco had him baffled, and it was getting less believable by the minute. Electrical blackouts, a news blackout, and now third-grade teachers seeing aliens walking the streets.

Another call came in. This time the small screen said, UN-KNOWN CALLER. It couldn't be one of those telemarketers of yore. They'd been shut down permanently by the Federal Trade Commission two years ago. Besides, Verizon's system of screening incoming calls had gotten so proficient these days, hardly anyone not on his good-guy list could get through to him. But now the second person in half an hour had.

He pulled the smartphone out of his pocket and punched *OK*. "Marshall. What can I do for you?"

The masculine voice wasted no time. "Is your line secure?"

"Ah, yes. It is," said Marshall, his forty-year-old brow scrunched in a mixture of indignation and curiosity.

"You using Verizon's GS-9?" That was the super-secure broadband Verizon offered only to government officials. The media could get it, too, at a healthy premium. Most reporters, like Marshall, who wanted to keep conversations with their *Deep Throat* informants private, felt it was well worth it. Besides, The Times paid for it, not him.

"Of course. Are you?"

"Yes. I'm a police officer."

"Okay. What can I do for you, officer?"

"My name is Jerome Willis. I'm a sergeant with the Iowa City Police department in Iowa City, Iowa. What I have to tell you must remain confidential. Never use my name, or anything about me. Agreed?"

"Okay. Strictly confidential," said Jacob. "What do you have for me?"

"Well, first of all, I'm not a kook. I've been on the force for twenty-two years, with a number of citations. I have a family, one kid in college, one in high school. I love my wife."

"Okay," said the New York Times reporter, "I understand you're not a kook. And I thank you for your service."

"Thanks."

"So, go ahead. What did you want to tell me?"

The officer drew in a breath and said a little quieter, "There's something going on around here that you should investigate."

"Something within your police department?"

"Well, kinda. But it goes far beyond us. Probably all the way up, if you know what I mean."

"The government?" asked the political reporter, getting more interested. This was his beat.

"Yeah. I'd guess at least the NSA or CIA. Maybe the military."

"Sounds serious," said Jacob. "What's it about?"

The sergeant paused, and then spoke even softer, "Two days ago my partner and I arrested someone who we both suspect is not...well, let's say may not be completely human...as in may not be from this planet."

"You're saying you arrested an alien?" There was no skepticism in Jacob's tone. This was the second phone call involving that noun in the past half hour. His interest was rising.

"That's what I'm saying, yeah. She had eyes the size of golf balls and a cranium to match."

Jacob Marshall was at full attention. He slipped out of his light-blue Ralph Lauren sport coat, and draped it over the back of his office chair. "Anything else that made her seem alien?"

"That's the strange part," said Willis. "Other than that, she was normal looking. Quite sexy, actually. Cute. Petite. Thirty. Spoke perfect English. Acted totally American. Had a driver's license. An Iowa City address."

"I trust you got her name."

"We did. It's Susan Hines. Lives at 306 North Clinton Street here in town. Birth year 1995."

"So why did you arrest her?" asked Jacob, writing all this down on his e-pad.

"That's the other strange thing," said Jerome Willis. "During the morning's briefing at HQ, we were given this hand-held device that registers infrared and body mass. My partner and I were ordered to do periodic scans around populated areas, like shopping malls. We were to look for anyone whose body temperature registered lower than normal and had a disproportionately large head. That device was so sensitive it could detect a difference of one tenth of one degree in body temperature, and any unusual head-to-body ratio. So, if it found someone registering below 98.6, plus with an oversized head, it started flashing."

"And it did when you scanned this Susan Hines person," offered Jacob.

"Exactly."

The Iowa City police sergeant went on to describe confronting the woman in the parking lot, removing her hat and sunglasses, taking her to the station to hand her over to the chief at the back door, and then being told to go back on patrol and discuss the arrest with no one, including his fellow officers.

"What happened to her?" asked Jacob.

"We were never told. The whole thing was on a strict, need-to-know basis. All we found out later was that a military chopper landed in our rear parking lot and took right off again. We assume she was onboard."

"Anything else you can tell me?" asked Jacob, scrolling through phone numbers on his wrist-phone.

"No. That's about it. The whole thing is real hush-hush. We are told nothing except to say nothing."

"So, why are you breaking the rules and telling me?"

"I don't know," sighed Willis. "I guess I'm kind of a sci-fi buff…UFOs and all that E. T. shit. If we do have aliens walking among us, I want to know all about it. And I think the general public has a right to know, don't you…being a reporter and all? That's what you guys do, isn't it: dig out the dirt?"

"We try," said Marshall, his mind mostly on finding that specific phone number, as he scrolled through the address book on his smartphone.

The conversation fell silent for a moment before Officer Willis said, "Well, all I ask is that you let me know what you find out. And please keep my name out of it."

"Will do," said Jacob. "And if anything more pops up at your end, you have my number."

"Roger that. Thanks. Bye."

Jacob Marshall found the number he wanted and wasted no time dialing it.

Chapter 18

Dressed in jeans and a white polo shirt, Jax Jackson flipped on the ceiling LEDs, illuminating his basement's workout room. He led Suzy and Captain Gregory Smith through and around the two treadmills, one NordicTrack elliptical, a Bowflex Home Gym, two exercise mats, and a rack of free weights.

"If you ever get the urge to work out..." said Jax, purposely ribbing their new house guest, whose slender physique under the tan slacks and forest-green Under Armor pullover suggested he and such equipment were not on intimate terms, "instruction manuals are tucked under each machine."

"Thanks," said Gregory, looking left and right at the various pieces of equipment. He was not as weak or out of shape as Jax would believe. The Desert had all these apparatuses in the latest state-of-the-art models, plus some incredible vitamin and protein supplements that added strength and energy without adding much muscle mass. These wonder drugs were still in the experimental stage and not yet ready to be leaked to the outside world. But they had worked wonders on the thirty-year-old captain.

"Don't listen to him, Greg," said Suzy, playfully squeezing the sinewy arm of her fellow one-eighth Mejan. "He hardly uses any of this stuff himself anymore."

Ignoring the jab, Jax flipped switches on a few machines to show off their various functions. Greg took the opportunity to look down at his hostess in her apricot boy shorts and white, strapless halter top. She looked up, her large copper-browns locking on his equally-sized baby-blues. He smiled. She smiled back. There was no denying the connection.

For him, she was a pixie-cute, kindred spirit, who shared all the pros and cons of being part Mejan...from being revered for their highly-intelligent lineage to hiding their abnormal features from the uniformed world. It was sad they had to fear being looked at, if not as freaks, at least as oddities not to be trusted and certainly not to become intimate with. It wouldn't matter to most people that in all other aspects they were just as human as the humans.

For Suzy, it was exactly the same. Plus, she found it so delightful to be looked at by a very handsome male, who saw her Mejan features as attractive—the way Jax used to look at her—rather than detractive. Even the cops that dragged her down to the station house seemed to find her pretty, despite their alarm at her atypical appearance.

The basement tour stopped at the far, windowless wall in front of a huge poster of Tiger Woods fist-pumping his win of the 2005 Masters Tournament. The framed print ran from floor to eight-foot ceiling and was anchored solidly to the ivory-colored Sheetrock.

"Tap Tiger's fist three times," said Jax, doing exactly that. The poster immediately shifted to the left with hardly a sound, clearing the entrance to a set of stairs and triggering a soft LED light inside. Greg and Suzy followed Jax down the ten gray-carpeted steps, landing in front of a door with a lighted keypad. "Two, zero, zero, five," said Jax, tapping the appropriate keys. "Same year Tiger won that Masters." The four-inch steel door opened on its hinges and The Mansion's panic suite came into view.

"It's actually a six-room apartment," said Suzy, stepping inside, the other two following. "It has everything up to eight people would need in case of an emergency lasting two months. There are three bedrooms, a kitchen with fully-stocked pantry, two bathrooms, and as you can see the living area is well-appointed with leather furniture, two wall televisions, computers, etcetera."

"Odett and Loretta know the code, and so do the kids," said Jax. "They are to use it only if there is an emergency or when okayed by Suzy or me."

Greg Smith was led farther in, past the kitchen, into a ten-by-ten room that obviously was an office. It had two computer workstations facing each other, a shared printer, a file cabinet, the works. Jax sat down at one of the computers and took it out of sleep mode. He typed a short something on the keyboard and the office's only bookshelf swung away from the wall with a hiss, revealing The Mansion's communications center.

"It's patterned after The Farm's," said Suzy, walking into the center of the room and doing a slow spin. "We had it and the panic room built right after we were married. The code is nine, star, eight, pound."

"I trust you used *local* contractors," grinned Greg, easing into the twenty-by-twenty room.

"Oh, yeah," said Jax. "There are more Mejan blue-collar workers in southeast Iowa than you may think."

"We know exactly how many there are," smiled Greg.

Jax and Suzy just shook their heads. Of course he knew; he came from The Desert.

On the north wall of the electronics-jammed room were four, eighty-inch, HD-3D television screens, three of them tuned to a major cable news channel. The fourth continually rotated among the major networks, stopping when it found something interesting.

Filling up the east wall were four more large screens, each a perfect square and not actual television sets. One was the National Weather Service radar, spanning all of North America. Two were live satellite feeds from space, one from The Desert's own Sentry 3, which had tracked Suzy during her perilous journey from shopping at the mall to hanging in a Regg spaceship. The other was perpetually hacking into the classified military satellite, USA-129.

The fourth square screen was connected to The Mansion's own radar in the backyard, hidden under an opaque dome of thin Mylar, sitting atop the three-story playhouse. Angled forty-five degrees skyward, its constant rotation scanned all horizons and vertically up to the heaven's zenith. With an effective range of some thousand miles, it could spot aircraft or birds or any solid object in the sky. Ten years ago its main purpose was to detect unique, heat-seeking infrared rays from Regg scanners, which limited its range to only ten miles or so on a clear day. But when that threat ended, it became the sentry for any flying object larger than a crow approaching The Mansion. If Suzy and/or the kids were outside and exposed, their smart phones beeped a warning to take cover, while the privacy roof over the pool area was automatically triggered to close. The screen's circular sweep over a green grid of concentric lines revealed no present activity within a hundred yards.

Turning another ninety degrees to the south wall brought into view the four computer work stations, replete with twenty-four-inch LCD monitors on short pedestals with their built-in lightning-fast processors, ten terabyte memories, plus standard wireless keyboards and mice. All were lined up along a fifteen-foot, beige-colored Formica table, free-standing on the hardwood floor by steel frames and legs. Suzy felt at home here, since it did so closely match the communications room of her childhood back at The Farm. This one, however, always smelled newer, plus with a touch of Jax's aftershave.

Greg looked all around the room, then said, "And I'd guess one of these walls opens to the fighter we sent you after construction here was completed."

Jax pointed to the east wall. "Right you are." He walked over and put his thumb on the lower right-hand corner of the television screen farthest to the right. "Jax Jackson," he said loud and clear. "Open." The wall split down the middle and folded in on itself. A soft green light revealed the backend of the two-man fighter, exactly like Fighter-One and Fighter-Two under the pond at The Farm. "There she is: Fighter-Three, our very own, under *our* pond. C'mon over and we'll program you in, in case you ever need it."

Greg walked over as Jax closed the wall with a simple "Close." He then pressed the same spot on the screen and said, "Jax Jackson. Program new user." He motioned for Greg to step closer, whispering, "Just put your..."

"I know how," interrupted Greg, putting his thumb in the same place. "Greg Smith, new user," he said into the screen. A green light above his thumb blinked three times. "Greg Smith, open," he repeated, and the wall reopened. "We use the same coding at The Desert."

"Jax Jackson. Close," said Jax, a little irritated. The wall obeyed. He spun around and walked over to the platinum-finished refrigerator in the far corner by the door. "Have a seat. Want anything to drink? Beer? Pop? Water?"

"Water would be fine," said Greg, pulling out one of the office chairs tucked under a work station.

"Honey?"

She was already seated in her own office chair. "Nothing. Thanks."

Jax handed a Dasani water to Greg and opened a bottle of Pabst Blue Ribbon for himself. He leaned against the computer table and said, "So, whadda ya think of our little set up, Captain?"

"Quite impressive," said Greg, looking around, although the room had nothing on his personal office space back at The Desert. "I love your house, if you can call it that. It *is* more of a mansion. I can see why you call it that. All the rooms. The massive kitchen and six-stall garage. Your guest bedroom here is three times the size of my bedroom back home. And your own personal maids. I could get used to this."

"You are welcomed here as long as you wish," said Suzy, patting the top of his hand. "We want you to make yourself at home."

"Speaking of which," said Jax, "are we still not allowed to know why you're here?"

"I'm afraid not," sighed Captain Gregory Smith. "It's better that you remain on a need-to-know basis, for your own safety and well-being."

Suzy squirmed in her chair. Her sense of foreboding was growing even more. "Can you at least tell us how long you will be here?" she said. "If for no other reason than we need to tell Loretta and Odett how to plan for meals and such."

"Fair enough," said Greg. "I will probably be here at least a couple days. They said I should get settled in and learn the lay of the land first. Then they will contact me."

"Well, just say the word and I'll drive you around town," said Jax. "Show you the sights. Get you orientated. Iowa City is only about sixty-thousand people, counting students at the university. The Iowa River has the streets all screwed up, but it won't take long to learn your way around…for whatever reason you need to."

Greg didn't take the bait. He just smiled and said thanks.

Chapter 19

Brady Leach had been waiting for a solid lead like this all his X-files-loving life. And to get it from someone of Jacob Marshall's stature was mind-blowing. He and the New York Times' top Washington, D. C. reporter had talked only once before, when Brady—the author of twelve books on UFOs and the publisher/editor of *Sightings Magazine*—called Jacob regarding a UFO sighting five years ago. A number of locals including two White House security guards reported three triangular-shaped lights in the night sky that hovered for about a minute over the area, and then simply disappeared. Andrews Air Force Base said they saw nothing on radar, and the raptors patrolling the skies saw nothing as well. So, the incident was filed away under *Unknown*, along with a dozen others around the D. C. area in the past eighty years. But Jacob Marshall had promised Brady Leach he would be the first to know if anything else regarding unexplained phenomenon came across his desk.

And here it was: 306 North Clinton Street, at the end of a col-de-sac in Iowa City, just one block from where he was parked.

He had been waiting and watching for six hours, when thankfully, at five-twenty in the afternoon, a green Ford Focus rolled into the driveway. The door of the two-car, attached garage opened revealing no other vehicle, before it swallowed up the Ford and swung closed. Brady had gotten a brief look at the driver as she drove by him. Her profile looked like a normal young lady's.

The UFO investigator wasn't really surprised. If it were Susan Hines, and she had ordinary head and eyes, the story of her abduction by the Iowa City policemen was just cock and bull. On the other hand, if the story and description were true, and Susan truly were an alien, she was probably hundreds of miles away right now, sequestered in some secret government facility, being examined by a team of lab technicians specializing in extraterrestrial physiology. There was no way in hell the abducted alien would come driving up home as if nothing had happened.

But this address Jacob Marshall had given him, along with a description of Susan Hines, were the only leads he had. He knew that going in. So, he was happy at least somebody had entered the residence. Even if she weren't Susan, the occupant had to know something about her. At the very least, he would gather some truth about this odd abduction reported to Jacob Marshall via an Iowa City policeman.

Brady ran a brush through his thinning chestnut hair and checked it in the flip-open mirror behind the car's sun visor. He grabbed the folding notebook off the passenger seat and slid out of his 2025 Mitsubishi Eclipse rental, looking left and right for anyone watching him. No one around or coming, he adjusted his white polo shirt to cover his ample waistline, checked his zipper, and plucked his black Haggar slacks from the backs of his legs. He hated the Midwest's humidity. He'd take the scorching dry heat of his Nevada home any day.

The paranormal fanatic sauntered the hundred yards along the curved sidewalk of the col-de-sac, and then ascended the two cement steps leading up to Susan Hines's front door to ring the doorbell. It was a full minute before someone opened the door. The woman was under thirty, petite, and quite attractive, as Jacob had described Susan Hines, and Officer Willis had told Jacob. But while her brown eyes were noticeably big and bright, they were hardly alien. And the size of her head seemed typically human, as well. But like everyone else, Brady was fooled by the woman's auburn hair being cut in a stylish bob to deemphasize the extra girth of the one-sixteenth Mejan's head.

"May I help you?" asked Deborah Collingsworth, keeping the screen door more closed than open.

"Susan Hines?" asked Brady, looking down at his opened notebook, then up at her.

"She's not here right now." Deborah made sure her tone was less than friendly, the impatient kind one uses with an unwelcomed solicitor, which this balding, beady-eyed, middle-aged man probably was.

"Oh," said Brady. "When do you expect her back?"

"I have no idea. I'm just her tenant. I live downstairs. We hardly see each other, and we certainly don't keep track of the other's comings and goings."

111

"Well, it's important that I speak with her," said Brady. "Do you know where she works?"

"No, I don't. What's this about, anyway?"

Brady pulled out his wallet and showed Deborah the fake identification. "I'm Frank Archer, FBI. A witness saw Susan being approached by two Iowa City police officers outside the Century Mall four days ago, and then placed in their patrol car and driven away. There are no records of her being booked or even brought in to the police station. She is now an official missing person."

"Who reported her missing?" Deborah knew that was a good question to this obvious phony, who knew nothing about the actual events of the past four days, including Suzy being safe at The Mansion as they spoke.

"I wasn't given that detail. I'm just supposed to try and locate her."

"I assume you questioned the arresting officers," said Deborah.

"Of course," lied Brady. "They said it was on suspicion of shoplifting. They don't know what happened to her after they brought her in."

"So, no one at the station knows anything, huh?" said Deborah with a theatrical sigh of sympathy.

"That's right," he lied again. Not enjoying being cross-examined, Brady Leach quickly flipped the interrogation. "May I have your name, ma'am?"

"It's Deborah Collingsworth."

Brady wrote it down. "And when was the last time you saw Susan, Deborah?"

"Like I said, we hardly ever see each other. I honestly don't remember. It could have been a few days. A week. I just live here...in the basement."

"Surely you have a phone number where I could reach her," said Brady, pleased to throw some snobbish indignation back at the hostile woman.

Deborah couldn't deflect that one. Of course she would have a number to call her landlady in case of an emergency. "Just a minute," she huffed, letting the screen door close on its pneumatic piston. She returned a minute later and without a word handed a small piece of paper to the man.

Brady Leach nodded his thanks, scratched his phone number on a corner of his tablet, tore it off and gave it to her. "Please call me if Susan shows up," he said over his shoulder, exiting the premises. Deborah just smiled and shut the door. *Some FBI agent; doesn't even have a business card.* But she would certainly be calling Suzy straight away with this disquieting bit of news.

Back in his rental car, Brady dialed the number supposedly connected to Susan Hines.

"Hi, this is Susan. Sorry I can't take your call right now. Please leave your name, number, and a short message."

Brady snorted. What did he expect? *"Hi, this is Susan, the presumptive alien you're looking for. Leave your name and number and I'll get right back to you, so you can expose me to the whole world and go collect your Pulitzer."*

Brady picked pensively at his nose. He may not have located an extraterrestrial directly, but the extended absence of one Susan Hines at her registered address, plus the possible cover-up by her so-called tenant, suggested this case was worth further investigation. The question was what to do now. Of course, he would call Jacob Marshall and report his findings. But then what… stay right here and wait for some long-gone alien with a fake name to show up at this fake address? That would require some serious thought.

Chapter 20

Jax was a hundred miles away at the Muscatine Pool of the Mississippi River, fishing his bass club's monthly two-day tournament. He wasn't sure he should attend, considering all that was happening these past few days with the blackout, the reappearance of some Reggs, his wife's abduction, and their new house guest. But Suzy echoed The Desert's urging him to go, saying it was important to maintain normal appearances. Besides, he needed a break. She and Greg would be fine.

And they were fine, lounging at the pool under the open roof, soaking up the sun, while Nicole and Nathan practiced summersaults off the low board, obviously showing off for their new guest, something extremely rare at their house.

Feeling more self-confident than she had in years, thanks to the fellow one-eighth Mejan beside her, Suzy had on no hat, no sunglasses, and almost no swimsuit. With her insistence, Captain Gregory Smith had reluctantly borrowed navy-blue trunks from Jax's personal walk-in closet, the price tags having to be cut off. The trunks' thirty-four-inch waist was four inches too big for his slender hips, but the draw string solved the issue just fine.

"So, did Jax show you everything around our fair city you needed to see?" Suzy asked from her supine position on the lime-green chaise lounge, rotating her head to look at their visitor on his secret mission.

"Yes, he did," said Greg, purposely not looking at her, as he had been avoiding as much as possible during his two-day stay out here. "It's a beautiful town. Green everywhere. Clean air. Bustling."

Everything about his hostess was bewitching, from her Mejan features to her sky-high IQ to her girlish charm. And now there she lay, virtually naked under the June sun, just half a reach away. There were plenty of woman at The Desert, some as Mejan as Suzy and himself. He was even in a semi-relationship with a pure human named Clarissa, with whom, if they ever got married, their offspring would be only one-sixteenth Mejan, virtually undetectable, like Nicole and Nathan. But just how serious he and Clarissa were was still in question. The slight difference in their heritage was an ongoing, unspoken riff that maybe wasn't so slight. It was sad, in a way, that even in The Desert's environment of futuristic technology and parity and harmony and tolerance, that racism could still be hiding in some dark corners.

So, if he weren't careful, this Iowa City woman could get real dangerous real quick. And that couldn't happen. She was married, and he was here for one reason only.

"So, what's it like living at *The Desert*?" said Suzy casually. "If I'm allowed to ask."

Greg took a moment to choose his words. He was under orders to reveal basically nothing about the clandestine organization and location…even to The Desert's most revered associates. It was for their own safety. "It's okay," he said straight forward. "We have everything we need. Busy every day. Exciting challenge after exciting challenge."

"I know you are underground, literally," said Suzy, prying a little farther. "But do you ever come up for air, so to speak?"

"Oh, sure," laughed Greg. "Quite often, actually. We're not moles. We are as free to roam the earth as you are. Some of us just have to be careful…" he reached over and patted Suzy's head, "as you know."

Suzy took the opportunity to quickly grab and squeeze his hand before he pulled it back. "Guess I wasn't so careful," she sighed.

"Hey, it was hardly your fault," he said, squeezing back, the electricity noticeable and ever-so pleasant. "With your hat and sunglasses, you were doing everything you could."

Suzy let go of his hand, but not because she wanted to. Nathan's holler for Mom and *Uncle Greg* to watch his next attempt at a one-and-a-half snapped her back to reality. "Go for it, honey!" she yelled back. Nathan's fifty-pounds barely bent the board, and he landed flat on his back with a loud smack. "You okay? Suzy called. The seven-year-old waved that he was, and climbed right back on the low board for another try. This time he rotated enough to hit the water feet-first.

"So, how do you hide your features," continued Suzy, turning her attention back to the captain, "when you go out among the ignorant?"

"Sunglasses, of course," he said, adjusting his black Ray-Bans. "And what my shaggy mop here doesn't hide, I deflect by wearing shoulder padding."

"Yeah, I do that, too, during cold weather," she said. "Not so easy in the summer."

The enigmatic Desert had always fascinated Suzy, and here sat one of its denizens, just as mysterious. Now that she had the captain opening up a little, she was really getting into him, in a way never before experienced...even with Jax during the early days. It wasn't sexual. Well, not intentionally so. She wasn't sure what it was...only that she didn't want it to end.

"How exactly do you come and go?" Suzy pushed on. "I mean, does the sand just open up and swallow you, like in the sci-fi movie, *Invaders from Mars*?"

"Hardly," laughed Gregory. "I suppose it may seem that way to you civilians. But we come and go as overtly as business men walking in and out of an office building."

Suzy's mind was racing. Of course! There had to be some kind of a façade above ground, masking the secret facilities below. The Desert may not even be in a desert at all. It could be anywhere. But it had to be at some out-of-the-way location easily accessible and clandestine enough to move a large, underground facility without being seen. General Middleton had mentioned that The Desert had moved since the first wave of Reggs had found it. That had to be some undertaking! They probably used ultrasound to burrow underground in some remote area late at night, just like when Suzy's Grandma Helen and family first came to Iowa over thirty years ago. They had buried their spacecraft under The Farm in only twelve minutes. The Mejans had long ago harnessed the incredible power of sound wave energy. The first group of Reggs used it too, but to a much lesser degree. They usually hid underwater.

"General Middleton mentioned you had to move The Desert ten years ago," said Suzy, knowing it was hopeless, but worth a try anyway.

"We did. After the Reggs hit us with those bunker-busters to destroy their spacecraft you had captured, we had no choice."

"That must have been quite an operation."

"It was. But we were successful. No one was the wiser."

"Don't suppose you can tell me where you are now."

"Sorry. Highly classified."

"Or where you were before."

"Sorry."

"Or what your mission is while here." *Worth a shot.*

Captain Smith's smile was wide and sympathetic. "Sorry, Suzy. I'd love to tell you. But I can't."

Suzy let out a big sigh. "Swing and a miss. Strike three."

"Don't take it too hard," soothed Greg. "You know it's for your own protection. Besides, you'll probably find out soon enough."

Two soggy little hands were pulling on Greg's wrists, while another pair from an equally-waterlogged sibling tugged firmly at Suzy's. "C'mon, Mom," pleaded nine-year-old Nicole, "let's play pool hoops."

"Yeah," said Nathan, just as adamantly to his new Uncle Greg, "you and me...guys against the girls. We'll kick their butts."

"No way, lil' brat-brother," countered Nicole. "You won't even get a shot off. I'll ram it down your throat every time."

It took another round of begging by the pair of one-sixteenth Mejans before the two one-eighth Mejans finally and reluctantly gave in. But once the game began, Suzy and Greg were well into it. It was the most fun Suzy had had treading water in the deep end of the garden pool in years.

Greg Smith was doing everything he could to keep from touching some part, *any* part, of his opponent. He knew it might lead to something he would enjoy far more than he was allowed to. But avoiding contact wasn't easy, considering he was sup-posed to keep her from throwing the soggy, yellow Nerf ball through the round rim and net attached to the end of the diving board. The first two times he purposely gave Suzy a free shot, Uncle Greg heard about it loud and clear from his competitive, young teammate. So, when the long-armed captain easily blocked the next attempt from the short-armed mother, he received cheers from Nathan and a face-full of pool water from Suzy. That's when the real game began.

Greg splashed her back. With an *Oh, Yeah?!* Suzy dived underwater, grabbing both his ankles and pulling him down with her. He opened his eyes to locate his aggressor, then quickly jackknifed to reach down and latch onto her wrists, pulling them away from his ankles. Suzy broke free from his grasp, and both pair of hands locked fingers, palms-to-palms, face-to-face. After a few playful push-pulls, they released bilaterally and headed for the surface and air.

"C'mon, Mom," whined Nicole. "Nathan scored while you were under water. It's not fair!"

"One, zip," smirked Nathan, tossing the yellow orb a little too hard to his sister. "Your ball."

The game of pool hoops quickly got out of hand. Nicole threw the waterlogging Nerf ball right back at her little brother from a distance of six feet, nailing him smack on his forehead. Instead of tears, Nathan lunged at his sister, pushing her under the water, like he had seen the adults do a moment ago. Joining in, Suzy surprised Greg again with another roundhouse, her open hand catching the surface of the pool just right to send a small tsunami into his unsuspecting face. He countered with a tidal wave of his own toward her face. But this time, as Suzy turned her head to avoid the onrush of water, Greg kicked forward, grabbed her shoulders and pushed her underwater. Figuring she would go for his ankles as before, he pushed himself away from her, keeping his feet far out of reach.

When Suzy didn't come up right away or make any attempt to retaliate, Greg assumed she was baiting him to submerge again. He could see her aquatically-distorted figure directly below him, apparently not moving. Maybe she wasn't able to take in a lungful of air before he shoved her under. Maybe she didn't know how to swim. Scratch that one.

Just in case Suzy was in jeopardy, Greg dived under, eyes wide open. He found her drifting lifelessly half way to the drain about seven feet down, her arms and legs limp at her side. Still suspicious, he frog-kicked to reach her and pull her into his arms. She didn't respond.

Before he could turn to drag her lifeless body upward, Suzy suddenly hugged her lifesaver right back. One big bubble of air with a question mark left Greg's mouth, followed by a second bubble with an exclamation point. Through the blur of the water he saw her mouth spread into a broad smile as her big copper-brown eyes flashed. In turn, Suzy saw Greg's face flicker from apprehension to relief...then to longing.

No one knows what might have happened next, because the suntanned bodies of two slender youths were suddenly among them, wanting to join in the subsurface fun. Suzy let go of Greg and wrapped her arms around both Nicole and Nathan. She gave each a smooch, then kicked for the surface, in need of oxygen.

All four bodies popped up one-by-one like bobbers, laughing and sucking 0-2. Above the ruckus, Suzy could barely hear her smartphone chiming. She checked her smart-watch: it was Jax. She swam to the pool's edge behind the diving board where her phone lay, blinking and chiming and buzzing.

"How's the fishing, sweetheart?" she panted, brushing water from her face.

"Pretty slow," said Jax. "The river's muddy and the backwaters are quickly clouding up. I managed a limit of five keepers before the mud-line overtook the slough I was working. I'm in second place."

"That's nice," said Suzy half-heartedly, turning to look back at the others.

"Is that Dad?" asked Nicole.

"Did he catch anything?" piped Nathan, purposely louder than his big sister.

"He got a few. He's in second place."

"When's he coming home?"

"I assume you still plan to be home tomorrow evening sometime," said Suzy into her phone, maybe a little too loudly. Her eyes shifted from her kids to Greg, who was still treading water.

119

"Yeah, I should be there in time for supper. Tell Odett her fried chicken would really hit the spot."

"Okay. We'll see you then. Good luck tomorrow."

With her free hand, Suzy hand-walked over to the ladder and climbed out of the pool, ignoring the protests from her scamps to continue the game. "You kids have been in there long enough," she called back, grabbing her towel from the chaise lounge. You look like prunes."

"Aw, Mom," pleaded Nicole. "Ten more minutes. Please. The score is tied."

"You heard me. Out, now. Hit the showers, and you both can have an hour of *Doom Extreme* before supper."

That sounded mighty good to Nathan and Nicole. It did to Suzy, too...the shower that is, in The Mansion's master bath with its five pulsating, temperature-controlled shower heads...hitting her from five different angles...rinsing the chlorine off her skin and out of her hair...while someone with the deft touch of a master masseuse washed her back in slow, gentle, soapy strokes...like she was the most precious creature on the face of the earth.

If only.

Chapter 21

Suzy had just finished blow-drying her hair and was putting the final touches on her brunette bob-cut with a brush when she thought she heard a soft knocking on the bedroom door. Completely naked, she quickly threw on her pink cashmere bathrobe and shuffled across the thirty feet of white berber carpeting. "Someone there?" she said, her hand pausing on the leveled door handle.

"It's me." His voice was barely above a whisper. "You decent?"

Suzy's heart quickened. A dozen scenarios flashed through her mind...all of them as exciting as they were impossible. Before her imagination could take over, she opened the door to find bare legs and feet sticking out from under one of her husband's cashmere bathrobes, this one in navy-blue with white trim. As she scanned upward, the man's slender build and then his handsome face with huge baby-blues and shaggy hair still wet from the shower made it perfectly clear this was not Jax, home a day early from his tournament.

Suzy's eyes grew rounder, wider, unblinking. Her tongue subconsciously moistened her lips. Her heart rate doubled. She knew her fellow Mejan had been holding himself in check for the past two days, just as she had, and especially during the semi-harmless flirting in the pool half an hour earlier. Had he succumbed to his obvious desire to be with her? Would she be able to resist him?

The sudden snap to reality almost hurt physically. *She was married! This was her husband's family mansion.* From the noise downstairs, *they still had kids,* obviously in the TV room playing video games, but capable of a surprise attack any minute. From the smell of sautéed garlic and onions circling up the stairway, Odett and Loretta were in the kitchen fixing dinner.

On the other hand, this bedroom door *was* quite soundproof. And its satin nickel handle had *a lock.*

Unfortunately, or perhaps fortunately, there were two things suggesting this was not a social call. One was Greg holding his smartphone up as if he wanted to show her something on its screen. The other was the stern look on his face, as if the news wasn't good.

"Sorry to intrude on your privacy, Suzy," he said, wagging his smartphone, "but I just got the call from The Desert. It's time for me to go."

Although Suzy knew this was coming, it blindsided her harder than she thought it would. She hardly knew this man on a secret mission, yet she missed him already.

Looking both ways down the hall, Suzy grabbed Greg's arm and pulled him into the bedroom. She eased the door closed, then spun to face the surprised captain. "When?" she said flatly.

"Tonight. After sunset."

"Where?"

"Someone needs to drop me off at the Century Mall."

The Century Mall! The quick-witted Suzy now knew for certain exactly why Captain Gregory Smith had come to Iowa City.

"You're setting yourself up to be abducted, aren't you?" she said, her voice trembling with both concern and anger.

Greg nodded and dropped his eyes. "You figured it out. I knew you would."

"I suspected as much the day you arrived," she said, walking over to sit down on the satiny white bedspread of the California king. "And starting at the Century Mall pretty much confirms it. It's the same mall where I was scanned with infrared and then arrested by the two police officers."

"I know," sighed the captain, joining her on the bed, his hands on his lap.

"You're going to let them take you, so The Desert can track you, so you can complete what I didn't."

He didn't look at her. He kept his head down. "Yes, we really need to locate one of their daughterships," Greg said, now laying one hand on the back of hers. "Hopefully, that should provide a clue to where the mothership is hiding. It is mandatory we flush the Reggs out. Things are going south quickly."

122

Suzy laid her free hand on top of his and craned her head to look him hard in his blue eyes. "Why? Has something else happened?"

Greg drew in a breath and said more business-like, "We're getting reports of one-eighth Mejans like us disappearing...all across the Midwest, and particularly in college towns."

"Oh, my God," groaned Suzy, squeezing his hand. "I was afraid of this. Just like last time."

"So far," said Greg, "none of the missing is in our network. They know next to nothing to tell the Reggs. So, we're safe in that respect. But..."

"But they don't have tracking transmitters in their scalps like we do," Suzy finished for him. "So, there is no way to find them."

"Exactly," said Greg, letting go of Suzy's hands and getting to his feet. He walked to the middle of the large bedroom and looked at the ceiling. "And no one has yet been returned. Nor do we expect them to be, considering the Reggs' known savagery."

Suzy's eyes narrowed to angry slits. "So, under threats of knocking out our cities, they'll just keep blackmailing our police and military to find us Mejans, then sort through them like a deck of cards until they find an ace who can tell them where The Desert is."

"That's what we assume," said Greg, bowing his head again. "The Reggs feel they must find and destroy our headquarters, before they can ever lay claim to the earth. We are their major stumbling block."

Suzy slipped off the bed and joined Greg in the middle of the room, his back still to her. She reached around and hugged him hard, burying her face in the soft robe above his shoulder blades. Neither said anything for a long moment.

Suzy finally released her hold and pivoted to Greg's front. She maternally smoothed the collar of his bathrobe, looked into his eyes, and said with manufactured sternness, "And how exactly do you plan to escape?"

Captain Gregory Smith looked down on his darling hostess and smiled, "Oh, I have ways."

"Yeah? Like what?"

Greg was hesitant to tell her. But her eyes kept insisting. He eased free from the hands still smoothing his collar and walked to the floor-to-ceiling curtains hiding the dual sliding doors leading out to the balcony. He parted the ivory-colored curtains and said to the late-afternoon sky, "Well, I plan to hijack a daughter-ship and get the crew to tell me where the mother is hiding."

"Oh, I see," scoffed Suzy. "Just like that."

"Yeah, just like that," he grinned, turning around to face her. "You ought to know. You and Jax hijacked that one ten years ago."

"Well, yeah, maybe," blithered Suzy, "but Jax did it while I was goofy on the drugs...and he got all the Reggs on the drugs, too...so it was fairly easy."

"So?" smiled Greg.

"So, how are you gonna do it without the drugs? You can't carry the spray bottles with you. If the cops don't take them away from you, the Reggs will. And either way they'll end up using them on you. You'll have no choice but to blab everything, including where The Desert is located. Game over!"

Greg stepped forward and cupped Suzy's face in his hands. "I appreciate your concern, sweetheart, but we've got it covered."

"How?"

Again Greg balked. He didn't want to come off as bragging, but how else could he? "Well, for starters it seems I'm master status in both the Marines' MCMAP form of martial arts and Israeli's Krav Maga. I can either kill or immobilize a Regg in five different ways. We know from the pair that kidnapped you, they have little concept of self-defense outside of lasers and sonic blasters and knocking you over with their bad breath."

"Okay, but you still need them alive to tell you where the daughtership is."

"Oh, I won't use anything on them until I'm on that daughtership," said Greg. "I'll just let the scout ship take me there like a good little captive. Once onboard, we assume they will immediately interrogate me. That's when I'll take over the craft and get all the intel out of the crew I need to find mother."

"How?" snorted Suzy. "By beating them senseless?"

Greg cocked a smile. "Drugs."

"Drugs?!"

"Drugs! You didn't think they'd send me in there unarmed, did you?"

Suzy's skeptical smile got even wider. "So, where are you hiding them on your body? Show me."

Greg held up both his thumbs. When he did or said nothing more, Suzy sneered, "Okay. I know you have it covered. C'mon. Can't you tell me?"

"I am telling you," laughed the captain. "The drugs are in a pair of fake thumbs back in my room, like magicians use to hide scarves and things."

"Clever," said Suzy, grabbing his thumbs, even though she knew they were still the real thing. "Tell me more."

Greg led her over and sat her down on the bed, while he stood before her to demonstrate. He held his right thumb close to his belly. "From the invaluable information you were able to supply us about your abduction last week, we have a pretty good idea how mine will go. I'll probably be handcuffed to my waist like you were. And since I'm considerably bigger than you, the Reggs will probably leave on my restraints throughout the whole ordeal, and tether me to a wall or the ceiling that way. No problem. At some point at least one of them will get his face within five feet of my stomach. All I have to do is squeeze the false thumb between my thumb and forefinger, and the stream of a lovely chemical cocktail floods his face. Within two seconds, he's mine."

"He'll do anything you say," said Suzy, nodding through the thought.

"Yep."

"As in, *unshackle me...*"

"Yep...if he has the key. If not, I'll tell him to go get it. This new drug is so fantastic, he won't appear to be drugged at all. Odds are any others in the room won't even know what happened to him. If they get suspicious and too close, spritz! It won't be long before I have the whole room of Reggs *under my thumb*, literally."

Suzy's mind was whirling with virtually the same scenario she had been through herself. So, she knew what Greg could expect. She didn't enjoy reliving it, but she was glad to help

125

with potential obstacles. "The daughtership Jax and I were on had a potential crew of about twenty," she said. "Are you gonna have enough sprays in that thumb to subdue all of them?"

"My right thumb is good for six doses," said Greg, holding up the thumb in question, then replacing it with his left. "My left hides a paste of the same compound. A dab on the snout renders the recipient equally as obedient, yet for a longer pe-riod...up to eight hours versus five from the spray. With my ever-growing crew of submissive minions to help, we'll have the whole ship under my command in no time."

"And you'll simply ask the captain or his communications officer where the mothership is."

"That's the idea."

"What if they don't know?"

"Then I'll have the captain make an urgent call to mother, saying they have captured a knowledgeable Mejan, but can't get me to talk. They want to bring me in to headquarters for more effective methods to get at the truth."

"If mother goes for it, what then? You aren't actually going to let yourself be taken aboard the mothership."

"Of course not. Once we know exactly where she is, we'll surround her just like we did ten years ago. She will have no choice but to surrender."

"And I'll bet while you're still aboard the daughtership," said Suzy sinisterly, "you'll fly it right up into Little Sister's belly, just like Jax did. Déjà vu all over again."

"Exactly. Dolly will be watching over me from the get-go, with Little Sis close at hand."

"I figured as much. And you'll be able to communicate with them while inside the Regg craft by raising its antenna."

"That's the plan."

Concern washed over Suzy's face. "It almost seems too easy, too pat," she said. "What if something goes wrong? What if these new Reggs do have truth serums...or they discover your fake thumbs and use the chemicals on you...or they torture you? How will you keep from giving away The Desert's location, or The Farm's, or The Mansion's?"

Captain Gregory Smith stuck his index finger in his mouth and tapped a rear molar. "A vintage World War Two false tooth. One hard flick with my tongue and…"

"A suicide pill?!" gasped Suzy.

"Gotta take one for the team," grinned Greg stoically.

Suzy suddenly hated everything: The Desert, the Reggs, General Middleton, the world. What in God's divine providence could have brought things to such a desperate point as this? Her emotions were torn between wanting to take Greg in her arms, kiss him passionately, and tell him not to go…and turning a cold shoulder to him, as if he meant nothing to her.

The bit of logic peeking out from behind all the emotion said one thing was clear: she would never see Captain Gregory Smith again. If he wasn't killed, he'd go back to The Desert and his secret, secluded life. There would be no reason for him to ever return here to The Mansion.

Logic lost. Emotions won. Suzy rose from her sitting position on the bed and almost ran into her fellow Mejan's arms, tears falling, heart aching with loss. "You be careful, damn it!" she sobbed into the open V of his bathrobe, her lips touching the hollow of his neck. "There aren't that many of us one-eighths around here."

Greg kissed the top of her head. "I'll be fine," he said as evenly as he could.

Suddenly, Suzy couldn't bear having two bathrobes between them. She flung hers open at the seam, and then just as rapidly undid the sash of his. She slipped her hands inside the cashmere robe and around to his back, pressing her bare breasts against his rib cage, turning her head to lay flat just under his chin. She squeezed his body hard. Greg wrapped his arms around her and squeezed back, bending his neck to brush his cheek softly against hers.

All control was quickly lost. Robes fell. Suzy threw her arms around his neck and pulled herself up to smash her mouth against his. His tongue thrusted hard into hers. Hands instinctively explored each other's bodies, desperately searching for whatever could satisfy this insatiable longing.

But it was when they returned to being lost in each other's embrace that both realized what was sending their emotions over the rainbow. It was this amazing sense of transcendence. A young male and a female from the same alien ancestry... their forefathers crossing dimensions eighty years ago to start a new life on a strange world in hopes of maintaining the precious Mejan lineage. Suzy and Greg didn't know each other that well socially or intellectually; but they did psychologically. Two mostly-human oddities with eyes, heads, and IQs too large to be considered normal in politically-correct society. Even in their own homes the lack of eye contact from their mates in recent years said it all.

Their souls melted together, feeling each other's pain and fears. The spiritual blending was stronger than physical sex could ever achieve. In each other's arms Greg and Suzy found the kind of kinship they could never experience with their pure-human counterparts.

Neither wanted the moment to end.

Both wondered why it should.

Chapter 22

Dressed in black jogging togs to fit her mood, Suzette Brookfield-Jackson sat on the edge of the office chair in The Mansion's communication room, her eyes glued to the large HD television screen on the far left. Courtesy of The Desert's secret spacecraft—Dolly—Suzy had a virtual bird's eye view of what might have been the same military helicopter that had transported her from the Iowa City Police Station to that isolated barn in the middle of agricultural nowhere five days ago. But instead of mid-afternoon, this time it was an hour before midnight. So, Dolly's camera was currently in infrared mode, making the copter's whirling blades look like a pulsating red disk, as they sliced through the humid night air, the friction generating a steady charge of static electricity. By adding in the red-to-orange heat plumes blowing out from the twin turboshaft engines, the aircraft's image looked like a solarized version of the starship Enterprise.

There was another difference, too. Instead of traveling east like last time, the UH-60 Black Hawk had settled onto a 304-degree, northwest course. The brain trusts at The Desert had quickly determined it was possibly heading for West Okoboji Lake in the northwest corner of Iowa. This natural glacier lake, with its maximum depth of 134 feet, would be a practical hiding place for a Regg daughtership. Nothing else on this course had that kind of ideal cover for something the size of four river barges.

Suzy knew Captain Gregory Smith was onboard the helicopter. So did her family five miles away at The Farm, as well as a whole team of Desert personnel, including General Joshua Middleton. Thanks to Dolly's eye-in-the-sky constant vigilance, they all had watched Gregory come out of the Century Mall just before closing to be accosted by two cops. He was zip-tied with his hands behind his back, placed into a patrol car, and taken quickly to the Iowa City Police Station. Through Greg's preset smart phone transmission, they also heard the traveling dialog between abductee and abductors, the latter of whom turned out to be none other than the same Officers Willis and Gonzalez. Bagging two aliens in less than a week might have set the fortunate policemen up for promotions. It did, however, prompt Officer Willis to make another secure call to Jacob Marshall at the New York Times. Willis felt this was an alien invasion, for sure.

Half an hour later two men in flight suits led Greg out the back door of the station with a hood over his head. But to everyone's dismay, his hands were still zip-tied behind his back. Since Suzy's hands had been fastened in front of her, The Desert assumed the same procedure would be used on Greg, thus making it much easier to administer the debilitating chemicals hidden in his thumbs. Now his ability to take over the daughtership was not so certain.

With the Black Hawk currently traveling at its top speed of 180 miles per hour, The Desert estimated it would reach West Okoboji at precisely 11:25 p.m., fifteen minutes from now. Suzy didn't know if she wanted the time to pass fast or slow. All she knew for certain was she had never felt so depressed in her thirty years of life.

Her mind kept flashing back to that impassioned, flesh-on-flesh encounter just a few hours ago. How she wanted to crawl inside her fellow one-eighth Mejan, become one with him, know his very soul. In a way they had, but not enough to violate either one's definition of fidelity. Suzy loved Jax: her imperfect, one hundred percent human husband, even if the honeymoon had ended years ago, and he rarely looked her in the eye anymore. She knew Jax loved her, too. He was caring. He was rich. He was the father of her children; and a good one, at that. Still, that groping, spirit-blending embrace she and Greg had shared in the bedroom left her limp and breathless.

And then the God-speed kiss in the mall's parking lot sent her crashing to the opposite side of the emotional spectrum.

Why couldn't a woman have two husbands?

Part of her depression was the gnawing fear for Greg's safety. Suzy understood the need and the urgency, and why the captain was the perfect choice for the mission. But none of those factors provided much comfort at the moment. One beautiful man taking on twenty black hearted Reggs on their home turf with his hands tied behind his back was enough to make her scream.

But at the center of it all was Suzy's sense of loneliness. There was no one else in the household qualified to be with her in the communications room right now. Before taking Greg to the mall, she instructed Odette and Loretta to make sure the children got to bed on time, and to stay in charge of them until further notice. She couldn't tell them anything more. The live-in housekeepers knew nothing about the secret communications room, let alone what sometimes goes on under their own roof. They knew very little about The Farm and absolutely nothing about The Desert. Nicole and Nathan were still too young.

She had already called Jax tonight, just to hear his voice. She couldn't tell him about Greg starting the mission, as much as she wanted to. Jax would come running home and get into the middle of it, when everyone agreed it was better for appearances if he finished fishing his club tournament on the Mississippi River. Besides, there was nothing Jax could do to help at this point, except hold Suzy's hand, while she tried to hide her distress over Greg's assignment. Jax would be home by late afternoon tomorrow anyway. Perhaps by then the mission would be completed. And successful.

A military-sounding voice broke in over the muted *whomp-whomp* of the chopper. "The Black Hawk is slowing and descending into a sand and gravel pit one click east of the lake." Suzy's focus snapped back to the television screen. Dolly's camera was zooming in to reveal the soft yellow glow of a ground-vehicle's warm hood a hundred yards in front of the whirling red disk. "It appears to be a double-cab pickup towing a boat," continued the voice.

No one was surprised. Knowing the Regg general level of intelligence, it was a reasonable assumption they wouldn't be stupid enough to hover over the daughtership out in the middle of West Okoboji Lake, and then try to lower its cargo on a tether. That would expose too much of the alien craft in a lake known for family vacationers and good fishing...even under the cover of a moonless night. That would also mean the United States Army crew onboard the Black Hawk would witness something they weren't supposed to. So, the Reggs had chosen a broad, flat plateau thirty feet down in an abandoned sand and gravel pit, where no passing cars would see the proposed midnight exchange.

Switching to whisper mode, the Black Hawk set down about fifty yards from the waiting pickup. Dolly immediately switched from standard infrared to The Desert's exclusive system of night vision that—with no more illumination than normal starlight—could turn the dark landscape to Technicolor daytime. Suzy had helped write the computer program that amplified and enhanced dark images, yet seeing *Day-Night* in action never got old for her.

No time was wasted, as two helmeted men in dark-blue flight suits opened the side door of the chopper and removed the hooded figure, who was wearing the same tan slacks and green pullover when Suzy dropped him off at the mall just a few hours before. Greg was hustled just beyond the spinning blades, then the two figures ran back to the waiting Black Hawk. It quickly lifted out of the pit and peeled away, leaving Greg all alone, some one hundred feet from the pickup.

Once the chopper was well out of sight, two hairy heads sticking out of black jumpsuits exited the pickup and ran to their captive. Each taking an arm, they quickly escorted him back to the black vehicle and shoved him into the back seat, settling in on either side. Dolly watched the shiny-new, freshly-stolen 2025 Ford F-150 with the twenty-foot Nitro bassboat in tow wind its way up and out of the gravel pit and turn left onto Linden Drive. Two miles later it turned right on Highway 71, driving through Arnolds Park for half a mile before taking a sharp left.

"It appears they are launching at Givens Point," said the voice from The Desert.

"Roger that," said another male voice. "Givens Point is only a mile from the lake's deepest water. Perfect place to hide a spacecraft."

It took the Regg a few comical tries to back the boat into the water without careening off the cement ramp, but it finally got launched at a precarious angle. The boat driver eased up to the dock to download Greg, a Regg still firmly on each of his arms.

Leaving the stolen pickup and jackknifed trailer right there blocking the double ramp, the bassboat gurgled quietly out into Smiths Bay. Once it reached the main body of West Okoboji Lake, the 200-horse Yamaha outboard roared to life, putting the boat almost instantly on plane.

Dolly widened the view to look ahead to see where the daughtership might show itself. She also switched back to infrared mode, knowing any part of the alien ship that surfaced would stand out like a sore thumb, since it would be much cooler than the surrounding water, having ascended from the colder depths.

It didn't take long before the infrared camera revealed the sharp contrast of a dark blue, circular shaft about thirty feet in diameter poking just above the dead-calm, dull-yellow surface half a mile ahead. The Reggs in the boat were probably using night-vision goggles with the same infrared mode, because they were heading straight for it.

A hundred feet from the shaft the twenty-foot bassboat throttled down, coming to a bobbing stop in its own wake. It then idled forward slowly, until the bow met the side of the shaft with a gentle bump. Without a sound, the black metallic cylinder re-submerged, allowing the boat to ease into the space it had previously occupied. Then just as quickly, it reappeared above the surface with the boat perfectly in its center.

Suzy held her breath. She knew this procedure all too well, even though she had been under the influence of a couple mind-altering drugs at the time ten years ago. The water level inside the shaft began to drop, taking the boat and its four passengers down into the daughtership. Ten seconds later the shaft retracted again, leaving the lake's surface smooth and barren, as if nothing had ever been there.

"That's it, folks," said the voice, now sullen. "There's nothing we can do but wait. Our prayers are with you, Captain Gregory Smith."

Dolly's camera clicked off, turning all receiving screens to black. General Joshua Middleton slumped in his office chair, his face stone blank.

Suzy dropped her head into her hands and began to sob.

Chapter 23

With all its underwater lights aglow, The Mansion's pool looked like a sparkling blue jewel against dusk's fading light. Nine-year-old Nichole—her flowered one-piece hugging her sopping-wet, willowy body, raced down the diving board and leaped into the air, reaching for the perfectly timed Nerf football. It bounced off her outstretched hands and landed in the water at the same time she executed a Vaudevillian belly-flop.

"You catch like a girl," hooted Nathan, her younger brother, climbing onto the board to take his turn as wide receiver with Dad as quarterback.

"I *am* a girl, brat-worst," Nicole sputtered, treading water and wiping the hair out of her eyes. She picked up the soggy football and flung it back to her dad, landing it with a splash three feet from his dry Nikes.

"Let's see if you can do better," challenged Jax, picking up the ball and pump-faking twice. Nathan took that as his cue, and padded down the board, his head turning to located the ball as he leaped. Jax threw this one just as perfectly, making sure it was two feet out of Nathan's reach. What the seven-year-old said just before hitting the water empty-handed cost him a dollar in the *Potty-Mouth* jar.

Watching from the sidelines in her chaise lounge, Suzy offered her fuming son a half-minded *Stick with it, Nathan*, then checked her smart watch for the tenth time in as many minutes. It had been over twenty hours since Captain Gregory Smith had been taken aboard the Regg daughtership, yet there had been no word.

If things had gone according to plan, he should have secured the spacecraft by now, raised its buoy antenna, and checked in with The Desert on the secure frequency. Maybe he wasn't able to squirt the chemical into the faces of his immediate captors. Maybe the Reggs were waiting a few hours before beginning the interrogation. Maybe Greg was able to subdue some of the crew, but it was taking time and considerable effort to corral the rest.

Maybe he was waiting until dark to raise the antennae on the busy lake. Maybe they discovered his phony thumbs before he could use them, and they turned the truth-powder on him. *Maybe they killed him.*

Only one thing was certain: the daughtership was still down in the depths of West Okoboji. Dolly had been hanging five miles up, keeping a sharp eye on the entire lake. She would have known if even a small bubble from a Regg fart had broken the surface.

On purpose, Suzy was not in any kind of swimwear. Neither was Jax, despite Nichole and Nathan's sincerest requests to join them in the pool. Both Mom and Dad had opted for casual shorts and tops with running shoes, knowing that at a moment's notice they might be sprinting for the communications room. Because it was nighttime, their excuse of not being able to catch some rays was lame, but adequate.

Jax was just as anxious as Suzy to be in the communications center, and he certainly wanted to learn more than the sketchy details from his wife about last night's events here and over West Okoboji. But he had just gotten home from his two-day fishing tournament a few hours ago, and needed to eat, spend some time in the shower, and now with his kids. Suzy needed some time with them as well, having sequestered herself in the comm all night and day and much of this evening, coming out only at noon for a quick sandwich a kind word to a whining Nicole and Nathan before disappearing again. The kids knew something was up, but they were reasonably appeased with the customary "Mommy has a lot of work to do in the office" defense. Besides, they were sure getting a lot of video game time lately.

Lounging beside Suzy was Loretta, their forty-something, Columbian nanny, ready to take charge of the kids in case Mister and Misses had to leave quickly. She knew something was up, too, yet wasn't about to pry. She and her mother, Odett, knew only that the Jacksons worked for some government organization, and no one, including the kids, was to enter the panic suite unless there was a dire emergency. And under no circumstance were they ever to try unlocking the Jacksons' private office in the back of the suite. What they didn't know was this so-called office was just a facade—the real one being the adjacent communications room hidden behind the wall and known only to Suzy and Jax. And lately Captain Gregory Smith.

Life at The Mansion had been fairly routine for the past ten years of Loretta's employment. But lately she and her mother were finding themselves being asked to watch the children more and more, and at the oddest hours. Neither nanny minded that particular duty. They loved Nicole and Nathan like their own. Besides, their annual salaries would outrage even the highest paid Southampton manservant.

The silent buzzing on Suzy's wrist snapped her focus to her smartwatch. The text read: *Antenna emerging.*

This was it: the very action they had been waiting for. Hopefully, Greg had taken over the ship and raised the buoy antenna to broadcast *mission accomplished.* He would say he was about to have the ship's drugged captain radio to the mothership that they had a Mejan captive, who seemed to know more than any of the others, and who needed to be brought to the mothership for more intense and effective interrogation. Then, under the cover of darkness, the daughter would leave West Okoboji and fly to wherever the mother was hiding. That's all they needed. Ka-boom! Game over.

"Jax," called Suzy, pointing at her watch, "we need to go."

Their eyes met. He knew exactly what his wife meant, because his watch had buzzed, too. "Sorry, kids," lamented Jax, tossing the football underhand to Loretta, who caught it quite nimbly. "Your mom and I have to go to the office for a while. Loretta can throw to you."

As long as somebody was still willing to play dive-ball, neither kid seemed to mind. And as far as Nathan was concerned, Loretta would probably throw better than his dad's last attempt.

Jax took Suzy's hand and both walked just slowly enough to appear in no real hurry. "It's almost ten," called Jax over his shoulder. "Just a few more minutes in the pool, then start getting them ready for bed."

Loretta waved in acknowledgement.

Once into the foyer and out of sight, Suzy and Jax broke into an all-out sprint for the basement.

*****

Jax typed *nine, star, eight, pound* on one of the computer's keyboards and the bookshelf swung away from the wall to reveal the opening to the communications room. The image of General Joshua Middleton, sitting at his desk, drumming his fingers, was already on the right side of one of the larger monitors' split screen. On the left side were Alan and Mary Brookfield, trying their best to look calm, yet coming off more like a pair of tense passport photos.

When Middleton's monitor showed Suzy and Jax entering, he remarked with both relief and annoyance, "Ah, there you are."

Jax said, "Evening, General. Hello again, Brookfields."

"Hi, Joshua. Hi, Mom, Dad," smiled Suzy.

Alan and Mary Brookfield nodded back. The four Iowans had already been conversing via a short video-chat late that afternoon, when Jax first got back from his tournament. Not wishing to stay on the subject of Captain Smith's plight too long, for fear of breaking down and have a lot of explaining to do, Suzy briefly briefed Jax on current events before insisting her fish-smelling husband take a shower.

"Sorry we weren't in the comm," said Suzy. "We were spending some time with the children at the pool."

"No apology necessary," waved off the general. "Family comes first." Then he set his jaw and said quietly and quickly, "Now remember all of you, until we know Captain Smith's status, you four go invisible and mute as soon as we get his transmission from the Regg craft."

"Got my finger on the button," said Jax, holding up the small remote that ran every electronic device in the room, including the four cameras with omni-directional microphones high in each corner of the room.

"Same here," said Alan from The Farm, raising an exact duplicate of Jax's remote.

"Good. In case things have gone south, we don't want the Reggs to know anything about you guys."

All four expressed their understanding and appreciation.

137

Middleton turned to look off-screen at another monitor, this one receiving daytime-type optics from Dolly via the ingenious *Day-Night* technology. She was high above West Okoboji, yet just below the cloud deck. "Looks like the antenna is starting to tip up towards our relay satellite," he said. "We should be getting a transmission any minute now. As soon as we do, our communications computer will automatically patch it through to all of you."

The words were no sooner out of the general's mouth than a squiggly head-and-shoulders image danced on the screen, flickering at first, then snapping to crystal clarity. Against a plain gray, metallic background that almost certainly was the inside of a Regg spacecraft were the head and shoulders of Captain Gregory Smith.

A cheer rose from all four Iowans. But the joy quickly faded when they realized Greg did not look victorious. In fact, still in his forest-green pullover, he looked sheepish, even a little pissed. "Hello, sir," he said.

"Hello, Captain," replied General Middleton. "Are you okay?"

As Captain Smith squirmed, it became obvious he was seated. "Yes, sir. I'm fine. I just need to go to the bathroom. But they've had *my hands tied behind my back the entire time*."

Message received. Damn it!

Just then, someone with virtually no shoulders, wearing a black jumpsuit with an orange belt and piping, walked into frame from stage right, no head yet visible. Coming up behind Greg, it turned around and placed a five-fingered, hairy hand on the captain's much broader shoulder. Some indecipherable foreign words were growled, presumably giving orders to a subordinate. The image of the seated Greg and the thing behind him trembled momentarily, as the camera was being handled. Then it smoothly pulled back to reveal all of both Greg and the Regg, including the latter's ugly head. It had the dark facial features of an Eastern wolf, but with no noticeable ears and a shorter snout with light-gray around the muzzle. No one could see its eyes, because it was wearing dark-gray shooting glasses. Jax recognized the brand as Wiley X. He had an identical pair, only in amber.

The most disturbing element of this picture was the proof that Greg's hands were indeed still tied behind his back. Their worst fears had become reality. The mission had failed, and Captain Gregory Smith appeared in double jeopardy. Tears formed in Suzy's big eyes. Jax leaned against the computer table, dumbfounded.

When the Regg suddenly spoke, it made Suzy jump. Until her own abduction last week, it had been ten years since she heard that unique, gruff kind of speech. She thought she would never have to hear it again. But there it was, a week ago, coming from one of her two captors, while her hands were bound and she was strung from the Reggs' spacecraft rafters like a side of beef. The Desert and Jax had rescued her and turned her captors into captives themselves. Now here was that voice yet again, over the airwaves, a slightly different tenor, yet just as grotesque.

"You are General Joshua Middleton, yes and no?" it asked with crusty words that were surprisingly articulate, if not lacking in grammatical acuity.

The general stiffened his shoulders and stoically nodded in the affirmative, forcing half a smile.

"Good," said the Regg. "And you are Mejan. Good. My name is Bruchelus Ronga. Call me *Bruche*. I command this vessel. Your officer here say you the Mejan we talk at."

"I am," said the general, his jaw muscles rippling. "We are pleased we have found this way to communicate."

"Good cover," nodded Jax.

The Regg chuckled, if you could call it that. It was more like a sneering growl. "Yes. We also want way to communications with you. Thank you for sending young Mejan and his device we use now to speak at you."

"That's why we sent him," said the general.

"Yes. Young Captain Smith tells us that," smiled Bruchelus, continuing his surprising grasp of the English language. "Capturing was too easy. And same place we captured young Mejan woman seven days ago."

"We assumed you would think so," said the general.

Even though no one else could hear, Jax leaned over to his wife sitting in front of him and whispered in her ear, "Do you think that's true? This was all a setup? This was the primary mission?"

Suzy was still running the general's words through the logical portion of her left brain. Greg hadn't said anything in this regard. But why would he? It would have been on a need-to-know basis. Fact was, he was reluctant to explain much of anything to her about his mission. And now that she thought about it...

"I doubt it," she finally said, gently chewing her lower lip. "I'm sure this wasn't the primary objective, but it could have been plan-B. Joshua is just covering, as you said."

The Regg commander put his other hand on his captive's other shoulder and split a toothy grin, "Yes. We appreciate it, General. Much to discuss."

Jax slipped off the table and moved closer to the television screen to get a better look. "With all that hair on his ugly mug," he said, "it's almost impossible to tell if the Regg is buying it,"

"I don't think he is, said the intuitive Suzy. "I'm detecting sarcasm under that growling fracture of the English language."

With a small flip of his hand, Middleton said, "So, where do you want to start, Commander? You undoubtedly know we have two of your people. Shall we do an exchange?"

The human faction held its collective breath. At least there was hope of getting Greg back. The Regg commander seemed to weigh the offer, before his black lips stretched into a smile. "Something to discuss, yes. But later. First, my superiors want we to talk your surrender."

Chapter 24

Temporarily taken aback by the Regg commander's statement, General Joshua Middleton gathered himself and said evenly, "Did I hear you right? You want us to surrender?"

"Yes."

Middleton's mouth cranked into a sneer. "What makes you think we would ever consider surrendering to you? That is ridiculous."

The Regg's toothy grin faded, disappearing completely behind the course hair of his graying muzzle. His black nostrils flared. He removed both hands from Captain Smith's shoulders and folded them across his own chest. "We control your president, General," he said haughtily. "We control your military. We control your nuclear weapons. We control your police." The Regg put both hands to the sides of Greg's face, and then he rested the underside of his elongated jaw on the top of Greg's chestnut-colored head. "And now we have one of you. We believe he knows all about you. Your home base. Your spaceships. Your weaponry. We have not interrogated him. But we will. And he will tell us these things."

The acid in General Middleton's stomach was churning to a boil. It was clear the primary mission was in deep trouble. What wasn't so clear was if the Regg commander believed the explanation that Greg was only a messenger. If the Regg didn't buy it and they started interrogating him, Middleton knew Gregory would bite the cyanine capsule before giving away any of The Desert's carefully-guarded secrets. That simply could not happen.

"I'm sorry to disappoint you, ah, *Bruche*," Middleton said, continuing the bluff, "but our young emissary there knows nothing. Surely you don't think us foolish enough to send you someone who knows any of our secrets."

"He is Mejan," countered Bruchelus. "He must know."

"Commander. As *you* must know, there are millions of people with Mejan ancestry all over the world. And virtually all of them know nothing about us. Captain Smith was selected from thousands of Mejan officers in our database. He is only one-eighth Mejan. He is single with no family. He lives in Iowa City. Only after he had volunteered for what he knew only as high-paying hazardous duty, did we offer him just enough details regarding the mission as a messenger. Previously, he knew nothing about your race. He only suspected something was going on, like most of the world these days, what with the blackouts in Washington and all."

The Regg seemed to study the prospect. Then he gave a short snort and replied, "Then we no use for him, yes?" He placed one hairy hand on the side of Greg Smith's throat, with the index finger extended like a knife blade.

"Of course he is still valuable to you," said the general, staying calm and collected. "You can use him to negotiate terms for getting your two colleagues back from us."

That brought a literal howl from Bruchelus. He removed his hand from Greg's throat and used it to fling away such a ridiculous suggestion. "We care nothing for them. Kill them, if you wish."

"You don't mean that," challenged Middleton. "Their lives can't mean so little to you."

"What good they now? You already tortured them. They tell you everything about us, yes? They stupid to get caught. Okay they die."

"Oh, my God!" gasped Suzy, balling her fists. "They're even more savage than the first batch."

"We have no intention of killing our captives," insisted Middleton. "We aren't barbarians."

That brought the widest grin yet from the Regg. "No? We watch your television broadcast for years, General. How you think we learned your language good? Earth always at war with itself. You have nuclear missiles aimed at each other. You assassinate world leaders. Terrorists kill women and children in the name of some god. Your police murder unarmed criminals, and criminals kill police. Your government workers care more about getting reelected than doing the job. Your news media care more about ratings than truth. I laugh, General. You are indeed barbarians."

142

"What you say has some small truth," nodded Middleton. "But those are the exceptions, not the rule. The vast majority of Earth's inhabitants are good, caring, honest people, opposed to any kind of violence."

"As are we, General," said Bruchelus, with a shrug. "We not want to hurt young Mejan here. But will if you no surrender."

The ensuing silence was gut-wrenching for everyone who wasn't a Regg. General Joshua Middleton appeared to be keeping it together, but his insides were executing a header into the abyss. All four Iowans knew their friend and leader was stuck in a deadly impasse. He couldn't give up any of The Desert's secrets, much less surrender to the barbaric invaders. Middleton had to come up with some kind of solution. Greg Smith's life depended on it.

"Surely the esteemed commander of the Regg spacecraft knows his demand for our surrender cannot be met," said Middleton flatly. "No general would sacrifice his entire command to save one soldier."

The Regg's reply came almost too fast, as if it had been predetermined and practiced beforehand. "Of course, General. We thought this your answer." The Regg commander concocted an overly-dramatic pause, and then said with a knowing grin, "So, we negotiate. You give up the spacecraft used to destroy our friends. You call it *Little Sister*. Your captain here for Little Sister."

That was an unexpected curve ball. General Middleton shrugged his shoulders almost as dramatically, and said, "Why do you want Little Sister? You know we could easily rig her to blow up in your face before you could retro-engineer her. She would do you no good."

"Please," laughed Bruchelus. "We not need her technology. We need her no longer exist. Without your best craft to oppose us, our weapons superior to yours."

General Middleton's jaw muscles rippled. "Forget it, Commander. That offer is no more acceptable than our complete surrender."

"Then we will have to kill your nice captain here," said the Regg, producing a straight razor from his black jumpsuit's hip pocket and holding it up high. "You like to watch?"

Alan and Mary at the farm gasped in unison. Jax froze in disbelief of what might be displayed right before his eyes. Suzy slapped both hands to the top of her head and screamed, No!"

That desperate scream caused Jax to turn his attention from the television screen to the back of his wife's trembling head. Her demonstrative display of horror for the possibility of Greg's demise seemed more suitable for one of her own children than for some captain from The Desert she hardly knew. Was something going on here?

Chapter 25

"Let's knock off the bullshit, Commander," said General Joshua Middleton, his attention fixed on the tense face of the young man sitting in the chair with his hands zip-tied behind his back, a razor at his throat, inside a Regg spaceship, at the bottom of Lake West Okoboji in northwest Iowa. The general's tone was direct and forceful. "You know damn well killing our emissary means your immediate and complete destruction. Surely you know we have tracked Captain Smith from the moment he was taken into custody by the Iowa City police to where he now sits with you at the bottom of Lake West Okoboji in 134 feet of water. None of us is a fool, Commander. So, let's quit the square dance and get down to it."

Here came that hideous, broad smile again from the six-foot Regg in the black jumpsuit with the ring on the zipper all the way up to his hairy chinny-chin-chin. He opened his hands in concurrence and said, "I agree, General. We have same goal today: open communication. That is done. So we talk now."

"Good," nodded Middleton. "Why don't we start with arranging a time and place for a prisoner exchange? Your two for our one."

Commander Bruchelus put one hairy finger to his pursed lips and said quizzically, "*That* most on your mind, General? A boring prisoner exchange? We have more important topics to discuss, yes?"

"It's a good starting point, Commander. A demonstration of good will on both our parts to show our willingness for open and honest talks."

"Hmm. Maybe. But General, you seem determined to get young captain back. He something special to you?" The Regg stepped in front of Greg Smith and twisted down to look him full in the face. Greg sneered back at him. "Now that I study you both," Bruchelus smiled, glancing back and forth between the captain and the general, "I see same. A relative? A son maybe?"

"No relation, Commander," dismissed Joshua quickly. "You know how we Mejans all look alike. Big heads, big eyes."

"Yes, hmm," said Bruchelus, straightening back up with a crocked smile. "Let's make prisoner exchange later. We talk now."

Jax looked back at his wife, who was quietly throwing up in her mouth. "He knows Greg is a key bargaining chip, hon. I'll bet they never let him go until these bastards get what they want."

Suzy could only nod.

"Okay," sighed Middleton. "But as a show of good faith, couldn't you at least untie the captain's hands so he can relieve himself? He looks very uncomfortable. Your fellow Reggs are being treated very well by us. They are even allowed to roam their environment freely, completely untethered. Like Captain Smith there, they have no way to escape."

"Good move, Joshua!" whispered Suzy mostly to herself through a soggy Kleenex. "That should do it."

Jax shot his wife another curious look. She sure seemed more into this mission than she should be. And now her mood had quickly flip-flopped from horror to informed hope. "Do you know something about this mission I don't, sweetie?"

Suzy rose to her feet in anticipation of what her fellow one-eighth Mejan could do if his hands were freed. Things were looking up. "I'm sorry, honey," she said, eyes fixed on the television screen. "Things were so hectic when you got home, I guess we forgot to mention Greg has a mixture of our *blue-be-true* and *gray-to-obey* powders hidden in a pair of false thumbs."

"Say what?" Jax's tone was a mixture of pleasant surprise and hurt feelings for being left out of the loop. "False thumbs?"

"Yeah. He obviously hasn't been able to use them with his hands tied behind his back. If they untie him…"

"Squirt. Squirt. Sit. Stay. Good dog," Jax mused, finishing for his wife. He liked that prospect. It reminded him of his own single-handed take-over of the Regg spacecraft years back.

The Regg commander seemed to contemplate the bathroom-break idea for a moment, before he shook his hairy head and said, "Maybe later. We talk."

"C'mon!" groan Captain Smith. "I need to go to the bath-room, like I told you hours ago."

"So, go," said Bruchelus.

"In my pants?!"

"Yes. Or my officers help you."

"For Christ's sake be reasonable, Commander," interceded General Middleton. "Let him keep some dignity. At least bring his hands up to the front so he can do it himself. You can retie them. He sure as hell isn't going anywhere."

The Regg considered the concept, and then said, "No. We talk."

Greg rolled his eyes.

"Have it your way," huffed Middleton with a purposeful lip-curl. He leaned against his desk and folded his arms. "So, let's get on with it. What are your demands?"

"I told you: destroy Little Sister."

"And as I told you: that ain't gonna happen."

"Then your captain here dies."

"Then so do you and your crew. As I said, the spacecraft we've had hovering over you the whole time will turn you into fish food."

Commander Bruchelus put his right elbow on the top of Greg's head and rested his hairy chin on the back of that hairy paw. "We not getting very far, hmm?"

"Not if you continue with such an unreasonable demand," said Middleton.

Bruchelus made his usual show of thinking hard for a mo-ment, then said, "Okay. How you like this? We join forces. You give us piece of Earth, you keep the rest. We want our own land to rule. We tired of living in spaceships."

That was nothing new. It was just about the same ridiculous proposal the first race of Reggs had offered ten years ago. It didn't fly then and it wasn't about to now.

"Give 'em the south pole," said Jax.

There was no reaction from Suzy. She didn't find anything about this amusing.

"Just which country would you like?" scoffed General Mid-dleton. "France? Germany? Ethiopia? I'm sure the Ukraine wouldn't mind."

147

"Any place where we grow food and animals," said Bruchelus. "This not much we ask."

"And what would become of the millions of people presently occupying that land?"

'They move or stay and help us grow crops and animals."

"As slaves."

"They would be well fed."

"As would you...if not on cattle, on your slaves themselves."

"We must live, General. We need meat. We are...what is the word... carnivals."

General Middleton wished he were in a different place under different circumstances, so he could laugh at the Regg's misuse of the word. But this dialog was far too serious for any kind of levity. "Don't take this personal, Commander," he said directly, "but you are out of your friggin' mind. You come to our planet. You blackout our nation's capital, and then threaten to do more to other cities if everyone from the president on down to the local police don't obey your commands to round up all the Mejans. Then by threatening to execute the very messenger we sent to you to establish communications between us, you think we are just going to hand over some part of our precious Earth?"

"Seems good to us, General," shrugged Bruchelus.

"You forget, Commander," said Middleton, "we have the superior firepower. Little Sister can wipe out any of your spacecraft that try to disable our cities. Eventually, we will find your mothership and either destroy it, or make certain your entire Regg nation leaves our solar system and never returns. We've done it before, we can do it again. Your choice."

The Regg commander stood motionless beside his still-seated captive. No one could tell if he was thinking or just being theatrical again. Bruchelus finally took in a slow breath and said, "Again, we not talk good, General. It important I go discuss with my superiors."

"Please do."

Bruchelus took a step back from his seated captive and opened his hands in petition. "We must leave this lake, General," he said, like a child asking permission to leave the dinner table.

"Why?" asked Middleton, although he knew the answer.

148

"No contact from here. Go to atmosphere."

That was bullshit. From right there in the lake the Reggs could use any of a hundred relay satellites to contact their high command. These canines just wanted to get the hell out from under the threat of being annihilated by the Mejan warship hovering above them. Once in the atmosphere, they'd have a fairly good chance of getting away.

But Middleton knew if he refused their request, the two factions would be right back to square-one. It would be better to let the daughtership go and wait for the next communication. After all, the Reggs had the most to gain from an equitable agreement. All he wanted was for Captain Gregory Smith to either get free enough to use his fake thumbs, or be released unharmed.

"Okay," said the General. "But on one condition."

"We leave now," said the Regg, purposely ignoring the general's upcoming condition. "You no destroy us. We have your captain."

"We won't destroy you. You have my word. And I want your word to not harm him. And also promise me you'll let the poor man relieve himself by himself."

"Yes," nodded the Regg commander. "And no follow us to atmosphere, where we open link to superiors."

"We won't follow you," groused Middleton, walking back to sit down behind his desk, mumbling under his breath, "Goddamn paranoid bastards."

"Good," said Bruchelus, as he walked toward the camera and then off the screen. "We use same frequency and touch back on you soon."

"Let's make that within an hour, okay?" said Middleton, calling after the disappearing Regg.

But the transmission was already cut.

"The sonofabitch is gone," spat General Middleton. He punched some keys on his iPad, making himself the only one now onscreen. "Go head, Iowa. Come back in."

Jax and Alan tapped their remotes, and all four Iowans were back in a video conference with The Desert.

"Jesus, General," groaned Jax. "Negotiating with them is like herding cats."

"I trust we going to follow them?" blurted Suzy, quick-stepping closer to the television screen. "They might lead us to the mothership."

"That will be difficult, sweetheart," said the general. "Their craft undoubtedly has stealth, so we won't be able to track it with radar. And we can't keep a visual on it if they decide to lose us by zigzagging through thick clouds at night at sub-light speed. Dolly will just have to hang in the atmosphere and hope she's in close enough proximity to catch the next transmission."

"Let's pray they untie his hands," said Alan Brookfield from The Farm.

No one said anything more, each contemplating the potential outcome that action could produce. Jax quietly poured himself another cup of coffee and one for Suzy.

"Hold on. Here we go," announced Middleton, punching more keys. "They are leaving the lake."

The *Day-Night* image from Dolly filled the right half of everyone's screen. As if it were high noon on a cloudy day instead of the actual midnight hour, they watched the antennae buoy disappear under the calm surface. A few seconds later a dark-gray shape slowly lifted out of West Okoboji Lake, water cascading off its smooth, oval-shaped hull. The first noticeable feature of the two hundred-yard-diameter craft was the ridge running the entire length of it down the middle like a wide spine of black glass. Being different from any of the daughterships belonging to the other bunch of Reggs from ten years past was no surprise, since the facial features of the two Regg types were also different. Reggland, or whatever they called their home planet, obviously had various ethnicities, just like Earth, and therefore different concepts of how a spacecraft should be constructed.

The huge Identified Flying Object hesitated above the surface a few feet, presumably checking for nearby boats and overhead aircraft. It then ascended into the night sky at a steadily-increasing velocity, penetrating the high ceiling of clouds in just a few seconds. That's when it escaped Dolly's camera, and the transmitted image became nothing but bright white. Dolly immediately launched upward herself, the white image becoming flashing streaks, until she broke above the cloud deck into the quiet backdrop of blackness, splattered with a trillion stars. Her

150

camera scanned in all directions, but the Regg craft was nowhere in sight. As expected, it was using the clouds and sub light speed for its getaway.

Middleton tapped a few keys to refill the screen with the familiar five faces. "That's it for now, folks," he sighed. "All we can do is wait for the call."

Chapter 26

Despite hourly attempts by Dolly to reestablish contact with the Reggs, there had been no word from them for almost eighteen hours. Suzy and Jax had given up sixteen hours ago, and gone to bed for some badly needed sleep. Jax suggested sex. Suzy declined, saying she had a headache. Jax went to sleep horny and pissed.

When they came downstairs blurry-eyed and famished at six in the evening, the ever-accommodating Odett fixed them a couple cheeseburgers with leftover mac and cheese. They found their abandoned kids so engrossed in the latest video game, *Call of Duty: Alien Invasion 3*, they hardly noticed their parents' reappearance. So, mom and dad joined them in the upstairs rec room, preferring to watch the news channels on the other television screen rather than seeing Martian zombies being splattered across Time Square. Besides, their smart wristwatches would let them know if and when something broke.

Wearing tan Dockers and an ivory pullover, Jax got bored with the lack of news on the networks and had settled deep in his black leather recliner to get back to reading his June issue of BassMaster Magazine. He had finished in third place out of nineteen at his tournament. He needed some tips.

Suzy had gone prone on the matching couch, comfortable in cutoffs and a black Hawkeye T-shirt, while continuing to flip back and forth among Fox News, CNN, and C-SPAN. There was very little concrete news in the paranormal category, just the usual rumors of missing persons, UFO sightings, and varied opinions regarding who or what had really blacked out Washington D.C. ten days earlier. Most people weren't buying their government's lame explanation of using themselves as a lab rat, and the White House had long since gone mum, leaving entire news groups scrambling to halt their falling Nielsen ratings with little more than speculation and uninformed fake news.

Suzy had just clicked back to CNN when she caught the tail end of some BREAKING NEWS flashing in big red letters across the telecast. The evening anchor, Carson Solidar, was doing his best to stay professional, as he excitedly repeated the announcement:

"If you've just joined us, at 7:00 p.m. Eastern Daylight Time tonight—in just over five minutes from right now and exclusively on CNN—a special address to the world will to be made by a faction calling themselves *friendly visitors from beyond Earth*. We don't know who they are or what they will say, but they claim to be responsible for the blackouts. Hoax or not, we will be broadcasting it live right here on CNN in just minutes."

Suzy sat upright. "Honey," she whispered with urgency, not wanting to alert the kids, "you'd better see this."

Jax had already dropped the magazine into his lap and was watching the television closely. The kids, both with virtual reality helmets covering half their heads, remained oblivious. Jax got up and moved over to join his wife on the couch. "Uh-oh," he said, taking Suzy's hand. "I don't like the sounds of this."

Carson Solidar lifted his eyes from the notes he had been reading to look straight into the camera lens and the teleprompter right beside it. "Normally, CNN would give no credence to any claim of such a wild and improbable nature. But the fact is that these so-called *friendly visitors from beyond Earth* just moments ago validated themselves by predicting and then actually executing a five-second blackout of Fresno, California. This was just like what happened in Washington D. C. back on June 10th.

"Moreover, we are now getting reports coming in from reliable sources that some kind of large craft has come out of the clouds and is hovering directly over the Pentagon. Our crews there are telling us they will have a live feed in just a few..."

Obeying his director's command in his ear, Carson looked ten degrees to his right at a separate monitor. His eyes got big. "Holy shit!" he gasped. When he realized his uncensored expletive, his face went crimson. "Er...we...er...we have that picture now. What? Okay. Yes, we're putting it up now."

A few million television sets across the world suddenly displayed the image of a long, dark-gray object, hanging motionless over the Pentagon, both building and craft bathed in an orange hue from the sun's low angle on the western horizon. The ground-level camera was about a mile away to the west, so the UFO was being viewed in a flatter profile, making it look like a huge lead pipe, tapered at both ends, with a black ridge running across its top. Based on its apparent proximity to the Pentagon, it was about twenty feet high and longer than the entire military complex with a block to spare on each end.

"Where have we seen that obnoxious monstrosity before?" sneered Jax, reasonably certain it was the same daughtership they had watched leave West Okoboji Lake eighteen hours ago with Captain Gregory Smith as its captive.

"I smell a betrayal," said Suzy.

Just then both hers and Jax's watches buzzed. No surprise, the text read, CONFERENCE. NOW.

Suzy instinctively checked the kids. They were still engrossed in their video game. She snapped off the other television and called out to Odett and Loretta, whichever one might be closest. It was Odett, hustling in from the kitchen, wiping her hands on her apron, a big question mark on her forehead.

"Watch the kids, Odett," said Suzy, walking steadily past her toward the stairs to the basement. "And keep them away from any live television for as long as you can."

"Why, what's up, missus?"

"There's a UFO hanging over the Pentagon," said Jax, right behind his wife. "It might be a hoax, but we don't know."

Just then Loretta was hauling her thin frame down the white carpeted steps of the curved staircase. "There's some kind of spaceship over the Pentagon," she huffed, almost out of breath. "What in the name of Heaven?"

"Keep the children away from the news," yelled Jax, now racing down the stairs behind Suzy. "We'll be in the office."

*****

The hands of the atomic clock on the wall of The Mansion's communications room said it was 5:58 p.m. Central Daylight Time, just two minutes before the purported special address was to begin. All four HD screens were on, mainly because they had never been turned off. The profile of General Middleton in a white wife-beater shirt was on the first one, obviously watching the same things that Suzy and Jax were seeing on the second screen: a CNN split screen between their anchor, Carson Solidar, and the Regg craft hovering over the Pentagon. The other two televisions were tuned into Fox News and C-SPAN respectively, showing two slightly different views of the same so-tagged *UFO Over Pentagon*.

"What are they up to, Joshua?" said Suzy, choosing to remain standing, Jax at her side.

"We'll know in a minute," the general replied, flashing a look their way from behind his signature aviator glasses, before turning back to watch the television in his private quarters at The Desert. "But whatever it is, it's no good."

"Is that the same ship at West Okoboji, General?" asked Jax. "It sure looks like it."

"Can't tell," said Middleton. "According to our Regg captives, that's their standard issue daughtership, one of many. They all look the same."

"So, Captain Smith may not be on it," offered Suzy, not sure if that would be good or bad.

"No idea," said General Joshua Middleton, shaking his large head with the graying crew-cut. "Let's see what happens." He checked his wristwatch. "It's almost time."

The final ten seconds were spent in silence, as Jax turned the sound down on the other two news channels, leaving it up on CNN and The Desert.

At precisely 6:00:00 p.m. CDT, the left side of the CNN screen switched from the silent, expectant visage of Carson Solidar to an obvious, almost comical avatar of a handsome man in his early-thirties, wearing a dark-brown pinstripe suit jacket, white dress shirt and pink tie. In the background was a pastoral scene of a green meadow and grazing sheep.

"Oh, my God!" moaned Jax. "Do you believe this? A friggin' *avatar*?"

"Well," said the general, "if they used their real faces it'd scare the shit out of everyone."

Then the audio began. As expected, the voice was computerized, using text-to-speech software to relay the message. The mouth moved in reasonably accurate diction. The accent was Australian.

"Hello. I speak to you from our spacecraft above your Pentagon. To prove this, we will now black out the Pentagon's power for a millisecond. This should do no harm to anyone or anything. Please have your cameras show both our spacecraft and the Pentagon."

There was a momentary pause. Then everyone watching saw the lights flicker all around the outside walls of the Pentagon, followed by the Regg craft doing a slow tip with its left side, as if nodding in proud self-recognition.

The mouth of the digital avatar sprang back into action. "I am Moses. We can be your friends, if you let us. We come from another planet near Earth. From our blackout of Washington D. C. you have seen how easy we can disable your infrastructure. We already control your president, your military, your defenses, your police, your media. We have thousands of ships like this one, with many more fighters. So, you are defenseless against us."

"*Thousands?* My lily-white buttocks," huffed Middleton. "They have fifty, at most."

The illusion of the handsome human paused, possibly to let the full implications of his threatening, earth-shaking words sink in.

"I gotta hand it to them," said Alan from The Farm. "They were smart to record their message beforehand, using text-to-speech software and careful editing. If they'd tried it live like last night at Okoboji, no one would have the faintest idea what the illiterate hounds of the Baskervilles were trying to say."

"Now we know what they were doing for the past eighteen hours," hissed Suzy, "while we sat around waiting for their promised call."

Jax opened his mouth to add something, but the avatar beat him to it. "We don't ask for much. We been living in spaceships for many years. We just want some land for ourselves. We not decided yet which land we will take. But it will be where the people did not cooperate with us, where they did not help us round up the real enemy of your planet."

The transmission changed to a series of still photographs, each showing Mejans. They were male and female, from thirty to sixty, all with their hair pulled back and glasses removed to reveal their large heads and eyes. If anyone were to check, they would find these were all *missing persons* from around the Midwest over the past ten days. And none were seen again.

"These are samples of the other aliens of Earth," continued the digital voice with the down-under accent. "The bad aliens. They have been here for a century, infiltrating your species, blending with you, procreating with you to eventually take over your planet. Note the big eyes and big heads. They are smart. They are clever. You need to help us find them and destroy them. You need to fear them more than you fear us. They have spaceships, too. And weapons. If we can stop them, you will give up only a small part of your land to us. If not, these Mejans will take it all from you."

There was another pause, as more mugshots of part-Mejans cycled through.

"They're trying to turn the world against us," said General Joshua Middleton. "They know they can't beat us on their own, so they're trying to send the populous out on a witch-hunt."

"Nobody's gonna believe them," offered Jax, although without much conviction.

"It doesn't matter," said Suzy. "They will out of fear. They are given no choice."

The image switched from the photographs to what appeared to be a live, shaky shot from a handheld camera. It was of Captain Gregory Smith in three-quarters profile, his face covered in a bright orange hue from the setting sun. There was fear in his large blue eyes, as wind blew through his shaggy chestnut hair. Directly behind him, with only the sleeves of their dark jumpsuits and orange latex gloves visible, were presumably two Reggs, each firmly holding one of Greg's arms. His hands were still tied behind him.

From The Farm to The Mansion to The Desert rose a conglomeration of groans and expletives, all unified in anguish and disbelief. Locked on Greg's fear-laced face, none of the five noticed the Fox News and C-SPAN broadcasts, presently able to show only the exterior of the Regg spacecraft. Now they were showing that the spaceship had moved. The silent crawl at the bottom of Fox's screen read, *"...now holding directly over Roaches Run Waterfowl Sanctuary about three-quarters of a mile to the southeast of the Pentagon."*

"They've moved," Jax blurted, pointing at Fox News.

Confusion was being added to the litany of Suzy's emotions, as she followed her husband's finger, only to snap back to CNN the moment the avatar continued, now in voice-over. "This is what one of them looks like in the flesh. See how they are almost human. See the calculating look in its eyes. This is the enemy. Find them. Bring one to your local police station, dead or alive, and you will receive a certificate stating you helped us rid your planet of this menace. The more certificates your state accumulates, the less its chances of becoming our homeland."

The voice paused, while Greg squirmed against his captors, his eyes wide and cast downward at something terrifying.

"And so you can better see what a Mejan looks like in the flesh..." said the voice.

With that the captain was unceremoniously shoved forward into the open air. Both Fox News and C-SPAN picked up on the action, the C-SPAN cameraman the quicker to catch Greg's leg-kicking, frantic free-fall. Suzy's eyes instinctively snapped over to watch in horror as her fellow Mejan plummeted the three hundred feet, ultimately disappearing behind a line of trees. Because of the low angle of the various news cameras, no one except a few passengers in cars driving along George Washington Memorial Parkway witnessed the hard landing in the shallow waters of the wildlife sanctuary, and the enormous splash radiating outward in the gruesome outline of a human form. One car instinctively hit its brakes, causing a four-car pileup, as the face-down body bobbed back to the surface in its quieting pose of still life.

Suzy Brookfield-Jackson never saw the splash-down, either. She had fainted dead away...Jax barely catching before she hit the hardwood floor.

Chapter 27

The cloudy veil blurring Suzy's vision slowly parted to reveal her husband looking down on her with a feeble smile and a puzzled brow. She had the sense she was being cradled in his lap, his strong arms supporting her upper torso and head, while her tailbone felt the hardness of the floor between his legs. She recognized the soundproof paneling of the ceiling and its five-bladed fan slowly turning above Jax's head.

"Welcome back," said Jax, his tone cautious. "You okay?"

Although Suzy knew she was in her communications room, she wasn't sure why she was on the floor and what might have caused her to lose an indeterminate number of moments from her life. She blinked hard and tried to shake some memory back into her brain. No luck. What suddenly did bring it back, however, was the impassioned voice of General Middleton bouncing off the walls in the background, "The USLAP range on Dolly is five miles, right, Steve?"

"Affirmative, sir," said Major Stephen Barron. "Effective at five, deadly at three."

Jax turned his head to see that Middleton's now-desert-camouflaged back was to the camera, his smartphone communicator pressed hard to his ear. The other half of the large monitor showed a stunned Alan holding Mary as she sobbed against his shoulder.

The stiff avatar was back on the CNN broadcast, mouthing more conditions and stipulations for finding Mejans and turning them over to local authorities. Both Fox News and C-SPAN were still locked on the Regg spacecraft hovering over the same wildlife sanctuary, where Captain Gregory Smith floated facedown dead.

All this competing chatter from the news crews and the Regg was barely audible above the ongoing dialog from The Desert, coming through loud and clear, thanks to Jax having the volume turned way up.

"What's your altitude, Steve?" barked Middleton.

"One hundred miles, sir. We've been here the whole time."

"How soon can you get Dolly into range?"

"Just say the word, General, and we're already there."

"Then do it. Do it now!" growled the general. "Blow those Regg cocksuckers to their rightful place in the burning depths of hell." With that he stormed off camera, leaving just a still picture of his unmade bed under the Claude Monet print, *Ships in Harbor*.

Suzy's memory was back, and just that quickly she wished it had stayed buried. The truth of Gregory Smith—her fellow Mejan and secret lover—being thrown out of the Regg spacecraft to his death, sent stabs of electricity through her brain and twisted her stomach like a coiled spring. Greg had come into her life like an angel of mercy to make her feel loved and desirable again. And now, just as quickly, he was gone, sacrificing himself to save Earth.

There was no preventing it. Suzy burst into tears, slapped her hands to her face, and rolled over onto her stomach in a feeble attempt to hide her grief and secret. Jax immediately grabbed her shoulders and pulled her back around to face him. "What's going on here, Suzy?" he asked with more suspicion in his tone than concern. "I can understand your being upset by the guy's death. But you're acting like it was one of our kids, rather than somebody we hardly knew."

Suzy was bawling so hard she couldn't answer. Or didn't want to answer. Jax shook her firmly. "C'mon. Get it together. This isn't like you."

With a couple deep breaths, her hysterics dwindled to sobs, then to some degree of composure. Her tanned face coated in shiny moisture, she offered a weak smile and simply shook her head sadly. "I...I'm so sorry, Jax" she gurgled.

Jax was stunned. That was all he needed to hear...or feel. He knew the answer to his question without having to ask it. The six-four, two-forty-pound handsome man with shaggy blond hair just sat there Indian style on the floor of their communication room, his beautiful, cheating wife supine across his lap, ashamed to look at him, neither knowing what to say.

Suzy jumped when Jax suddenly put both hands to the sides of her face and bent his head down closer. "Tell me you didn't have an affair with Smith while I was gone," he demanded, almost squeezing the truth out of her. "Tell me!"

Suzy's eyelids closed slowly over her big copper-brown eyes, pushing out the next wave of tears. Her lips trembled, trying to find the words that would make all of this go away. But there were none. She hadn't had an affair with Greg the way Jax was insinuating. There had been no sex. But what there had been was, in many ways, far more forbidden. She and her fellow one-eighth Mejan had connected in a way that most pure humans never could. "I...I don't know how it happened," she sputtered. "It just did. I didn't mean to hurt you. That's the last thing I wanted."

Jax pushed her off his lap and scrambled to his feet, turning his back on the infidelity. He had heard her say it. It was true. Yet, he couldn't bring himself to accept it. Not Suzy Q. Not his beloved wife. Not with all the tears and joys, ordeals and delights they had been through in their lives together.

Suzy wanted to be someone else...anyone who would have a scintilla of happiness in their heart. She had just lost a lover, a friend, a fellow Mejan who understood things about her that no human ever could. And now she was about to lose her husband, the father of her children, the man she loved from the moment they met that glorious day at The Farm's hilltop pond in May of 2015.

In a moment of clarity, common sense stepped in and kicked her grief to the curb. Greg was gone, but Jax wasn't. He was still here. Alive. Mad as all hell, but alive. So, there was hope. She pulled herself to her feet and took the three steps to slip her arms around her husband and pull herself tight to the back of his ivory pullover. His reaction was to pull away. But his effort was less than determined.

"Please, honey," she peeped, her lips between his shoulder blades. "It wasn't what you think."

"Oh, yeah?" scoffed Jax, without turning around. "What do you call *cheating*?"

There weren't many things that could divert Jax and Suzy's attention away from the heated exchanged that was about to happen. But the live audio-visual report from Fox News on the monitor was one of them:

Ladies and gentlemen, this is incredible! It appears the UFO has been hit by something from above...maybe a laser, maybe lightning. We don't know. There was a flash of light and a small explosion on its top. Now, as you can see, it is rocking side to side and losing altitude. Oh, my God! There it goes. It's falling!

The video cameras from both Fox News and C-SPAN must have been handheld by people who feared for their lives, because the video of both telecasts suddenly jumped and flipped so badly all the viewers saw was flashing streaks of sky, grass, and buildings, as the operators presumably hit the ground in self-preservation. The pictures had no time to stabilize, now quaking from the ship hitting the ground with such force it put cracks in some of the Pentagon's outer walls.

"Jesus Christ!" gasped Jax, now recalling General Middleton's orders from a minute ago. "We did it. We blew those cocksuckers right out of the sky!"

Suzy slipped around to Jax's side so she could see what she was hearing. The cameras had steadied now, and through clouds of dust and debris the viewers saw the upper half of the Regg daughtership poking serenely above the treetops, a small stream of smoke lofting from where Dolly's USLAP beam had struck. CNN's broadcast feed from inside the alien craft had gone silent and dark. The Ivy League avatar had departed to byte heaven.

Suzy had the urge to throw her hands up in victory and yell, *"Hallelujah! You alien savages deserved it. I hope you're all dead."* But she decided to keep the celebration to herself. It would only further demonstrate to her cuckolded husband how much Captain Gregory Smith meant to her.

And yes, Jax was still very upset by his wife's affair. And he really wanted to have it out with her. But as far as reality television was concerned, this was really good stuff. The domestic fight could wait a few more minutes.

While a grounded C-SPAN reporter was trying to estimate the downed ship's dimensions, Fox News had switched from the ground-level long shot to a live action feed from a local affiliate news helicopter. The aerial view proved just how massive the downed craft truly was, its cracked and bent hull stretching from Long Bridge Park soccer field to blocking the south-bound traffic on Interstate One, well over two hundred yards. Chaos was

fighter escorts, while delivering enough damage to bring down a Regg daughtership, as she had just proven.

The audio-video cameras in Middleton's office were on maximum wide angle to show his five assistants and advisors, sitting in chairs, one slumping in a corner. The general was leaning against the whiteboard behind his desk, face down, rubbing his grayish-red crew cut with both hands. There was a low murmur and occasional cough in the room, but no one was actually speaking.

Suddenly, a graveling voice said, "Hello." It came from that one portion of every one's monitor that had purposely been left open to the special frequency linking The Desert to the Reggs. Every head from Iowa to that other place turned to see the live image of a grinning Regg, donning a white admiral's cap, complete with the navy insignia on the crown and gold braiding across the bill. The matching uniform was actually wearing him, as it hung loosely over his nonexistent shoulders. Reggs had obviously raided a navy surplus store at some point.

The mood of everyone watching turned from devastation to utter disgust.

"Hello!" the Regg said again, now saluting with his hairy fingers crooked at an awkward thirty-degree angle. "Good to talk at you. I see there many of you. You call me Admiral. Not my name. I command our ships. Oh, there are you, General Middleton. I know you from talk you had with my officer, Bruchelus. He dead now. So be many of you."

Middleton used his handheld remote to zoom the camera in on himself. "Yes, I am General Middleton" he growled, standing erect, his fist out in front. "And you are all conniving sacks of shit! Bruchelus and I were negotiating peaceably, when he broke it off saying he was going to consult with his superiors and get right back to us. Instead, you sneaky fugitives from a dog pound go on CNN with our Captain Smith, who, by the way, was our emissary, sent to establish communications with you. You expose us to the world, saying we are Earth's enemies. Then for no good reason under God's bright Heaven you kill him on live TV."

The grin on Admiral's fur lined jowl stretched even farther. His yellow eyes twinkled. "And you fell in our trap, yes, General? We...what be the word...*sacrificed* our spacecraft to kill your Little Sister. You are now of no defense."

Middleton's locked-and-loaded reply stopped cold in his throat, a thousand thoughts raced through his mind. Back at The Mansion, Suzy was the one who put the revelation into words: "Jesus! They think Dolly was Little Sister!"

General Middleton was thinking fast. If the Reggs thought Little Sister was out of commission...

"We still have fighters," he said meekly, purposely acting like a boy with a slingshot despondently defying a man with a shotgun. 'We can still fight you."

"Do no good," said Admiral, waving off the concept. "What you call our *daughterships* are many. We can burn your cities before you blink. And we shoot down your fighters."

Middleton acted distressed. His lips mouthed words unspoken. He then shrugged and asked quietly, "So, what do you want, Admiral?"

"You surrender," the pretentious Regg said with an off-handed gesture, as if it were a foregone conclusion.

"And if we don't?"

"We start destroying your cities with electromagnetic pulses. Not for a minute this time. For good. Many die. Your economy ruined. And we blame it on you Mejans."

There was a long silence before Middleton finally nodded slowly and asked with a defeated sigh, "How do you propose we enact this surrender?"

"Simple, General. You bring all your spacecraft to here in the Sahara Desert." The Regg turned his tablet to the camera and pointed with one claw to the map it was displaying. "We will give you the coordinates. Leave them there. We take care of them. You go home. You no threat to us. We not kill you. Too many Mejans. Not worth our efforts."

"How would you know that we surrendered all of our ships?"

The Regg officer was back to grinning, this one more sinister. "If we see one, we kill a city. You get blame. Earth people hate you more. Come after you more. No peace for you."

166

Continuing his dramatics, Middleton took a deep breath, let it out with exaggerated sigh, and said, "I need to confer with my superiors. I'll get back to you shortly."

"You have one..."

The general clicked the *Off* button on his remote and the Regg was cut off in mid-demand. Payback!

"Come back in, folks," motioned General Joshua Middleton, as he walked over to his desk and sat down in the tan executive chair. All four cameras in the room followed his movement, the one with the red light indicating which one was on. Jax and Alan hit their respective remote buttons to activate their own cameras and microphones. The video conference was back in session.

"Okay, everybody," said the general louder than was necessary, tapping a stylus on his smart pad, "the dumb-ass bastards think Dolly was Little Sister. They think we are defenseless. We most certainly are not." He glanced down at his tablet, poked it a couple times with the stylus, and then continued, "We know from our two, dog-faced captives, Hose-A and Hose-B, the Reggs have approximately fifty daughterships and twice that many fighters, considerably fewer than the first group of Reggs. But all of them stay inside the mother. Unlike their predecessors, they haven't been here for a millennium, staking out areas and hiding in deep waters all around the planet. This bunch lets out just enough craft to do a job, like they did to ambush Dolly. We can assume those ships have already run back home to mommy."

A female voice came from off camera, causing the camera to swing sharply in its direction and its red light click on. It was a pretty ensign of about thirty in standard desert camouflage, sitting in a chair to the general's right. "That means, sir, if we can destroy the mothership, we can destroy them all."

"Yes," said another advisor, this one a male with big eyes and head, on the other side of the room, "but we have no idea where she's hiding. And they aren't about to bring her out so we can blow her to kingdom come."

"General, if I may." It was Suzy, holding up her hand.

"Certainly, Suzy," chimed Middleton. "We'd love to hear anything you have to say."

167

"I'm just brainstorming here," she said, still organizing her thoughts, "but can you ask your engineers how much energy it would take to completely burn out an entire city? I'm just wondering if the Reggs really could do what they're threatening."

"Well, let's see," said the general, leaning back in his chair. "Dulcie, give me Darnus in Electronic Engineering."

"Getting Darnus in Electronic Engineering," said the sweet female voice.

In a moment, Middleton was sharing the split-screen with the darling, eighty-year-old, fifty-percent Mejan with her huge green eyes poking out of her distended and wrinkled bald head. She was wearing her usual white lab coat, and her tiny mouth was already wearing a frown. "Things not going well, Joshua?"

"Afraid not, sweetheart," sighed Middleton. "We need your help."

"That is why I came to your dimension," she joked.

"And we thank you," nodded the general, playing along for the briefest of moments before getting serious again. "Listen, Darnus, is it possible for a Regg daughtership, or even something twice as big, like Little Sister, to permanently fry every electronic circuit in a large city with an electromagnetic pulse?"

"No."

"That was fast," said a surprised general. "You sound pretty sure."

"I am. Neither reactor is powerful enough to completely destroy circuitry over a wide area. At best, they could only disrupt the electron flow for about one minute...as the Reggs have demonstrated quite clearly."

"How about their mothership? If she is the same size as the last one from ten years ago, could she fry an entire city?"

Darnus did some quick calculating on her pad. Without looking up she said, "Possible, but not likely. Needing approximately twenty percent to maintain anti-gravity, it would require channeling all the rest of its resources into the pulse generator, and even then the target area would have to be less than five miles in diameter."

"General?" The screen switched to Sam Pierce, Darnus's pure-human assistant, wearing the same style of white lab coat.

He was sweeping an index finger repeatedly down his smart-pad, obstinately searching for something.

"Yes, Sam."

"If I remember correctly…yes, here it is," he said, now reading what he had found. "Our two Regg captives told us that when they started their trek to our solar system at half the speed of light—which is their maximum speed—all the daughterships had their black matter-antimatter reactors literally plugged into the mother's to boost the energy needed to reach that initial velocity."

"Yes, I think I remember something about that," said Middleton. "Go on, Sam."

"Well, I was thinking that if that's true, and if Darnus's calculations are correct…"

"*If?*" challenged Darnus.

"Sorry, your royal Mejan hiney," bowed Sam to his boss. "*Knowing* her calculations are correct, then to make good on their threat to fry a city, wouldn't they have to have all their daughters at home and plugged in?"

"Hmm," mused Darnus. "Interesting question. They have about fifty daughters, correct?"

"Yes, about fifty," said Sam. "Minus one, now."

The tiny half-Mejan did some more tapping, then said, "Yes, with that extra energy force, they could permanently disorder the flow of electrons of every electrical device within that maximum five-mile diameter."

"How long would that take?" asked Middleton.

That answer required only two taps. "At least forty-five seconds of a sustained, maximum pulse."

Suzy's analytical mind was clicking. She couldn't help it, she had to interrupt. "Darnus? Hi. Suzy Brookfield-Jackson here. Could the mother maintain her protective shields during that time?"

Darnus cocked her head at the sound of the faceless, new voice. She liked the female's sound, and the good question. "Please to meet you, darling. I can't see you, but you sound nice."

"Thanks. I can see you. You remind me of my grandmother, Helen."

"Helen?" Darnus mused. "Helen? Was her Mejan name by any chance Ursalu?"

"Yes, it was. You knew her?"

"I knew her. We were in the same sector of our mothership until she left to live outside in Iowa. We went to the same exercise and cooking classes."

"Ladies, please!" interrupted the general. "You can catch up later. We have a slight crisis on our hands, if you don't mind."

"Yes, yes," huffed Darnus. "Keep your tighty-whities on, General. To answer your question, Suzy, shields alone require a forty percent drain of Little Sister's resources, so we can presume the same for a Regg spacecraft. Therefore, maintaining their anti-gravity and their shields while *frying* a whole city—as my Cro-Magnon coworkers so delicately put it—would be impossible.

"Thank you, Darnus," said Suzy, her mind still miles ahead. "And if the Regg's mothership has her shields lowered, would Little Sister's USLAP cannon have enough punch to bring her down?"

Across this video conference, a dozen mile-high IQs were spinning, beginning to follow the pretty Iowan's spitball.

Darnus tapped to bring up the schematic of the Regg mothership from ten years ago. She did some more calculations, paused, thought, and tapped some more. She looked into the camera and said, "The laser would have to hit dead center in the ship's lower quadrant where the reactor is. Anyplace else and it would just blow holes in the hull, maybe taking out some random electronics or other such peripherals."

Suzy Brookfield-Jackson took a big breath, held it, then let it out. "General, if we could bait the Reggs…"

Chapter 29

Back on the screen was the laughable figure of the Regg leader calling himself *Admiral*, the white navy togs still hanging on him like an adolescent wearing daddy's uniform. But there was no humor in anyone's face or in the proceeding dialog.

"Ten minutes we wait for you, General," he growled.

"Sorry, Admiral. But we had our engineers do some calculating. And one of the conclusions they drew was that you do not have the capability to destroy the electronics of a Walmart, let alone an entire city."

That was clearly a jolt to the Regg. His face folded into a sneer. "You not watch what we did to Washington and Pentagon?" he challenged. "That only a specimen of our power."

"*Specimen*?" snickered Jax. "I think the dufus meant *sample*."

"You're bluffing, Admiral," said Middleton. "Short interruptions of electronic flows are all you've shown, because that's all you can do. Hell, we can do that. We are not impressed."

The Regg's yellow eyes stared hard into the camera for a moment, then his right hand jerked upward. His half of the screen went blank.

"I don't think he was expecting that response," smiled the general.

"Ten to one he's having his engineers do the same calculating," said Sam Pierce.

"Do you think he'll bite?" asked Suzy.

'It's hard to know the mind of these aliens," said Middleton. "They aren't like us. Some of them are smart enough to build intergalactic spaceships and all. But they still look and act like timber wolves. I think they will accept our challenge. The question is how long we have to wait now."

The wait was about the same length of time it took Darnus to do her calculations: barely three minutes. When the Admiral's hairy mug returned to the screen, his expression and words were decisive. "We not want to do this, General, but now no choice. We permanently blackout a city. Then you believe us."

General Middleton was elated, but he was careful not to show it. Instead, he acted indifferent. "Well, we still don't believe you, Admiral," he said with a sigh. He counted to three and then added, "But if you can, you'll have to show us."

"And if we do, what will you do in return?"

Middleton stepped closer to his camera until his pocked face and reddish-gray crew cut filled the screen. "If you really can fry an entire city," he said slowly, "that would demonstrate you have a most powerful weapon, in deed. So, we will join forces with you and rule the Earth together...as you offered earlier. With both our races having superior technology and weaponry over these ignorant humans, there would be no stopping us."

The phony admiral could not conceal his glee. "Wonderful, General!" he yelped, jumping into the air like a golden retriever after a Frisbee. He landed on all fours, then bounced back up to lupus erectus.

There was considerably howling. Not from the Reggs, but from the six Iowans, who could not be seen nor heard by the Reggs or The Desert. "Give him a Milk-Bone," quipped David Brookfield, "and maybe he'll roll over."

"We thought you see it that way," the Regg leader continued. "We divide the planet. We not need much land. Just much meat and some slaves."

Middleton pulled back from the camera and wagged a finger, "Let's not get ahead of ourselves, Admiral. We still don't be-lieve you can destroy an entire city with an EMP. We have to see it happen."

"You will."

"And we want it to be a particular city, one of our choosing."

"Certainly!" grinned the Regg leader. "Name the city and..." He was suddenly distracted by low growls coming from off-screen to his right. He listened, nodded, then turned back to the camera and said, "What city, General?"

"Pyongyang."

"Where is that? Name is familiar."

"North Korea."

"I see," laughed Admiral. "Clever. Use us to kill your enemy."

"They are your enemy, too, Admiral. It would do us both a big favor."

The Regg looked to his right again, getting more advice. "My officers say city is quite large. It better to send pulse to small section. Not want to destroy too much."

Again, no surprise. As Darnus had determined, the scope of their EMP weapon was limited to about five miles across. "We agree," said Joshua Middleton. "We don't want to disrupt the lives of too many innocent people."

"Yes, said the self-proclaimed admiral. "We need innocent people. What part of that Korean city would you like us to target?"

Middleton pretended to think on it, before saying what his group of advisors had already determined, "Let's key on the North Korean's military, say, their navy's east coast fleet at T'oejo-dong."

"*T-dong* what? Where?"

"We'll give you the coordinates."

Chapter 30

Suzy Brookfield-Jackson felt pulled in four different directions at once. She desperately wanted to continue grieving for the death of Captain Gregory Smith, her fellow one-eighth Mejan, her friend, and for a few glorious minutes last night, her spiritual lover. But her current surroundings would not allow even one more tear.

She also wanted to scream in dread for her husband, who walked out on her a few hours ago to pilot The Mansion's only fighter and help protect Little Sister. General Middleton had told Jax he should stay home with his wife and kids, that The Desert had enough fighters to do the job. But Jax insisted on coming, despite Suzy begging him to stay. She had watched him open the hidden door just off the comm to the small hanger that re-sided under their five-acre pond. At the last moment, as he had turned back to face her, she would never forget the look on his face. It was a wordless compilation of emotions and logic she could clearly sense:

Why not go? You obviously don't love me anymore anyway.

You were so distraught at losing your lover, let's see how you feel about losing your husband.

I'm born-again brave and I need to do my part.

Deep down I'm terrified.

Tell the kids I love them.

Suzy wanted to stay in the communications room, monitoring the feed from the camera on the nose of Jax's fighter, *Iowa Three,* so dubbed the day it was delivered from The Desert ten years ago. But the image was of slowly rolling dark-gray clouds. From Jax's last communication to The Desert before going mute, Suzy knew he was doing as told, hiding inside a cumulus cloud two hundred miles east of North Korea over the Sea of Japan.

Having her husband in harm's way was bad enough, yet join-ing him were her father, Alan Brookfield, in Iowa One, and her

brother, David, in Iowa Two, also insistent volunteers. Middleton had told all three to stay out of the mix unless the mission
went south, and even then to think twice before engaging the
enemy. The Farm and The Mansion were The Desert's two most
important satellites. He needed them to remain intact and unknown.

Even if she couldn't hear or see what the most important men
in her life were doing on the other side of the globe, by staying
in the comm Suzy could at least be monitoring all the news reports, and especially CNN and Fox News, which had been on
the scene since the murder of Greg and the two spacecraft crashing near the Pentagon last evening. The Marines and Corps of
Engineers had quickly moved in, having a slow go of cracking
the hull of both downed spacecraft with acetylene torches and
lasers. Once inside Dolly, Suzy knew they would find a human
crew of about ten, some with enlarged eyes and heads, all wearing standard-issue desert fatigues, all probably dead from the impact. And once inside the Regg craft…well, just imagine what
the world will think of a pack of dead werewolves in black
jumpsuits and orange boots.

Suzy had seen more than enough replays of her soulmate's
body being fished out of the small lake by the local fire department. And if CNN wasn't looping the goofy avatar's rambling
message to the world about the evil Mejans, there was the never-
ending snaps of Greg's oversized head and eyes just before being shoved out of the portal. Thanks to being scooped by CNN
and Fox News, the other major networks were trying to stall their
plummeting viewership numbers by parading a plethora of ex-
perts from every conceivable branch of science, trying to explain
the unexplainable.

Still, the most important tug on her heartstrings at the moment was, of course, her two children. Ever since this crisis
started with her own abduction ten days ago, it had been a series
of mommy and daddy having to *go to the office* at all hours and
for longer and longer periods. Thank God for Odett and Loretta.
But job-one for Suzy was still to be a good parent. And part of
that role included being there with them, playing with them,
sharing their lives. And especially at this uncertain time in history, it was to keep them safe.

175

"C'mon, Mom, it's your turn," said an impatient Nathan. "Roll the dice."

"Sorry." Suzy picked up the red dice and rolled a nine. She landed on Free Parking, which had a couple hundred Monopoly dollars in it. But she didn't claim it. She just stared right past it. Nichole and Nathan looked at each other. *Mom's losing it.*

Okay then. Nathan rolled a six and landed on his mother's Marvin Gardens with two green houses. He waited for her to demand the rent. It never came. He wasn't about to say anything. He quickly shoved the dice to Nicole, who definitely *was* going to say something.

"Mom," Nicole whined, "Nathan landed on your Marvin Gardens. C'mon. Make him pay."

"Why, yes," Suzy muttered, blinking back to reality. She checked the yellow card's rent. "That will be three hundred and sixty dollars, please."

"Thanks a lot, Nicole!" sneered Nathan, fisting his sister's shoulder none too lightly.

"Mom, Nathan hit me!"

With all things considered, Suzy felt it best to have all five of the remaining people of The Mansion sequestered in the panic room. That included their live-in nannies, Loretta and her sexagenarian mother, Odett. Suzy didn't want any of them to know what was going to happen in a matter of hours, especially her two adolescents, and especially since it involved their missing father.

Still, Suzy couldn't help herself; she had to have both HD televisions in the living area of the panic room tuned to one news station or another, in case something prematurely broke regarding North Korea, and she would have to slip back into the private office. She kept the sound muted, and made sure both kids had their backs to the screens. Odett and Loretta knew about the UFOs and the murder of their one-time houseguest, so they were almost as interested in any breaking news as was Suzy. They both sat on the tan suede couch, nervously knitting nothing in particular, one eye on the same silent screens, the other reading the scrawls at the bottom.

As the game of Monopoly continued, Suzy kept thinking about the so-called compromise last night between General Middleton and the Regg commander calling himself *Admiral*. It lasted over four hours, with frequent pauses for both parties to consult with their advisors regarding anything from what the other side was trying to say to what they were actually thinking and not saying. Neither side trusted the other as far as they could spit.

Middleton insisted on having some of his spacecraft present for first-hand observation of North Korea's east naval base going into permanent midnight. The Reggs said he could have one fighter, which meant the Reggs would have two. Middleton said he needed two fighters for perspective from two different angles; the Reggs said okay, but they would then have four fighters. And so it went.

When the smoke cleared, the two sides had reached a disagreeable agreement at best. Zero-hour was set for midnight of the following day (tonight), weather permitting. The Regg bragged they would need only one of their *thousand* daughterships to deliver the killer electromagnetic punch. The Desert played along, knowing full well it had to be the mothership with virtually all of her *fifty* daughters plugged into her black matter-antimatter reactor to generate enough energy to maximize the EMP's effect. As Sam Pierce commented, one daughter by herself wouldn't have enough electromagnetic power to cook a Thanksgiving turkey.

The Desert's two designated observers were to hover no higher than one mile above North Korea, while the Reggs refused to disclose the exact altitude of their killer craft. The Desert didn't push it. Thanks to Darnus's calculations, they knew almost exactly where the mother would be hanging.

The Reggs thought they had come out on top with the negotiations. They were confident that after witnessing North Korea's east navy go dark, the humans/Mejans would have to admit the Regg's superiority, and have no choice but to join forces with them and rule the planet together.

On the other side, Middleton and his staff felt they had outsmarted the Reggs, who still believed they had destroyed Little Sister, thereby eliminating The Desert's only superior weapon.

But they had only brought down Dolly, at best a little sister to Little Sister. So, the plan was for Little Sister to wait in the weeds until the Regg mothership lowered her shields to divert all power to the EMP device, then hit her hard with the USLAP in just the right place to knock out her reactor.

That, of course, would start the dogfight. Hopefully, the bulk of the Reggs' one hundred or so fighters would still be inside their respective daughterships, which in turn were still having incestual couplings inside the mother. If everything went according to plan, the Reggs wouldn't have time to launch any of the daughters or fighters. The entire Regg nation would tumble into the Sea of Japan and be lost forever.

The self-proclaimed admiral said they would have only four fighters escorting the daughter with the EMP device, but Middleton didn't believe it. He figured the Reggs for at least six others hiding in the wings, so he wanted all eight of his remaining fighters on the periphery, too.

Even if some daughters and fighters managed to belch out of mother on her way down, it wouldn't be a fair fight. From the dogfights ten years ago with the first group of Reggs, it was clear The Desert's fighters were faster, more agile, and the built-in USLAPS had far more kill power and range.

It seemed like certain victory.

*****

Bedtime mercifully came at ten. Suzy gave Nicole thirty minutes of iPad in bed, while she finished the Stephen King short story to Nathan. Kisses all around, then Suzy quick-stepped the forty feet from the sleeping area of the panic suite to the office in the rear of the living room. Inside and door locked, she typed in the code, and entered her home-within-her-home for ninety more minutes of agonizing watching and waiting.

The rolling office chair was right where she left it, as was the half full bottle of Dasani on the PC counter. She grabbed the latter and plopped down in the chair, centering herself in the action like a wide-eyed new customer in the middle of Best Buy's entertainment section. Every one of the six HD television screens was glowing with a variety of images. The half-screen from Jax's Iowa-Three camera was still a fuzzy dark-gray and the audio was still mum. The other half of the same screen showed General Joshua Middleton leaning back in his office chair, talking casually to a female assistant, both still in their desert fatigues. His office microphone was also off. So, the only sound in the communications room came from two talking heads, one from CNN, the other from Fox News. Suzy listened to each one's speculations for a moment, realized it was all redundant and boring, and turned the sound down to a whisper.

Now things were eerily quiet. With no distractions, her mind jumped immediately to thoughts of all the men in her life, three of which were out there in the dead of night, over the Sea of Japan, ready to take on a force of aliens, who outnumbered them fifteen to one.

Chapter 31

When the main screen flashed to life, Suzy jumped, her eyes instinctively snapping to the fuzzy, infrared image of the Regg mothership filling the frame. It was being transmitted from Little Sister, ten miles above the mother in the atmosphere, slightly off to one side, above the clouds. Like the Reggs, all of The Desert's spacecraft had state of the art stealth. None could be detected by radar, sonar, laser or any electronic-based wave. The only way to detect them was visually. So as long as Little Sister was above the cloud deck, and the lower-altitude Iowa fighters stayed out of sight inside clouds, the Reggs had no idea they were around.

Of course, with a layer of clouds between Little Sister and the mothership, Little Sister had no optics on her, either. Thus the need for infrared, which could detect even slight variances in temperature levels. And since mother was using considerable energy to keep her shields up, she was shimmering like a rising sun.

Graduated black lines ran horizontally and vertically across the screen, accurately measuring the monster alien craft down to the millimeter. She was basically round, over two miles across, identical to the mothership from ten years ago. No doubt it was built in the same plant on Reggulus, or whatever the name of their insidious home planet was.

But what made Suzy's skin crawl was the off-color outline of the alien craft's most distinguishing feature. There, spanning almost the entire length and breadth of its topside, was the last letter of the Greek alphabet: omega. She couldn't make out the features from the infrared transmission, but she remembered that the U-shaped, raised portion was made from some type of translucent, tinted glass on most of its sections. This was the location of the bridge, the command center, observation decks, and any other onboard area requiring a live view. From cameras aboard a squadron of choppers and Little Sister herself ten years ago,

Suzy had watched the earlier mothership rise out of the Pacific Ocean off the coast of Oregon in surrender, to be escorted out of the solar system. Everyone thought that would be the last ever seen of the Reggs. No such luck.

"T minus one minute," squawked a voice from Little Sister, coming over the highly-secure, continually-encrypted channel Suzy had helped develop long ago. It was a completely different frequency from the one used to converse with the Reggs, so all the humans/Mejans could talk freely among themselves.

On the adjacent screen General Middleton's head and shoulders were already front and center with his headset on. "Copy, Little Sis," he said. "Wait until she starts dropping her shields, then close on her fast."

"Roger that. We'll come in just under Mach-Three with guns a-blazin'."

Middleton laughed, "If the sonic booms don't make Kim Jong-un crap his pants, the exploding Regg reactor certainly will."

Darnus had calculated that the Regg mothership needed about five seconds between lowering her shields and converting that energy to charge the EMP cannon to full power. The idea was to hit her before she could fire, so that even if the North Koreans were awakened by all the noise, they would never know just how lucky they were to avoid a total electronic Armageddon.

Little Sister and all the fighters had a sub-directive: if possible, they were to take the action away from the Korean Peninsula and out over the Sea of Japan, where the splashdown of a spaceship the size of a small island would keep damage and eyewitnesses to a minimum. God help any ships at sea; some collateral damage was unavoidable.

Holding the remote that controlled every piece of electronics in the comm, Suzy clicked the button that reopened the audio channel to Jax. They had been maintaining radio silence, as instructed, but time was rapidly running out. She asked tentatively, "You there, Jax?" He didn't respond. "C'mon, honey. You gotta talk to me. It's about to go down."

There was a continued silence before Jax finally said, "Not now, Suzy. I gotta stay focused."

Suzy. He called her *Suzy*. Not *Suzette*, like he often did when perturbed at her for something. At least this was a good sign. But Suzy had to admit her husband's tone was less forgiving and more toward nervousness, maybe even fear. Who could blame him. The fate of the world was about to be decided, and Jax could easily be right in the middle of it.

"I just want you to be careful up there, baby," said Suzy, her voice soft and shaky. "Don't take any chances. Your kids need you."

"I will. Kiss them for me."

"You know I will…"

Suzy's sniffling reply was cut short by the commander of Little Sister, announcing, "Mother is going dark. Shields coming down. We're one mile and closing."

"Squadron, Go!" barked General Middleton, talking to his eight fighters. "Close with Sister, protect her flanks. Watch out for EMPs from their fighters. You Iowans stay put. That's an order!"

A concerto of *Copy* and *Roger* filled the airwaves, as the fighters deserted their positions in the nearby clouds and raced to where the Regg mothership was hovering five miles above the North Korean navy. The TV monitor that had been showing Middleton in split-screen now flashed to full-view from Little Sister's nose camera, as she closed in on the rapidly-growing U-shape. Infrared showed she was losing her red glow, as the shields came down.

The instant the glow was completely gone, Little Sister fired the Ultra Sonic Laser Accelerated Pulse cannon from five hundred yards above. The bullseye was at the base of the U right between its two arms, where her black matter-antimatter reactor was running everything from its anti-gravity to its Electro-Magnetic-Pulse weapon that was just about to fire.

But just as a small red dot burned into the mothership's hull, the large craft twitched, as if it felt the sting. The red dot shifted slightly to the left, carving a slash in the hull, more than drilling straight in. The ship began rocking like a boat in rough water. Fighting to stay upright, she slowly moved westward away from the Korean Peninsula.

Two Regg fighters coughed out from an open portal on mother's right side to join the other four fighters serving as escorts. All six turned to face the oncoming desert fighters, which were closing fast, already firing their own USLAPs. One Regg fighter cracked open like a snap pea. Smoke came from the cockpit of another. Both tumbled seaward out of control.

As Little Sister's cameras switched to Day-Night mode, the mothership and everything in view became pseudo-daytime. Suzy sat transfixed, her mouth open, her eyes wide, as she watched Little Sister in pursuit of the mother, firing again and again into the hull, but doing little if any damage. A quick check by Little Sister's infrared revealed the mother had raised her shields. Not good. Not good at all. But at least that was keeping any more fighters from belching out from her side ports.

The audio inside The Mansion's communications room became a din of elevated voices, reporting hits, near misses, and the ever-changing locations of the targets. Much of it was laughter and war-whoops, as our superior fighters continued dropping the inferior Reggs without losing any of our own. But when a crush of two dozen Regg fighters unexpectedly poured out from the heavens, our pilots found themselves heavily outnumbered, unable to keep track of them all. The sneaky bastards had broken the agreement with extras hiding in the clouds...just like The Desert had.

"I'm hit! Going down," said one of the good guys.

"Losing power..." said another, apparently being hit with an EMP.

The tide seemed to be turning. Then things got even worse. Suzy heard what she hoped she never would:

"They need us," said Alan Brookfield, her father.

"Let's go!" replied her brother, David.

"I'm in," said her husband, Jax.

Suzy's heart fell into her stomach.

Chapter 32

In equal quadrants on the HD screen, Suzy could see everything Little Sister saw through four of its twelve exterior cameras. The half-mile-wide craft stayed in pursuit of the wobbling, two-mile-wide Regg mothership, repeatedly firing the USLAP cannon with no apparent effect against its shields.

But that action no longer held Suzy's interest. Her vision was now locked on the HD screen to her right, devoted entirely to the view from Jax's nosecone camera, as he sped out of his cloud to join the dogfight. Her hand was shaking so much she could barely punch the correct buttons to tune down Little Sister's audio and bring up the running interchange among Jax, her father, and younger brother.

Alan was reminding the other two that their fighters had that built-in collision-avoidance feature, so they never had to worry about colliding with each other or with a Regg spacecraft. Nor could they accidentally shoot each other, only Reggs, and at a maximum effective range of one mile.

Suzy remembered from the interviews with the two captured Reggs, their fighters had none of these capabilities, just like their wolfen brothers from ten years ago. Their cannons were strictly laser-based hole-burners with an effective range of only a thousand yards. Also, each Regg fighter carried an EMP devise that could disable the electronics of another fighter, if it could maintain the beam for a solid three seconds at close range. In a sense, it was a more effective weapon than their laser cannons.

The fighters of neither side had shields.

"I'll go in first and draw their attention," squawked the elder Alan Brookfield. "You two follow me in and take them when they aren't looking."

"Roger."

"Roger."

The Day-Night camera on her husband's fighter showed her father pull ahead and increase his distance from the other two. On the horizon was the massive Regg mothership, lumbering left

184

and right, with Little Sister hot on her heels. Shortly, the images of the much smaller fighters became visible, as they buzzed in and around each other like bees on a hive.

From a distance, it was hard to tell the good guys from the bad, as both types were about forty feet long, countershaded with dark tops and lighter undersides. But as the action drew closer, Suzy could see the difference. The Regg fighters still looked like classy, oversized Lamborghinis, while ours had the low-slung styling of curvy, ergonomic, television remote controls. The Regg canopies were set low and farther back, butting up against a raised portion of the fuselage like a headrest. So, their view was limited to the sides and straight ahead. Our canopies were raised, oblong bubbles, set far forward on the sleek fuselage for an advantageous, three-sixty view.

As Alan Brookfield drew within range, he locked on one of the Regg fighters that was trying to bring down a Desert fighter. When he pulled the trigger on his joystick, a small puff of smoke appeared on the canopy of the unsuspecting Regg, and the craft plummeted downward. Alan managed to drop another one, before three of them broke away from the adjacent dogfight and turned on him. Being more agile and quicker, Alan was able to avoid their scattered laser fire, as he spun upward into the heavens.

Instantly, Jax and David joined the action, each taking out one of the Reggs trying to follow Alan. The third Regg fighter, seeing he was outnumbered and outclassed, retreated for the comfort of his two dozen buddies still trying to kill the remaining five Desert fighters. All three Iowans pursued him into the fray.

"I'll take the ones on the right," yelled Jax, his adrenalin pumping.

"Okay, I got the left side," said David, just as excitedly.

"I guess that leaves me the middle, huh boys?" said a calmer Alan.

Suzy's screen showed a group of six Regg fighters quickly grow larger, as Jax raced into them. The telltale alarm of his radar locking on one filled the room, then the sight of it exploding filled the screen. Jax war-whooped.

With only the jerky images from her husband's camera now, plus an occasional glance at Little Sister's equally-erratic transmissions, Suzy was having trouble following the action visually. The audio wasn't much better, as she strained to filter anything meaningful from the shouts and vulgarities among her three men.

"Got another! Die, mo-fo, die!" called one of them, now coming in more clearly.

"Yeah! Me, too. Splash number three."

"It's a turkey shoot, boys."

"Oh, shit! I've got four on me,"

"...keep twistin'...jivin'," yelled another. "They can't out-maneuver..."

The next transmission stopped Suzy's heart cold.

"I'm being pulsed! I'm..."

Static. Then yells from two of the other Iowans, impossible to tell which ones.

Who was hit with the EMP? In one nanosecond, her mind raced through the short list of her three loved ones, trying to logically decide which one she hoped it was...or wasn't. Her father was older, sixty-something, he'd had a good life. She loved him. Her brother, David, was still young, only twenty-eight; he had a wife and new son. She loved him, too. Jax was her husband, the father to her children, her daily companion, her emotional shoulder, her financial security. And, oh, yeah: she loved him deeply. But considering her recent infidelity, would he ever take her back?

That's when Suzy noticed the HD screen that had been receiving the video feed from Jax's nosecone camera was now nothing but white noise.

Oh, dear God in Heaven. It was Jax!

"Jax!" she screamed. "Jax! Are you there?" No reply. "Dad! David! I can't raise Jax. Somebody speak to me!"

"Can't tell, punkin'." That was definitely her father, Alan. "A little busy here. Jax, you there?" Static. "David?"

"I think it was Jax," yelled David, obviously with his hands full, as well. "I don't see him or hear him. Jax? You okay?"

Static. Continued white noise on the screen.

186

Blinking away the mist coating her eyes, Suzy found the right button to bring up the dialog between The Desert and Little Sister. Maybe they knew something.

The commander of Little Sister, Major Charles Westbrook, was yelling. "...can't penetrate mother. Her shields still up. And their fighters have knocked out our shields while we were firing."

"What's your status, Chuck?" said General Middleton.

"We can still keep up with mother, but we are losing our fighters, our protection. They're hitting us hard."

"Forget it, Chuck," said Middleton. "Break off. Get the hell out of there. That goes for you fighters, too. Break off. Get out of there, now!"

"Might be too late," puffed Chuck Westbrook. "Scanners show only two of our fighters left. It's the Iowans. Two of them, anyway."

Middleton's radar screen verified the fact. He wasted no time. "You Iowans, break off now! That's an order. Execute the exit strategy. Now!"

"Roger."

"Copy."

"Chuck, what shape is Little Sister in?" said Middleton, trying to stay military calm. "Can you outrun the Reggs?"

"We're hit pretty bad, General," said a weary Major Westbrook. "We've lost a lot of power. No speed. And they keep hitting us."

"Satellite shows you are one hundred and forty miles east of Seolak, South Korea," said Middleton. "There's a large forest just north of its airport. Can you make it there?"

"No way, sir. Instruments show our anti-gravity engine is shutting down as we speak." Crackle. "...losing altitude. Five hundred feet. Four. Mark our location...full of laser holes....probably sink. Hundred feet.

"Oh, God!"

Two of Little Sister's cameras showed small whitecaps coming on fast, then a solid gray-blue, then blackness. The audio followed with a high-pitched whine, then steady static.

"Chuck!" yelled Middleton. "Major Westbrook? Do you read?" His voice dropped to a defeated whimper. "Goddamn it, Chuck. Talk to me."

Suzy Brookfield was bawling so hard tears were literally flying out of her eyes and onto the floor. Fortunately, her fingers remembered which button to push to bring the audio back to her Iowa fighters. "Dad? David?" she blubbered. Then a heartbreaking, "*Jax*? Anybody there?"

It was her dad who answered after an agonizing five seconds. "We're here, honey. David's flying beside me. We're in the stratosphere. We're safe." Alan paused to get the next words out of his throat. "We still don't know about Jax. He might be behind us, baby. We just don't know."

"He was hit, wasn't he?" choked Suzy. "I heard him say he was hit with an EMP. Did you see it? Did you see him?"

"Sorry, Sis," added David quietly. "We heard it, too. We were just too busy to locate him."

In complete denial, Suzy consider only two possibilities. The best one was that only Jax's communications system was knocked out by the Reggs, and he had flown to safety somewhere away from the action. He'd be back here at The Mansion within the hour.

The next best scenario was that his fighter had been disabled, and he ejected, landing in the Sea of Japan. And because he was certainly wearing his puffy, Michelin man spacesuit to counteract all the high-speed, G-force twists and turns during the dogfight, he would be floating on the water at this very minute like a big marshmallow. Some passing ship would eventually pick him up, and she'd be hearing from him in a day or two.

Those were the only two scenarios she would consider.

Chapter 33

It was about to become the worst day in human history. To the horror—plus a certain degree of fascination—the entire world had watched recent events unfold on their home televisions and mobile devices, broadcast by every news station with a license to operate and every smart-phone user who knew how to upload to social media. Then yesterday (Sunday, June 21) a charcoal-gray spaceship the size of a small city had set down in the agricultural region of north central Iowa, callously crushing four farmsteads, ten people, a wind farm, a cell tower, and an undeterminable number of livestock and cash crops.

Its initial landing was a bit rocky, as the mothership seemed damaged, teetering right and left, a narrow plume of smoke trailing skyward from someplace atop its three-story structure. By the end of that day the smoke was gone, but not the ever-growing crowds, which were now ringing the perimeter along country roads and trampling down even more green crops to gawk at the massive monstrosity from outer space.

No one got *too* close. They didn't know for sure which one of the aliens this ship housed or their motives. The masses had seen the telecast from CNN and Fox News two nights ago, showing that smaller spaceship hovering over the Pentagon, while an alien-generated avatar told everyone about the evil Mejans, one of them even being pushed out the hatch to his death. But that spaceship was a toy compared to the size of this one. And they had seen enough sci-fi movies to fear killer-rays could come streaming out from the craft any minute, vaporizing every biologic in a ten-mile radius.

With their red and blue lights flashing, dozens of Iowa Highway Patrol and county sheriff vehicles were circling the adjacent county roads in an attempt to establish some kind of security for something no one yet understood. Two local news choppers, one from Des Moines and one from the Twin Cities, had arrived, along with two twin-bladed Chinooks from the National Guard in Mason City...all four buzzing above like hummingbirds, but staying on the fringe just in case. The horizons were splattered with more of everything coming in from all directions.

That was yesterday.

Today, the area was filled to capacity, with hardly anything moving. Hanging ominously above the still-grounded mother-ship were four of her daughters, as if daring anyone to try anything foolish. These counter-shaded, saucer-shaped UFOs were identical to the one that had crashed near the Pentagon two days ago, just before another, considerably larger spacecraft (Dolly) also fell to earth a few miles away near Chevy Chase, Maryland.

No one knew much of anything. But at three o'clock this afternoon, all speculation and much of the curiosity came to a gasping halt. Once again the Reggs had linked up to CNN to get their message out to the world. And it was not what the world wanted to hear. Nor was it what it wanted to see, as the plastic human avatar was replaced by a true-to-life, wolf-faced, cat-eyed, earless Regg. The only banal facial feature was his Clark Kent-type, black-rimmed glasses. But even they quickly lost their humanness by framing yellow cat eyes, while resting on a short snout tipped with a pitch-black nose.

Cloaked in a floor-length robe made of patchwork Guernsey cow hides, the Regg spokesman was standing at a gun metal po-dium in the observation deck of the mothership. In the back-ground through the clear, floor-to-ceiling windows were the em-erald-green corn and soybean fields of north central Iowa, still ringed with people and vehicles, the mid-afternoon sun flashing off windshields and the occasional circling helicopter keeping its distance. This movement told the world the panorama was real, not a painted backdrop.

About the only good thing that could be said for him—if it were a him, as both sexes looked and sounded about the same—was his surprisingly excellent grasp of the English language. It was apparent he had been training for this moment for months, if not years. And now it had finally arrived. You could hear the fervor in his raspy voice.

"Hello again my fellow Earthians. I am talking to you from our magnificent spacecraft many of you have come to admire here in this region of green and plenty you call I-o-wa. We felt it was time you saw what we really look like and where we have

190

been living for years in this ship, so we can get to know each other better.

"We ask you to stay back and not approach our ship for any reason. And as a warning to your military, do not attempt any kind of strike against us. Our force field makes us impervious to any attack. We would be forced to retaliate with our spacecraft, which are patrolling the skies above us, as you can see.

"But onto happier things. My name is *Rouchearc Straxdra*. I know that is difficult for you to say or remember. So, you may call me *Ambassador*. Okay? We want to make things easy for you, as you can see. And we want to be your friends."

The Regg spokesman paused to look down at his notepad and adjust his glasses. "We are pleased to inform you that despite a sneak attack on us, we have defeated the evil Mejan race, which has been preying on your planet for eighty years. Their weapons and deceit can no longer hurt you. Their leaders are dead. Only their underlings still walk across the land. They still must be found and captured. But more of that later.

"We hope you are not too troubled by our appearance. We realize we look similar to your fictitious wolfmen of horror films. And you probably think us akin to some of Earth's canines. But obviously we are much smarter and more erect. The only thing we have in common with the wolf and dog is our love of fresh meats. As you love your chocolates, pizzas and seafoods, we love meats. And that is why we have landed our ship in this beautiful agricultural region of your world…which is now our world, too.

"We will be asking some of you to be our friends and keep us well supplied with meats. Black Angus and Hereford are some of our favorites, but we like all cattle. Sheep, too. Pigs. Deer. We feel chicken and turkey are edible, but one needs to develop a taste for them, don't you agree?" Ambassador looked up and offered a quirky smile, before returning to his notes.

"Those of your local farmers and ranchers who bring us fresh meats each day will be highly rewarded. There are over a thousand of us: males, females, and offspring, so we need approximately twenty thousand pounds of meats each day. Some of these meats can be already processed, provided they are processed no more than two hours before and not frozen. We prefer, however, for the animals to be brought in on the hoof, as you say, so we can do our own slaughtering and quality control. This we have been doing for years without your knowledge. We apologize for stealing your livestock. We had no choice. Now with our new partnership, things can become more open and amicable.

"We do eat things besides meats, such as grains, fruits, and vegetables. But, again, we have little desire or means to grow and process these ourselves. So, those who bring us truckloads of these items will be highly rewarded, as well. We will need approximately a thousand pounds of grains and fruits and vegetables each day. Don't make us have to keep raiding your grocery outlets, as we have been doing for ten years now."

Ambassador turned to look behind him at the people and vehicles on the distant perimeter. He smiled broadly and continued, "You are a curious race. That is interesting. So, enjoy watching us while you can. Soon, we will be expanding outward from our craft to inhabit most of this countryside in private. We will take over and live in the farms, and we will build other structures to inhabit." He laughed, then added, "But of course, we will call upon you our friends to do the actual constructions. You will be highly rewarded."

Ambassador leaned forward against the podium. "We *do* want to be your friends. It will be the best for everyone. Please do not make us shut down or destroy your cities again. We want them to keep functioning as much as you do. We did it only to get your attention and demonstrate our capabilities."

He held up his right paw, which was actually more a hand than paw. It had four elongated fingers and a very short thumb. He grouped the longer digits in twos, forming the Vulcan symbol for *live long and prosper*. "Peace to our friends," he said. Then he signed off.

Chapter 34

Suzy couldn't ask the others to turn off the nauseating telecast with its occasional cutaway to again show the video of Captain Smith's death. So, she turned off her senses and drifted back into depression. She curled her arms around herself in the pink terrycloth bathrobe and slumped deep into the black leather couch of her youth. She didn't even notice the sympathetic pat on her leg from her one-quarter Mejan mother, Mary, sitting beside her.

Suzy's one-night, tantric tryst with Captain Gregory Smith seemed like a distant memory now, like something she had read in a Harlequin romance novel as a teenager. But this non-fiction story had ended with her Mejan lover being shoved out of a spaceship to his death in an act of pure barbarism by a bunch of black-hearted heathens bent on ruling the earth. That was more like a Stephen King tale co-written with Arthur C. Clarke.

Heart-wrenching as that was, it had become overshadowed by the loss of her husband two nights ago somewhere over the dark Sea of Japan. His fighter—Iowa-Three—was presumable hit by a Regg EMP, which was when all communications ceased. It had to be an electromagnetic pulse, because even the homing chip in the back of Jax's head had stopped transmitting its signal. Thankfully her dad and brother had made it back safely, but they could shed no light on what might have happened to Jax; it was night, and they were in a hectic dogfight with more Regg fighters than they could handle.

If only she had kept her quasi infidelity a secret from Jax, like she had from everyone else so far. Maybe he wouldn't have stormed out of their communications room so determined to go help The Desert fight the Reggs. And now he wasn't here anymore, the second man to evaporate from her world in as many days. Gregory being murdered was the gut-wrenching loss of a countryman, a kinsman her spirit badly needed at the time. But he had occupied only a few short days of her life and an even shorter hour of her love. Losing her husband of ten years, her daily companion, her confidant, the father of her children…that had Suzy's heart lying dead in the pit of her stomach. And it was all her fault. She would trade a hundred nights with Gregory to have just one more with Jax, if only to tell him how sorry she was and how much she loves him.

Suzy's kids—Nicole and Nathan—were currently downstairs in The Farm's rec room, playing with their cousins, still oblivious to most everything. They had asked where dad was, as it had been over two days since he *had to go to town on business.* That was later modified to *out of the state for a while longer.* Sooner or later she would have to tell them the truth. The problem was Suzy didn't know what that truth was.

She was sure Little Sister had gone down into the sea, too, along with all its fighters. She heard firsthand accounts of that. Little Sister was The Desert's best weapon. Now they were defenseless. General Middleton hadn't been seen nor heard since. The monitor in the communications room stayed on, but it was only white nothing for two straight days.

The Reggs had won, and they were bloviating all over the airwaves about it. Life—as the people of Earth had known it— would never be the same. And that was all the more true for any part-Mejan woman who had just become a single mother in a world about to be run by a bunch of alien sons and daughters of bitches. *Literally.*

Suzy's wristwatch vibrated, nudging her out of her misery. She slowly glanced down to see it was her father, Alan, on watch with Mike in The Farm's communication room downstairs. With little enthusiasm, she plucked her communicator from the pocket of her bathrobe and punched OK. "Dad?"

"Honey," said Alan cautiously, "it seems a black Lexus sedan is coming down the lane. You drove the silver Lexus SUV, right?

"Yeah...."

"Well, this looks a lot like your other Lexus. Whoever it is opened the gate with the pass code. Surely you didn't give the code to anybody...maybe Loretta or Odett?"

"No," said Suzy, just as cautiously, "they don't even know about our farm. They think the kids and I are at Six Flags."

"Well, we tried hailing the vehicle with no reply. The silo camera is zoomed in on the driver, but the angle is too high up to see his or her face. Infrared shows only one person. Pretty good size person."

"*Pretty good size* as in short and fat, or big and tall," breathed Suzy, optimism beginning to swell in her throat.

"I'd say big and tall," said Alan. "But be careful now, sweetheart. It could be anything. We've got the silo's laser zeroed in, just in case."

Suzy didn't hear her father's warning. Her communicator was doing a single bounce on the couch, as she ran through the foyer toward the front door on rubbery legs. She hit the outside security lights switch on the wall and peered through the bulletproof glass, as the black SUV pulled up front in full view.

It just sat there, engine off. No one got out. The heavily-tinted glass hid the profile of the driver, so no one could see his head was down, perhaps praying, perhaps giving thanks, perhaps summing strength for the upcoming encounter. By now Mary, Alan, and David were in Suzy's orbit, more than two sets of supportive hands on her back and shoulders.

Suzy's intuition insisted it was Jax. She unlocked the tandem deadbolts, opened the steel reinforced door, and despite her father's second *Be careful*, she headed down the cobblestone walkway.

The driver watched her approach. He drew in a deep breath, then slowly opened the car door. He slid out of the black leather seat, closed the door, and leaned against it, his hands at his sides.

It was Jax.

Suzy stopped ten feet short, her bare feet gripping the cool texture of the flagstone slabs. The trill of summer insects seemed exceptionally loud in the silence, as she studied her husband's face, partially shadowed under the sodium light. Was he glad to see her? Was he okay? Injured? Confused? He just stood there in his navy-blue jogging outfit, looking at her blankly.

Suzy's lips quivered with the words she wanted to say, but couldn't. She clutched her bathrobe's lapels and pulled them even tighter to her chest.

195

In slow motion, Jax pushed away from the car to stand up straight. The shortest of smiles cracked his lips as he opened his arms halfway.

Suzy hesitated. He *was* beckoning her, wasn't he? She eased forward, cautiously. His arms spread open a little farther. She quickened per pace. Crossing onto the asphalt, Suzy stopped three feet from her husband, never taking her eyes off his shadowed face. With her indigenous, enhanced night vision, she could see his expression as clearly as if it were daytime. But it was as noncommittal as the vibration she was feeling. He seemed to want her in his arms as much as he didn't.

Jax extended both hands, placing them on her shoulders and drawing her gently toward him. Suzy easily obeyed, folding herself into his arms. Nothing else mattered now. Her husband was different, but he was home and safe. Suzy hugged him hard and allowed herself to cry.

Chapter 35

Just because he was home didn't mean Jax had forgiven Suzy her indiscretion with Captain Smith. That wasn't the kind of thing a man can toss back in the water like an undersized bass. But his reticent heart couldn't help but warm when his two adolescents sprinted across The Farm's recreation room screaming, "Daddy!" Nicole bear-hugged his waist, while Nathan got him around the knees, and all three went down to the floor in a giggling heap.

After a short bout of WrestleMania, the kids decided all was right with the world again, and went back to bowling with their cousins. Alan and David quickly helped Jax off the floor. They were dying to hear what exactly happened to him and his fighter while battling the Reggs, and how he managed to get home from halfway around the world.

But what Jax really wanted at the moment was to get alone with his wife, even though he wasn't sure why. What would he say? What would she say? What could they say? Would talking about the affair only make things worse?

Jax's dilemma was put on hold by Alan's fatherly arm around his shoulder, leading him over to the wet bar. "Let's hear it, son," coaxed his father-in-law. "Every detail." He deposited Jax on a bar stool, then went around behind the bar to help his wife and son serve up a round of cold Pabst Blue Ribbons and various snacks. Suzy, meanwhile, stayed standing at her husband's side, clutching his arm like he might float away if she dared let go. Jax found it difficult to look at her.

The man of the hour munched on the pretzel Suzy had stuffed in his mouth, swallowed, and said, "Well, as you two well know, we were outmaneuvering the Regg fighters, like we did ten years ago. It was almost fun. Then all of sudden there were so many buzzing us, my auto-avoidance system couldn't handle them all. So, one of them I didn't see must have hit me with its EMP long enough to knock out all my power."

197

"He's right," nodded David. "They were everywhere, and more seemed to be coming from nowhere. Sorry we couldn't help you, bro."

"Yeah," said Alan, "we didn't even see you go down. So, what the hell did happen?"

Jax took a long sip on his longneck bottle, and continued, "I was in free-fall. No control at all. Spinning. Tumbling. I sure hated to abandon Iowa-Three, but she was dead in the air. I pulled the manual eject lever and the next thing I knew I was floating on the wind, still seated in my cockpit chair. Its parachute had deployed automatically. It was so dark I couldn't see the water, so when I hit it, I got a hell of a jolt."

"But you were wearing your Michelin man suit, right, honey?" said Suzy, fresh tears on her cheeks. "So, it cushioned the impact, and then you floated on the water like a big bobber, right?"

"Exactly," smiled Jax, giving her a glance, then back to his bottle. "The weight of the chair kept me upright, and the inflated suit kept me buoyant. It worked just the way The Desert geniuses designed it."

Suzy smiled to herself. It was exactly as she had envisioned the less favorable of the two acceptable scenarios. The other was Jax flying home within hours, unhurt. "And eventually a boat came along and picked you up," she added.

"Yeah, I don't know how long I was in the water, because I was stunned, and the rolling action of the waves kept rocking me to sleep. But I opened my eyes to find it was daylight and I was looking up at a line of oriental faces staring down at me like I was…"

"…from outer space?" laughed Mary.

"Yeah, in my puffy flight suit and helmet, they must have had second thoughts about hauling me aboard that sixty-foot fishing trawler, especially with all the UFO action over the Pentagon and the Reggs barking orders on the airwaves. But they did, despite my not remembering who I was or what I was doing out there on the ocean. I guess it didn't matter much, since none of them spoke English anyway. When they got my helmet and suit off, they saw I was human and seemed to relax. They must have assumed I was an American, because after a day and a half of lying in their sickbay while they fished for tuna, they dropped me off at the U. S. Army base in Okinawa."

"That was what, *yesterday*?" challenged Mary with furrowed brow. "Dear boy, why didn't you call?"

"My communicator got fried, along with everything else."

"Doesn't the army base on Okinawa have *telephones*?"

Jax squirmed on his stool, using a thumbnail to pick at the label of his beer bottle. "Like I said, I had amnesia. They had me in the army hospital quite a while for observation. Things were really fuzzy for a while."

Suzy knew Jax was lying. The truth was he was in no hurry to get home. He was still mad at her. He needed time. And at this moment in The Farm's downstairs rec room, he certainly wasn't going to tell the family about his cheating wife. He felt it was none of their business, thank goodness. Suzy could only hope they were buying this lame amnesia story.

"So, how'd you get back to the States?" asked David Brookfield.

"Well, apparently they were already on high-alert from the sketchy reports of our dogfight near Korea, plus all the crap the Reggs were broadcasting over CNN. So, based on my high-tech spacesuit, they assumed I was something special. Enough of my memory came back that I told them I worked for a secret government agency that was fighting the aliens. I knew I was based somewhere in Iowa. So, they put me in the copilot's seat of an F-22 Raptor, and flew me to straight to Offutt Air Force Base at Omaha. Again, my spacesuit was like carte blanche to get anything I wanted. I asked for a cheeseburger and a cab to take me home, which I now remembered was in Iowa City. They even prepaid the driver three hundred bucks."

"So, when did you get all your memory back?" asked Alan, popping the cap off his second Pabst.

"Just a few hours ago, on the ride back to Iowa City. The closer I got, the more I remembered. By the time he dropped me off at my front gate, I remembered everything."

Jax took a long pull. Suzy didn't say a word.

"Well, you still could have called from your house," chided Mary. "Suzy's been sick with worry for days."

"I know," said Jax. "But after the gushy, welcome-back greeting I got from Odett and Loretta, I thought it'd be even better to surprise all of you in the flesh." Jax slid off his stool and took Suzy by the hand. "And speaking of which," he said, leading her toward the steps, "I want to be alone with my wife for a while now, if that's okay with you folks."

"Of course, it is," said Mary with a throw-away gesture. "How thoughtless of us. You two run along."

"Just don't be too long," called Alan after them. "Middleton is gonna want a report from you."

*****

Reaching the top of the stairs to the main level, Jax led his wife down the long hallway to her old bedroom. He had no sooner locked the six-panel oak door, when Suzy spun around and said, "Jax, listen. I've got to tell..."

A finger to her lips cut Suzy off at mid-sentence. "Let me go first," he said, taking her gently by the shoulders. Without turning her around, he pushed her slowly backwards to the four-poster bed and sat her down on the white goose-down comforter. He then backed off a step and stood before her, gathering his thoughts, like a man about to present his case to the Supreme Court.

"First off," he said, "I didn't really have amnesia."

"I know that, honey," said Suzy with a maternal half smile.

"Yeah, I didn't figure you were buying it. I didn't call because I needed some time to think things over."

"I know that, too."

Jax fought to regain his thought pattern. "Look," he finally said, hands on his hips, eyes on the floor. "What you did was wrong. And I'll admit I was very upset when I stormed out. But having a near-miss with death, and then having time to think on it, I came to realize just how much our lives intertwine. We have two beautiful kids. You are their mother. And for that reason, I will always love you, no matter what you do. Nicole and Nathan represent everything that's good between you and me. That can never change."

200

Suzy started to say something, but an insistent stare and an erect index finger stopped her again.

"And now, with all that's going on with the Reggs trying to take over the planet," he said, "I think you and I need to stay together, for their sake, if nothing else."

"I feel the same way," nodded Suzy, moisture coating her eyes. "The kids mean everything. But I want to stay together for us, too. I love you, Jax."

Suzy stared hard into Jax's azure eyes. Those last words were a definite opening. How would her husband respond?

"I want that, too," he said, his mouth and eyes revealing he was sincere. "Despite what you did, I love you, too."

Suzy's heart skipped a beat, but it didn't leap with joy. While his words were what she wanted to hear, the emotion behind them lacked a noticeable degree of passion. Who could blame him?

When Jax said nothing more, Suzy presumed her husband was done talking. "Is it my turn now?" she asked softly.

Jax tipped his head, giving her the go-ahead.

Suzy's big copper-brown eyes remoistened. "It wasn't what you think," she said, starting to get up from the bed. But Jax's outstretched hand signaled for her to stay seated. It seemed he wasn't done after all.

"Well, let's see if it *is* what I think," he said evenly, with no anger. "I think it was because you felt a strong bond with Gregory. Why wouldn't you? You're both part Mejan. You understand each other in a way that no pure human like me could. You both know what it's like to have to hide from the world, for fear of being laughed at or at least stared at for your unusual features. As you told me the other day at the pool, all you want is to be able to walk down the street with me and the kids without getting racial epithets thrown at you like you are some kind of circus freak."

Jax moved in closer and put a gentle hand on each side of his wife's face. Suzy looked up into his eyes, barely able to make them out through the blur. "I know I don't compliment you like I used to," Jax said honestly, "…that I don't look at you like I used to, and see just how beautiful you are both inside and out. I love your big, beautiful eyes. I always have. I love your big

201

head: it reminds me how smart you are. There are volumes in there that my tiny brain could never handle. I've always loved you for how special and unique you are."

Those same copper-browns were so filled with tears now, the overflow was running down her cheeks in rivulets. She put her hands on his and blubbered, "Oh, Jax, thank you!" She latched onto his upper arms and pulled herself to her feet. Wrapping her arms around him, she said, "That means everything to me."

Suzy wiped her facial liquids on his jogging suit, and then pushed away enough to look up into his face. "But there is something you have to know, Jax," she said, her voice dropping to a more serious level.

"What?" Jax asked, caution and concern in his tone. He wasn't sure he really wanted to know. Did more happen between them than he had already imagined? Did Mejans have a secret sexual position they would never think of doing with humans? Had his wife already filed for divorce? Was she going to have Gregory's baby? *What*?!

"We didn't have sex," said Suzy with a pacifying smile, like a doctor telling a patient he didn't have cancer.

Her words came from so far out in left field, Jax wasn't sure he had heard her correctly. His ensuing "Huh?" was as much from *please repeat,* as it was from *are you serious?*

"Greg and I just hugged," she said, bringing her hands up to frame her husband's scrunched up face. "We hugged like we were long-lost siblings. I never felt love for Greg the way I feel love for you. I felt…ah…*acceptance* with him. *Understanding*, like you just so wisely said. I felt his pain, as I knew he felt mine. We were kindred spirits, who needed the connection, if only for a few moments."

Twenty pounds of anguish lifted off Jax's heart. He couldn't have asked for a better explanation. Without a word, he sat down beside Suzy on the bed and lifted her effortlessly onto his lap. They both hugged and squeezed and sobbed for many minutes.

"Can you ever forgive me, baby?" Suzy finally whispered into the front of his tear-soaked jumpsuit.

"I just did," said Jax, his chin on the top of her brunette head. "Can you forgive me for being so blind to your needs?"

"Of course, I can," she replied, giving him an extra-hard squeeze. "I've never loved you more, Patrick Bernard Jackson. Never."

The couple jumped to their feet and began tearing at each other's clothing like they were on fire. Their naked bodies smashed together so hard there was danger of their flesh fusing into a single mass. As they fell back on the bed, every terror, tribulation, and torment of the past weeks since Suzy's abduction were sent skyrocketing into the atmosphere at sub-light speed.

A soft knock at the door broke the spell. Jax none too politely asked who it was and what the hell they wanted.

"It's Mike," came the voice on the other side, not about to try the door. "Welcome home, Jax. Sorry I couldn't celebrate with you in the rec room. I was manning the comm."

"We know, Mike," sighed Suzy impatiently. "Is that all you want? We're kinda busy here."

"Oh, sorry. No. General Middleton just called about something. We told him about your return, Jax. He's excited. He wants to talk to both of you right away. He's waiting onscreen."

"Shit! Can't it wait?" sighed Jax.

"No, the general says it's urgent."

"We'll be right there, Mike," conceded his sister, slipping back into her pink bathrobe, as Jax pulled on his pants.

Mike's reply was mostly an embarrassed apology. "Okay, see you down there."

Suzy rolled on top of her frustrated hubby and gave him a wet kiss on the cheek. "I guess we'll have to consummate our born-again marriage a little later," she said coyly.

Chapter 36

General Joshua Middleton didn't look good at all. The worry lines crisscrossing his face and the extra droop in the corners of his small mouth aged him ten years. If it weren't for his signature aviator glasses, his eyes might have revealed a high degree of despair over the recent catastrophes.

He was in his private office, sitting behind his mega-cluttered desk. With the volume turned down, only snippets of the rambling Regg could be heard in the background.

When Middleton saw Jax and Suzy come into view, his face lighted up. "It's so good to see you, Jax!" he said with genuine elation, rising to his feet. "We thought we'd lost you out there. You Iowans must live charmed lives. You're the only ones to make it back alive. Welcome back, my friend."

Jax smiled and nodded. Good to be back, General."

"And you, sweet Suzy," the general continued, lifting his sunglasses momentarily for a better look. "I imagine you're pleased to have your man home safe."

"I'm over the moon," she grinned, squeezing Jax's arm.

With words and gestures, Middleton told everyone to sit, then his face turned serious. "I trust you've been listening to our friend back there," he said, motioning with his thumb. "*Ambassador*, my ass. These hairy bastards know as much about diplomacy as they do bikini waxing. Just because one of them can speak decent English doesn't mean they understand diddly squat about us."

"There must be something we can do," said Alan Brookfield, crossing his arms across his bib overalls. "We can't just sit back and let them dictate conditions like that. Jesus! They want to make slaves out of us farmers and ranchers."

"But what *can* we do?" shrugged Mike Brookfield. "With Little Sister and all but two of our fighters destroyed, we got nothing."

"Could we get the military involved?" asked Mary Brookfield, knowing the answer before she asked.

204

"General Middleton shook his head. "Sorry, Mary. They couldn't penetrate those shields any more than we can."

"Can't nuke 'em, either," added Alan. "Even if it worked, there'd be too much collateral damage."

Suzy had been basking so much in the physical and emotional reunion with her big brave forgiving husband, it took a moment before Middleton's words and projected despondency began to sink in. Something wasn't quite right. She started running his statements through her mind, while studying his face and demeanor intuitively. She was sure the good general knew something he wasn't telling them. And was that a glimmer in his big Mejan eye before he put his aviators back into place?

"What are you thinking, Joshua?" she said, walking closer to the television screen, the closest camera following her. "You didn't call this special conference just to welcome Jax home and then get us all depressed again, did you?"

Middleton smiled impishly. "That's my girl," he said, giving her a one-finger salute. "There *is* something. Listen to this." He picked up his iPad, tapped it a couple times, and a throaty voice filled the Brookfield communications room, overriding the rambling Regg.

"I must speak to you," it said, quietly, on the down low. "My name is Saltok. I am...your term for us...a *Regg*. I am female. I am a historian. Unlike my military, I am peaceful. Please, quickly find the right military person to talk to me. Contact me on this secure channel with video. I must see you. You must see me. I am not inside the ship. I am outside with a crew to survey the area for dwellings. I am alone in a shed with farm equipment. Please call soon. I have very little time. I am sincere. Peace."

"Whoa!" breathed Jax. "Was that for real?"

"What do you think, Suzy?" asked General Joshua Middleton. "Is she?"

Closing her eyes, Suzy Brookfield-Jackson refocused her thoughts and feelings on the echo of the recording for only a moment, and then replied, "I feel like she is. And it seems logical. I don't see what the Reggs would have to gain by trying to sucker us into some nefarious plot at this point."

"So, you say..?"

"I say call her back, General. "Let's hear what she says is so important. It's all we've got at the moment anyway, right?"

"You all agree?"

A chorus of approval.

"Okay," said the general. "But I want you in my ear, Suzy. Keep telling me what that radar of yours is picking up about her."

"Sure. No problem," said Suzy.

"Great," said Middleton, putting his hand to his ear. "I'm sticking in my earpiece, so she can't hear you. And I'll keep both channels open so you all can hear and see our conversation."

The Brookfield farm's communication room was a rustle of rolling office chairs and cleared throats, as everyone settled in closer to the large HD screen.

On the left side of the split screen were the narrow shoulders and broad head of General Joshua Middleton. He was purposefully not wearing his aviator sunglasses, so his big blue eyes would draw the Regg's attention. On the right side of the same screen, also looking straight ahead, was the Regg calling herself Saltok, claiming to be a historian. Sticking out of the standard black jumpsuit was her wolfman head and yellow cat eyes, topped off with of all things a Chicago Cubs baseball cap. She was leaning against the huge rear tire of a red McCormick tractor. Behind that was a single, load-bearing wooden pole with a coiled rope hanging from a nail. A pigeon could be heard flapping in the rafters. She was indeed inside a machine shed.

"Ah! I was hoping it would be you, General Middleton," said Saltok, her voice just as raspy as before and less secretive. "I know you from your earlier communication with our officers. Because I have studied and know your language well, I was enlisted to write the scripts our officers used. I hated doing that," she said with a wave off of a five-digit paw. Then she looked hard into her handheld commination device and said, "You are a good man, General. You are a leader of your people, yes?"

"Something like that," said the general, his tone feigning disdain. He wanted to play the superior party in this dialog until he

206

could figure out the Regg's angle. "So, what can we do for you?"

Saltok's reply was short and quick. "You must stop us from taking over your planet."

Middleton wasn't sure he had heard the Regg historian right. The best he could muster was a puzzled "Say again?"

"I have studied your culture for many years," continued Saltok. "I know from your history that you would not allow this. You despise tyranny. Especially you Americans would rather fight to the death than come under our rule."

"Sounds about right," said Middleton with a shrug. "So, what do you care what happens to us?"

"I fear in trying to stop us you would defeat us. You humans outnumber us by billions. Even with our superior spacecraft and weapons, you would eventually destroy us all. I cannot let this happen to my race. We want to survive, just as you do."

"That's very noble of you, Salt Lick," said Middleton, acting impatient, but getting interested. "So, how are we supposed to stop you?"

Saltok ignored the intentional mispronunciation of her name and said, "I can do very little. It is our hope you have some means of doing so. My fellow peaceful Reggs outnumber our violent military ten to one, but we have no weapons. Only the officers have weapons. And only they fly the ships."

"Are their weapons lasers?" Middleton already knew all about the Regg's meager arsenal from the interrogation of the two Reggs captured weeks ago. Their lasers were the shape and size of a baton used in relay races. They had an effective range of only a couple hundred feet, similar to the ones built into The Desert's and Iowan's own communicators.

"Yes, lasers. And a few have guns they stole from your sporting stores. They pretend they are cowboys, like in your old movies."

Middleton shook his head slowly in disbelief. Was this goofy alien for real? He pulled on his ear lobe: the signal to hear from Suzy.

"I know she sounds a little pathetic," she whispered to the general. "But I'm sure she's telling the truth."

Joshua Middleton moved over to plant his butt against the edge of his desk, the camera in the high corner of the room dutifully following him. "Sure, we have all kinds of firepower," he said, folding his arms across his chest. "But it does no good. Your spacecraft have shields that even our most powerful weapons can't penetrate. Believe me, we tried."

"I know," nodded the Regg historian. "And you were successful, at least somewhat. While our mothership was sending the electromagnetic pulse down on the Korea navy, her shields were down, and your Little Sister managed to damage the reactor."

"Really?" said Middleton, pleasantly surprised by the news. "We thought we had missed the reactor and just damaged the navigation system or something."

"No, you did hit a major part," nodded Saltok, looking around nervously, as if one of the militant Reggs might come into the shed at any moment.

"But apparently not enough, since you got away," said the general. "And then your daughters destroyed Little Sister, our only hope."

"Yes, we got away," said Saltok, "but our shields were losing power, along with our anti-gravity engine. We barely managed to set down here in the corn."

Middleton had to keep himself from doing a fist-pump. "You mean you're sitting in our cornfields because your ship can't *fly?*"

"Yes. Our technicians are working feverishly to repair the reactor."

"So, she's vulnerable."

"Oh, yes."

Middleton started pacing. "So, *that's* why so many daughters are hovering above her."

"Yes. To protect her while the repairs are made. Her shields are completely down."

Middleton pulled on his ear lobe.

"Still telling the truth, Joshua," Suzy reported excitedly.

"But your daughters all have shields, too," said the general, his mind racing.

"Yes."

208

"So, what good does that do us?" shrugged Middleton, acting defeated, when he knew the vulnerable mothership meant there was hope. "Their laser cannons will neutralize any aircraft or bomb or missile we send."

"I don't know," sighed Saltok. "We were hoping you had some means to disable our mothership before the repairs are made. Without her, our military would never be able to take over your planet."

"You'd still have all fifty or so of your daughterships."

"True. We hope you could disable them, too."

Middleton's large brow wrinkled. He put his hands on his narrow hips and queried accusingly, "So, what's in this for you, anyway? You'd be homeless, if not defenseless."

Saltok's reply was quick, indicating she had it locked and loaded. "My fellows and I would humbly ask that you give us a piece of land to cultivate and raise livestock. A sanctuary. Allow us to live on Earth peacefully. We are only a thousand souls, with very few children to ensure our continued existence. Because we have been cramped in our spacecraft all these years, we have had to issue a moratorium on births."

"She's still being truthful," volunteered Suzy in Middleton's ear.

Joshua Middleton began a dramatic, circular pace around his office, the camera following along. "Well, this is all academic, anyway," he growled. "You bastards destroyed the last weapon we had that even had a chance of knocking out your mother."

Saltok's hairy head dropped. "I am sorry to hear that, General," she said softly. "Sorry for your race...and for mine."

No one said anything for a few moments. Everyone in the Brookfield communications room was feeling the hopelessness, as well. Jax literally scratched his head. Alan steepled his fingers and pressed them to his lips. Mary seemed to be praying. There was no solution.

From his office in The Desert, General Middleton broke the silence, a thoughtful finger tapping his thin lips. "How long did you say it will be before the reactor is fully functional?"

"The engineers who are working on it thought about two days from now," said Saltok.

"Are they your friends...I mean, non-military?"

"Oh, yes. Certainly. They are part of my talking to you."

Now Middleton rubbed his chin in even more exaggerated thought. "Can you get your engineer friends to stall for at least one extra day?"

"Yes. I suppose that could be done. Why?"

"Well, I'm not saying there's anything we can do," he said, stopping to look square into the camera. "But we can at least put our heads together here to see what options there may be. Meanwhile, I suggest all of you stay inside the ship as much as you can. If there is anything we can do, being anywhere around her perimeter could be dangerous. Call us only if you have vital news."

"We will hope for the best," said the Regg, a hint of optimism in her smoky voice. "Zexic be with you."

Both parties signed off. Saltok disappeared from the split screen, and once again General Middleton's countenance filled both halves. "Whadda think, troops?" he asked with a straight face.

The Iowans' halfhearted chatter among themselves indicated a sincere lack of ideas. What could they do without Little Sister?

Suzy walked front and center. She had been reading Middleton right along with Saltok. "I'll tell you what I think," she said loudly above the others, one big eye half closed, the other riveted on the top man at The Desert. The room fell quiet. "I think you aren't telling us something, General. You were playing dumb with the Regg, weren't you? You've got something up your sleeve, don't you?"

General Joshua Middleton cracked a Cheshire cat grin. "Maybe."

David jumped out of his chair. "What? What?" he pleaded, his one-eighth Mejan eyes larger than normal. "Do you have another warcraft...another Little Sister?"

"Yeah, c'mon," said Jax, joining his wife's side. "What is it? Tell us."

"Don't go getting too excited there people," cautioned the general. "Yes, we do have something we could use. But without a foolproof plan, it's worthless." He studied the six Iowa faces staring back at him, five in open-mouth anticipation, while Suzy's head was cocked to one side in an *I-thought-so* sneer.

"So, go get some refreshments, troops" he said. "Then let's sit down and see what we can come with."

Chapter 37

Janice and Stewart Gilbert were nine miles down Kansas Highway 283 in their aging 2017 Ford pickup. Janice had had her annual dentist appointment up there in Ness City at eight o'clock that morning, and it actually felt good to do something normal in these crazy weeks of blacked out cities and aliens pushing other aliens out of UFOs. And now that god-awful creature yakking away on virtually every radio station for the past week.

"Bring 'em meat, indeed!" spat Stewart, punching off the radio. "I don't see why the air force don't just blow the shit out of them pricks. They're just sittin' over there in the corn asking for it."

Janice took a sip from her water bottle to rinse away the last of the mint-flavored pumice the dentist had used to polish her sixty-year-old teeth. "Goodness, Stew," she said. "Didn't you hear that alien say their spaceship was surrounded by a force field? Bombs would just bounce off. Besides, that would kill all those innocent onlookers."

"I don't care," hissed Stewart. "We need to do something to get rid of them. We ain't about to kowtow to no outer space moon men."

"At least we're lucky to live out here away from all that," said Janice, turning to glance out the window at the flat fields of never-ending crops. "Those lazy aliens would never find enough of us around here to wait on them hand and foot like they want."

Janice's focus sharpened somewhat as they came upon the Pioneer Seeds test plots on the left. This was about the only thing of interest way out here on the Kansas plains, seeming to pop up almost overnight ten years ago. Each ten-row plot was marked with a different number on a white post, designating what type of hybrid corn or sorghum had been planted there.

After another half mile, right in the middle of the sea of green, came those six, nondescript, one-story buildings themselves. It was just assumed this is where all that research took place, agriculturalists always looking for ways to grow it taller, quicker, cheaper. Each of the evenly-spaced structures was about a hundred feet wide and made of cinder blocks, painted over in a glossy white. The monochrome monotony was broken only by young maple trees in and around the complex, plus a black asphalt parking lot out front with about fifty cars glistening in the morning sun.

No one knew exactly how many people worked there. Some of them would come into Ness City to shop at Walmart and Target and frequent the restaurants, but never the bars. They seemed friendly enough, normal enough, except some wore big sunglasses even inside. And they never volunteered much about the complex, how it was built so fast, or what they were currently working on. That was okay, because the locals weren't all that curious anyway; seed test plots were commonplace in the Midwest. And no one was too surprised that the entire country mile out there was protected by a fifteen-foot-high chain-link fence, topped off with razor wire. Hybrid seeds was a multi-billion-dollar business. Excessive security was not unusual.

Just as the Gilberts were passing the buildings, their Ford 150 started to shake and the highway seemed to tip to the right. "Jesus Christ!" yelled Stewart, fighting the steering wheel while slamming on the brakes. "It's an earthquake!"

The white-haired Kansas farmer managed to bring the blue pickup to a full stop, just as the road leveled off again. The Gilberts frantically looked right and left to see what might be causing the trembling and tipping. On their left and through the dust they gasped at the sight of the Pioneer Seeds complex rising a few feet in the air, the ground around it bulging beneath it. The white cinder blocks began to crack apart as if made of Legos. The cars in the parking lot slid into each other, setting off dozens of car alarms, as they piled up against the security fence.

What the Gilberts could barely make out through all the dust was some kind of enormous object slowly lifting out of the ground. Spanning the entire square mile, the spacecraft took every plot of corn and sorghum and soybeans and oats with it into the blue sky, along with most of the buildings.

Then, at an altitude of five thousand feet, it suddenly stopped its ascent to rotate a hundred and eighty degrees on a horizontal

213

axis. Now upside down, it sent the tons of topsoil, bricks, fencing, and greenery cascading back into the mile-wide crater it had just created.

In all the turmoil, one thing the Gilberts didn't notice falling back to earth was the complete lack of anything related to the inside of a normal research facility. There were no desks, or office chairs, or file cabinets, or coffee machines, or microwave ovens, or test tubes. Nothing, just white bricks, six white doors, and the Pioneer Seeds sign. It would be a few days before the sheriff of Ness County suggested that the buildings were only a façade.

The highway concrete was full of fissures and still trembling. But Stewart Gilbert wasn't about to wait, because a black-dirt tsunami was rolling toward them. He hit the accelerator, and the pickup bounced off to the south as fast as it dared, determined to get the hell out there while its driver could still see the white lines of the highway.

It wasn't until they were two miles down the road that Stewart and Janice Gilbert felt safe enough to stop the vehicle and fulfill their burning curiosity. A massive black cloud was still roiling a hundred feet above the entire section, the top of it now catching the summer breeze and drifting northward.

Looking up higher, they saw the massive UFO was still hanging in the air. It seemed to be round or possibly oval shaped, at least ten stories thick, and shaped like a spice cake sandwiched between two dinner plates. Beyond that it was impossible to make out any colors or definition, as the craft was silhouetted against the bright sky.

Then, just that quick, while maintaining its horizontal plane, the object shot straight up and disappeared into the cloudless ether. All that remained were a few wisps of light brown dust where it once had been.

The sexagenarians looked at each through their respective bifocals, eyebrows raised.

"Janice?"

"Stewart?"

Having been married for thirty-eight years, they both knew what the other was thinking. They jumped back in the Ford 150, turned it around in the middle of the highway, and drove back toward what used to be the Pioneer Seeds complex. They slowed down just enough to circumvent the new bumps and fissures in the highway, then sped up again, back toward Ness City, Kansas.

This had to be told.

Chapter 38

The late-morning sun was finally high and hot enough to burn off the layered mist hanging lazily above the corn and soybean fields. The cars, trucks and news vans were parked bumper-to-bumper and two-deep, making travel along any county road virtually impossible. The only vehicles moving were the occasional ATVs, noisily navigating the six-foot-deep ditches or the tents and campfires spread out across adjacent fields.

Jacob Marshall was sitting on a gravel road in a fold-up lawn chair beside the Chevy Tahoe rental, thumbing a text to his girlfriend, White House Press Secretary Georgia Roman. His job as The New York Times' bureau chief for Washington D. C. was basically political. But almost every journalist across the globe these past weeks was clamoring to cover the greatest story in modern history. And in just the past two days the bulk of them were crammed into this square-shaped perimeter around the Regg mothership, which had come to rest dark and dastardly in the agricultural region of north central Iowa.

Yesterday at this time, by order of every law enforcement agency from the Attorney General on down to the Floyd County sheriff, he and the rest of the global media horde had been forced to move back at least two miles from the mothership, thus causing the impassible logjam. While that sudden directive suggested something big was about to happen, it had been almost twenty-four hours with nothing new to photograph or report. The four daughterships hovering sinisterly above the mother were still there, just as they were only moments after the two-mile wide spacecraft thumped down here two days earlier.

Jacob's text: *BORING. BUT WISH U WERE HERE. C'MON. I'LL WEDGE U IN TWEEN MY PRAVDA AND BOSTON HERALD BUDDIES. LOL.*

Georgia: WISH I COULD. BUT POTUS WANTS ME CLOSE FOR SOME REASON.

Jacob: WHY? SOMETHING UP?

Georgia: DON'T KNOW. BUT LOT OF ACTIVITY AROUND HERE THIS A.M.

Something moving in the sky reflected off the glassy face of Jacob Marshall's smart phone. His eyes lifted from the text to see the four daughterships were now being joined by many others, and in a most rapid fashion. Some of the black disks were pouring out of the mothership's main portal like huge, round bats out of hell, while others swarmed in from the wild blue yonder. The commotion was eerily quiet, as the aerodynamic objects displaced the humid air in mere whispers. Within seconds at least four dozen identical spacecraft were in a tight defensive stance over and around the mothership. Since each was the length and width of two football fields, the morning light was not so much anymore, as if ominous clouds had moved in before a storm.

Jacob rose cautiously to his feet. "You getting this, Shooter!" he said quietly to his cameraman, knowing he had mere seconds to scoop his adjacent competition. Shooter was sitting on top of the SUV beside his video camera on a tripod, also texting to someone. "Dude! Fire up," Jacob Marshall hissed louder. "Something's happening."

Shooter looked up and blinked at the unfolding scene. With a "Holy shit!" he jumped to his feet and stabbed at the *Record* button, taking the video camera out of the standby mode it had been in since dawn. Jamming his right eye into the soft rubber eyepiece, he zoomed the lens back to as wide an angle as possible. "Damn, Jacob," he said. "I can't get them all in. I should've brought the fish-eye."

The words were no sooner out of his mouth, when a barrage of Hellfire missiles and Hydra 70 rockets streamed in from all directions, a couple passing barely twenty feet right over Shooter's head. Ducking instinctively and almost falling off the roof, he managed to keep the tripod in place and the camera rolling just as simultaneous fireballs all around the perimeter lit up the landscape. The silence-shattering explosions arrived seconds later, the closest ones first and loudest, the others trailing in from as far as five miles away, each a little quieter than the previous.

That was the first barrage. The second came in before the echoes and the flares of the first had subsided. Then came the third. And the fourth.

Unfortunately, none reached its target: the mothership. The daughters' laser cannons were more than adept at targeting the warheads of all oncoming projectiles, causing them to explode at a harmless distance of a thousand yards. The battle was life and death for each daughter, because in order to fire its laser canon, its protective force fields had to be down, making it defenseless. So far, the Reggs were batting a thousand.

The missiles and rockets kept coming, and the lasers kept destroying them, the shafts of white light splaying outward like hundreds of tightly-spaced spokes on a wheel. The Reggs' shotgun tactics meant many lasers missed their target, passing harmlessly over the heads of the bystanders. But occasionally one was angled low enough to put a clean, round hole an inch wide though a news van, a patrol car, or a luckless reporter.

A spectacular ring of mottled fire, smoke, and falling debris formed around the outer perimeter of mother and her overprotective daughters, which now numbered at exactly forty-nine, the entire Regg flotilla.

Curiosity forcing Jacob Marshall to take his eyes off the action and look all around, he found the source of the onslaught. It was a circle of army Apache helicopters, hundreds of them, keeping their distance at some five or six miles. They seemed to know the Reggs' lasers were ineffective at that range. But it didn't matter. The daughters were doing just fine circling the wagons and mowing down every incoming projectile.

That's when an even more remarkable thing happened. The three-sixty streams of white laser beams radiating out from the daughters suddenly stopped as if a switch had been thrown. Simultaneously, so did the rocket barrage, no more arriving. For a few seconds, the landscape stood frozen in time, the halo of multi-colored smoke around the mothership hanging soft and quiet. Gasps and exclamations began to rise from the crowd, followed by a few people cheering and honking their horns, without having a clue as to why. It was impossible to tell who had won. The U. S. military? The Aliens? Both? Neither?

218

Then, as if someone released the pause button, all forty-nine of the daughterships began a slow, wobbly decent toward earth, picking up speed as they fell. They covered the fifty-to-one-hundred feet in only seconds, and landed none too gently, each sending its own seismic tremor and cloud of green debris across the land.

When all were down and nestled in the corn and soybeans, from his lofty perch high above, General Joshua Middleton leaned closer to his monitor and remarked, "Would you look at that! Looks like raisins sprinkled in a ring around a chocolate layer cake, sitting on a green table cloth."

"What the hell is happening?" breathed Shooter, dislodging from the camera's eyepiece to scan the terrain with both natural eyes. "This is nuts!"

"They've either lost their anti-gravity ability," said Jacob Marshall, watching through binoculars, "or they saw your biceps and decided to surrender."

"Well, I vote for getting the hell out of here," said Shooter, now looking hard at Jacob. "Their storm troopers could come marching out any minute to take their wrath out on us. I ain't about to be one of their goddamn slaves."

The impossibility of that was just possible enough for The New York Times reporter to take a nervous look around. To his left he saw his Russian counterpart, Ivan Spatski with Pravda, easing back a couple steps. On his right, Richard Pennon and his camera crew at The Boston Herald were looking back at him, fearful, questioning.

Yeah, maybe it was time to leave.

Just as Shooter was folding up his tripod, someone down the line yelled, "Look! Up there."

All eyes went to the heavens, finding and focusing on yet another spacecraft, descending from ten thousand feet directly above the Regg mothership and her entourage of disabled daughters. This one was about half the size of the mother, yet still massive enough to draw another round of shock and awe from the observers. Silhouetted against the once-again bright ten o'clock sun, no details could be made out. She was just another

219

dark, mysterious, cookie-shaped, alien spacecraft with no visible means of support.

The question on everyone's mind was whether she was friend or foe.

That got answered when the nervous cease fire was shattered by the sight and thump-thump-thump of dozens of CH-47 Chinook transport helicopters racing in low, barely above the crops. All stopped well short of the downed daughters, holding just a few feet off the ground, waiting for something.

Scant seconds later, as if well-coordinated, two relatively small, two-man space-fighters shaped like DIRECTV remote controllers came gliding down from the bigger craft. Hovering about ten feet off the ground, each picked a disabled spacecraft and pointed at its closed portal.

"Whadda ya say, Suzy-Q?" said Jax. "Dead on?"

"Affirmative," said his navigator. "Fire away."

With its USLAP bean set to *Wide,* Iowa-Two fired its cannon, and the fifty-foot-wide portal blew open with a loud, smokeless blast.

"One down, twenty-three to go," chimed Suzy into her mouthpiece inside her helmet. "How you and Dad doing over there, Mom?"

"Yep, there goes the first door," replied Mary Brookfield, from the other side of the perimeter in Iowa-One. "This is more fun than I thought it would be. Good shot, dear."

"I seldom miss at this range," quipped Alan Brookfield, sitting beside her in the captain's seat. "Moving to number two, Jacksons. Try to keep up."

At opposite ends, the two Iowa fighters continued circling clockwise around the fallen daughters, blowing each one's main door open with their ultra-sonic-laser-accelerated-pulse cannons. It was partly an act of compassion, because with all their electronic functions permanently destroyed from above by The Desert's massive EMP, the Regg crews had no way to get out of their spacecraft before the oxygen expired. That is, if any of them were still alive after their not-so-gentle crash landings.

But the door-busting was mostly to allow the two hundred Navy Seals access to the approximate two hundred Regg militants for capture and confinement...if not bagging and burying.

220

This commenced immediately after the Iowans had begun blowing open the portals. One Chinook choppers set down by each disabled daughtership, a four-man team of Seals pouring out to secure their respective objective. Canisters with sleep agents were first fired inside the craft, rendering any who were still alive into a deep slumber. That would be sufficient until each of the skeleton crew of three or four Reggs could be bound (or bagged) and dragged away into the open air, where the living would recover to find themselves prisoners for the rest of their lives.

Meanwhile, the remaining dozen choppers flew directly into the gaping portal of the mothership herself, from where all those daughterships had previously belched. No sleeping gas should be necessary. These choppers were loaded to the brim with a mixture of riot-control teams armed with Tasers, workmen with blow-torches and dozens of battery-operated lamps, sanitation engineers, computer technicians, social workers, interpreters, and a few veterinarians. This was to be a much larger yet safer task, corralling and documenting some seven hundred other Reggs, almost all of whom would be nonmilitary scientists, technicians, agriculturalists, educators, females, males, and children.

Oh, yes. And one helpful historian named Saltok, whose intel was critical to the success of this mission.

Chapter 39

It had been over a year since the Regg mothership had crash landed in the corn and soybean fields of north central Iowa. Yet the whole alien invasion saga was still a hot topic on many news fronts, social media, and over-the-coffee conversations from Buffalo to Bangkok. The super-secret Mejan mothership—previously code-named *The Desert*, with all its onboard-geniuses of various hat sizes—was no longer a secret to anyone. General Joshua Middleton and his cadre had decided the time had come for the world to know about the Mejan history and all the health, security, and technology contributions they had been making to the planet for the past eighty years. There was no sense in trying to hide it anyway, what with that mile-wide spaceship suddenly erupting out of the Kansas subsoil, leaving a ten-story-deep crater, so it could hover over the Regg mothership to demonstrate some of its otherworldly capabilities to half of the Earth's open-mouthed media.

She was quickly tagged "Mej-America" by the State Department, making sure everyone knew what country the alien craft had chosen to hide in for the past eight decades. The White House and The Desert both agreed Mej-America should tour the world, setting down and staying in major cities for one week at a time. Ostensibly to lessen people's fears about the Mejans, free tours were conducted throughout many levels of the magnificent craft, including living quarters and communications centers, the bridge and navigation area. Of course, certain floors and areas remained verboten.

But it was obvious to a few key cities—namely Moscow, Tehran, Beijing, and Pyongyang—that the United States was serving notice. The Americans owned the most powerful weapon the galaxy had ever seen, and bad behavior would not be tolerated. Such threats were never voiced or written, yet within weeks Putin gave the Ukraine back to Ukraine, Iran cut off all financial aid to ISIS, China forgave the U. S. half of its twenty-trillion-dollar debt, and North Korea's imperial leader was told by China if he tested one more nuclear device of any kind, he would be summarily executed in the public square. The impossible had become possible: World Peace.

Of course, it was anybody's guess just how long it would last before Mej-America would have to relaunch on that four-city reminder tour.

The Reggs were given their requested sanctuary. Fanning out from where the mothership still sat in grounded defeat, a hundred square-mile section of Floyd county in north central Iowa was purchased by the Fed from the local farmers for ten times what their land and buildings were worth. Besides the thirty farmsteads she hadn't crushed, other buildings were constructed to supplement the Regg housing, schools, warehouses, and so on. Mejan engineers came in with their superior technology to fire up a small proportion of the mothership's reactor, so the ship could still be used for a variety of services, including a hospital, fire department, a small college, malls, offices, a town hall, and a prison. The engineers made sure that even if the Reggs wanted to, they would not be able to re-energize the reactor beyond its current minimal level. This was of little concern, since the only Reggs who were capable of this were the non-military, peace-loving Regg engineers. In fact, there were only five remaining militants who had survived their crashes, and they were gracing the aforementioned prison cells with no hope of parole.

Although the displaced Iowa farmers were now multi-millionaires, some still resented being forced from their homes, many of which had been in the family for generations. At first, about half of the townspeople joined in with said displeasure, knowing hundreds of werewolves from outer space were out there howling at the moon, eating meat and defecating on what was some of the richest topsoil in the world. The electrified fence the Corps of Engineers had erected around the entire perimeter kept the races separated, but it didn't stop the occasional bullet or bottle rocket aimed at a nearby Regg dwelling.

Once that fence was completed and the surrounding area was opened back up to the public, that anger quickly transformed into dollars. The good folks of nearby Marble Rock found their sleepy little town suddenly deluged with thousands of Earthlings wanting to drive around the Regg sanctuary to see the actual mothership and maybe some real live Reggs hoeing a garden, scratching their ears, or making puppies. Within days, Marble Rock, Iowa, became the world's number-one tourist destination, as well as America's most overwhelmed, chaotic small town.

Things were no less calm for Suzy, Jax, and Joshua Middleton. After being awarded the Congressional Medal of Freedom by President Henning at the White House two weeks after the defeat of the Regg nation, every correspondent of every news agency from every country wanted them for interviews, photoshoots, or as talk show guests. The prickly General Middleton had no desire to chat with any of them, and told them exactly that. He had all he could handle making the transition from his once highly-secret operation into a more transparent one, and didn't have time to play games with what he considered the corrupt, gold-digging, highly-biased, liberal media. Besides, Middleton knew audiences would just be staring at his alien features and not hear a word he said.

But he still wanted the message to get out. So, he encouraged Jax and Suzy to be the spokespersons, as Suzy was only one-eighth Mejan to his one-quarter. Besides, she was certainly more intuitive and even-tempered, and a hell of a lot prettier. Jax was pure human, tall, handsome, and articulate. They could tell the story better than anyone. The world would eat them up.

And therein lay the problem. Five seconds after it was known Jax and Suzy were husband and wife, everyone in Iowa City knew exactly where they lived. Ten minutes after that, the whole world knew. The news vans with their microwave dishes ringed the property, much as they had the Regg mothership a hundred miles to the north weeks earlier. Swarms of drones constantly circled above, so the roof over the pool area had to be closed indefinitely. Jax did have fun shooting many of them out of the sky with his scoped M-16.

The Jackson family's tans faded to pasty pale. Their cell phones buzzed incessantly. Suzy had to tell *Dancing With The Stars* flat-out *No!* six times before they finally gave up. But she couldn't resist the offer to be on Jeopardy. It was no contest. She set the record for total winnings in only two weeks, after which she gracefully bowed out and gave all the money to the new foundation, "Mejan Lives Matter."

The press agent who Suzy and Jax were forced to hire said they had to agree to an in-depth interview soon or the usual we-have-no-life protestors would be picketing Capitol Hill, and the world would think maybe they weren't such good aliens after all.

Of the myriad offers, they narrowed it down to two news shows. *Sixty Minutes* wanted them so badly they offered a king's ransom for a one-hour interview. Jax and Suzy liked Jane Pauley, but CBS's ratings—along with most of the other major networks—had been on a downhill skid for fifteen years, never recovering from their biased handling of the Donald Trump phenomenon from campaign through his eight-year presidency, and then carried through to President Henning. Could they be trusted with something even more radical and important?

So, they chose *The Furman Factor* on Fox News. Besides Fox being the most-watched network on television for the past five years, its news channels had long been known for being more fair and balanced in its handling of any controversial news story. The arrogant Bill Furman still interrupted his guests if they weren't agreeing with him, but he remained one of the most knowledgeable and in-touch correspondents in America, even at age seventy-seven. As far as Suzy and Jax viewed the news media in general, he seemed the lesser of a hundred evils.

Chapter 40

The Furman Factor wanted the interview to take place on location at The Mansion in Iowa City, but the couple flatly refused, saying Fox's studios in New York City would be just fine. People didn't need to know any more about them than was necessary, and that definitely included an intrusion into the sanctity of their own home. Besides, once the interview was over, Jax and Suzy preferred the idea of making a run for it in the bedlam of a big city crowd, as opposed to fighting off the paparazzi pole vaulting over The Mansion's wall.

Before the taping, Bill Furman did what he claimed he never did: he graciously went over most of his questions, so Suzy and Jax had time to prepare their responses. They appreciated Bill agreeing to that deal-breaking condition.

Suzy wanted to wear her large, Prada sunglasses and floppy hat, but the producers said that might make viewers think she was ashamed of her big eyes and head, or even worse, she was basking in her new-found celebrity. A more sympathetic female assistant suggested going with smaller, slightly-less opaque sunglasses, while using only lateral lighting and extra shoulder padding to deemphasize her large head. After Jax reminded his wife that the purpose of this coming-out interview was to show the world the Mejans were nice and friendly and just as human as everybody else, Suzy agreed. But just the same, she expressed feeling almost naked without her usual disguises.

Despite Furman's calm reassurances and a lowered thermostat in the studio, once the taping began, both Suzy and Jax were nervous and sweating. After hiding from the public for over a decade, they were about to be exposed for who they were and the instrumental part they played in this whole sci-fi adventure. They wanted the world to know they were just as normal as any other couple; but now that the cameras were rolling, they worried that they might not come off that way. After all, exceedingly handsome and filthy-rich Jax had almost single-handedly once defeated the entire Regg nation, while the great-grand-mother of drop-dead-gorgeous, 230 IQ Suzy had come to Earth from another dimension. Nothing abnormal there.

After a brief introduction in which Bill Furman took his turn at making sure the viewers knew The Furman Factor had secured the first exclusive interview with the now-famous and very-illusive pair of Earth-saving superstars, he smiled warmly at them and began, "Welcome, Suzy and Jax. It's an honor and a privilege to talk with you both."

Suzy and Jax replied with nods and "Thank you, Bill."

Bill dived right in. "From our preliminary discussion before this show, I must say I am amazed by what you two have been through." He checked his notes. "First, eleven years ago in 2015, you both were abducted by the Regg aliens, and taken aboard one of their spacecraft. Can you tell us about that?"

Suzy looked expectantly at Jax. He was more awake during that ordeal than she was and certainly more contributory. It was decided he should tell the tale.

"Yes," started Jax. "They broke into our house during the night, drugged us, and took us to their ship that was hiding on the bottom of the Coralville Reservoir."

"So, what did they want from you? Did they do experiments on you?"

Jax shifted in his chair, keeping his fingers interlaced on top of the table. "They were mostly interested in Suzy. She is part Mejan. Only one-eighth, but enough for the Reggs to believe she would provide them with many answers."

"They saw Mejans as a threat to them," offered Bill.

"Yes, but they weren't sure why or how much. As you know, their goal was to take over the planet. They feared the Mejans had superior weapons and intelligence."

"Which you obviously did have," said Bill, looking at Suzy. "Especially intelligence."

"I guess so," blushed the pixy-cute woman behind her down-sized Prada glasses that barely hid her large, copper-brown eyes.

Chuckles rose from the crew behind the cameras. They loved her.

"So, how did you two get away from your Regg captors?" asked Furman, directing his question to Suzy, when it should have been to Jax.

"That was all my husband's doing," she said, grabbing Jax's arm and looking at him. "I was heavily drugged and hardly knew what was happening."

Bill turned to Jax. "So, what did you do, Mr. Jackson?"

Jax shifted again, remembering his pre-editing words. Middleton had warned them to keep explanations to a minimum; there were still many things the world did not need to know. "Well, I was drugged too...with the same drugs and dosage. But being twice the size of Suzy, the effects were far less. And when they came at my pregnant wife's stomach with a foot-long needle, well, I kinda lost it. I guess it was a surge of adrenalin, but I broke my restraints and knocked the shit out of all four of those sonsabitches!"

Due to ever-relaxing restraints on the use of vulgarities over the airwaves, neither expletive would be later bleeped out, nor was the entire crew's laughing and whooping behind the scenes. Suzy just beamed and nodded in affirmation.

Jax went on to explain how he used the same drugs to subdue the entire Regg crew, which then helped him fly the craft into the hands of the good guys. He left out any part of the Reggs' assault on The Farm, fervently wishing to keep it completely out of any narrative. The Reggs had their sanctuary. The Brookfields needed to keep theirs. Besides, Jax was hardly proud of how he had folded under pressure that one night weeks before.

"And then you, Suzette Jackson," continued Bill Furman, "were captured again by the Reggs, just a year ago."

Looking down, Suzy nodded sheepishly. "Ah-huh."

"My goodness, but the Reggs sure seem to like you," quipped Furman. He looked into the camera lens. "Actually, I can't blame them." (Affirmations in the background.) Back to Suzy, he asked, "Can you tell us about *that* one?"

Without giving out too much sensitive information, Suzy carefully scratched the surface of how infrared was used to detect her unusually low body temperature, and how she was taken to a barn where some Reggs were waiting. But thanks to the tracking devise in her smart phone, the good people at The Desert, along with her brave husband, came and rescued her. Then in turnabout, they captured the Reggs and their spacecraft.

Per their agreement, Bill Furman didn't push the Jacksons to reveal anything about their backgrounds, family, or other delicate material. And when they came back from commercial messages toward the end of the interview, the Iowa couple were given the final three minutes to tell the world anything they wished to say. But true to form, Mr. Furman had to go first.

"The entire planet Earth," said Furman straight into the camera, "from the Middle East to the Midwest, owes you two and all those connected with the good ship Mej-America, our most profound gratitude. Working behind the scenes for eighty-some years, without our knowledge, we have been protected from forces that would do us harm, including ourselves. And all down the chronological line we have been given a wealth of technology that otherwise might have you all listening to this program on vacuum tube radios. That is, if you hadn't already died from any number of diseases, or lack of transplants, or live-saving medicines, or surgical equipment or machines."

Bill paused to shake his head. "Somehow, the Congressional Medal of Freedom you folks received just doesn't seem to do you justice. As far as I'm concerned, you should be given the keys to the everlasting kingdom." He turned back to his two guests. "Suzy, Jax, you have the last word. What would you like the world to know?"

As prearranged, Suzy went first. Still looking at her host instead of the camera, she said calmly, yet firmly, "We just want to be seen and treated as equals, Bill. Many across the world...millions, in fact, have some Mejan blood in their veins. A few are still alive who are a full one-half Mejan. Just a few. And they are precious. Their IQs are off the charts. They are the ones responsible for most of the good things you now enjoy in life...from the vaccines and the integrated circuit to the internet and smart phones.

"I'm one-eighth Mejan. That makes me seven-eighths human. If it weren't for my slightly bigger eyes and head, you wouldn't even know the difference. My blood is red, just like yours. I laugh and love, just like you. I have two beautiful children, who look so normal you wouldn't suspect they are one-sixteenth Mejan. We as a family haven't been able to walk down the street of our home town, for fear of being..."

Suzy and Jax had been given the last word, but in true Furman fashion, the opinionated host cut in. "That is such a true and sad commentary on our society these days. You are an extremely attractive young woman, and yet because you have a couple physical features slightly different from the norm, you are open to racists remarks. Yes, I do mean *racist*, in the sense of disparaging anything out of the ordinary or that doesn't fit with one's personal views. In our schools it's called bullying, which runs rampant, despite ongoing petitions by parents and legislatures to punish the bullies. But it just keeps getting worse, especially over the social networks. And why wouldn't it, when you look at the kind of humor, if you could call it that, the so-called comedians are using today. The worst are the late-night, far left-wing hosts. Remember how they literally *attacked* Donald Trump nine years ago when he ran for president, and then it only got worse all throughout his presidency? And now they're doing the same thing to President Henning, another Republican. Since they don't agree with their politics, they make the cruelest jokes about them, that quite frankly, folks, aren't even remotely funny. They are just mean for mean's sake.

"What in God's name are we teaching our kids? That kind of humor used to be considered slander and open to litigation. Then back in the nineteen sixties the courts ruled that since it was presented in the context of humor, the comedians and networks could not be liable. So, now it's okay to use mass media to make fun of someone who looks different from you or has a different point of view. And not just make fun, but exaggerate even the slightest malformity to the extent of hyperbole, so the person can be laughed at like a freak in a sideshow until they have no self-respect or dignity left. How many children have we lost to suicide because of this kind of *humor*?

"We can only hope that after the world sees you two tonight on The Factor, and especially you, Suzette Jackson, and how truly beautiful you are both inside and out, this era of bullying can come to an end. It's been going on for decades. Enough is enough.

"So, go head Suzy, or Jax. You have the last word. What? Oh. Sorry, but we are out of time. Again, thank you both for coming on The Factor. Please, come back again soon. Hannity is up next."

Jax and Suzy had only enough time to smile.

Chapter 41

The silver, 2026 Lexus SUV took what looked to be the last empty spot in the asphalt parking lot of City Park. No surprise. It was a beautiful, sunny Sunday in the middle of summer. The populous of Iowa City often flocked to the twenty-acre park on weekends with their offspring for its large swimming pool complex, carnival-type rides, softball games, concessions, and three ponds full of ducks and geese you could feed. Judging by the mass of people already there at eleven-thirty in the morning, the Jacksons were lucky to find this spot.

Jax punched off the engine and turned to address his two adolescents in the back. "Ready, gang?" he chimed.

"Ready," both said, although neither shared their father's enthusiasm. Sure, going to City Park could be fun, but they'd been here just two years ago with Mom. Of course, that was before anything was known about aliens versus aliens versus Earth. At least this would be the first time with Dad tagging along, which seemed to be the main reason for today's visit anyway. That was pretty cool, but a movie would have been better.

Jax turned to his wife in the passenger seat. She was darling in her cream-colored chino shorts and half-sleeve lemon top with extra ruffles around the shoulders to draw attention away from her large head. But she looked nervous. He couldn't blame her. This was to be a day like none other.

"Ready to do this, hon?" he asked, tongue-in-cheek.

Suzy slipped on her oversized sunglasses, then turned to give Jax a crooked smile that said she wasn't anywhere near ready to do this.

"It's gonna be okay," he said, reaching over to give her spray-tanned thigh a reassuring squeeze. With all the extra public interest in their lives, the louvered canopy over the pool area at home had been locked in place for a year. The whole family loved being tan. But lately it had to come from a bottle.

"I'm not so sure," said Suzy, suddenly digging into her tote bag to produce her favorite floppy hat.

"C'mon, hon," scolded Jax. "You don't need it. We talked about this."

"And I said I'd feel naked without it," whispered Suzy soft enough so the kids couldn't hear. "Not wearing it on TV is one thing. But out here in the real world…"

She didn't need to worry about the kids. Nichole and Nathan had already unbuckled their seatbelts and were sliding out of the car.

"You kids wait for your mother and me," ordered Jax, just before the doors slammed. "Stay right here."

"Well, hurry up," groaned eight-year-old Nathan, barely audible from outside. "You were the ones who wanted to come here in the first place. Whataya waiting for?"

"C'mon, Suzy Q," coaxed Jax. "Lose the hat. It was yesterday when you needed it. This is today, and you don't. Be proud of your brains. I am. And by now I'm sure the world is, too."

Suzy lowered her huge Prada sunglasses and gave her husband the look. "You know damn well it's not my brains I'm worried about."

"Nobody will be looking at your head anyway," smirked Jax. "They'll be looking at your legs. We both know that's why you chose to wear those short shorts in the first place."

Busted.

With a chuckle and a muted *Okay*, the one-eighth Mejan stuffed the floppy hat back into her tote bag. But she made it clear the sunglasses were to remain firmly on the bridge of her button nose.

Obeying orders, the kids stayed close to mom and dad, as the foursome left the safety of the SUV behind and began their maiden voyage as a family into the land of the normal. Back at The Mansion, Nicole and Nathan had been gently schooled on why the family was doing what it was doing, and on what they might encounter here in the park. The kids, of course, didn't see what all the whoop was about. So what if Mom has a big head and eyes? They seem perfectly normal to them. If anybody said anything gross, Nathan said he'd kick their ass. It cost him a dollar, but Jax couldn't have been prouder.

Being two years older and a relatively mature ten, Nichole understood only slightly more…that for a very long time Mom and Dad had hidden the fact they were married, because they feared some people wouldn't understand about Mom's Mejan features, just like the kids have, yet to a lesser degree. But now that their secret had been out for over a year—thanks to Mom and Dad being all over the news, talk shows, and even a game show—enough time had lapsed that hopefully the Jackson family could be accepted around their home town as regular folks. Today was to be the first test. City Park seemed like a good place.

The kids had already made it clear it was lunchtime, so the Jacksons set course for the closest taco stand about a block away through a crush of people. Suzy especially was well aware of the facial expression and body language of every person they passed. Most were oblivious, their eyes cast downward, or their minds focused on their kids or some personal, trivial matter at home. But those who did notice her paused to stare, whisper to each other, or smile and wave in wide-eyed recognition.

It wasn't long before the brashest stepped right up and blocked their path.

"Well, if it isn't Jax Jackson," grinned the tall, thin, white-haired man of sixty, thrusting a welcoming hand toward Jax, yet finding it difficult to stop staring at the main reason he was interrupting their day.

"That I am," said Jax, his hand being pumped like a car jack.

"I'm Fred Cox," the man said. "I don't know if you remember me, but I'm on the city council. I was the one who handed you the scissors at the ribbon-cutting ceremony for the new football stadium you built for West High five years ago."

"Oh, sure," nodded Jax, recalling the event but having no recollection whatsoever of the man.

Fred's impatient wife quickly stepped to the fore, she also quite tall and anemic. "And you, Suzette Jackson," she gushed, reaching to squeeze Suzy's hand, "we absolutely loved you on Jeopardy. My goodness, sweetheart, you set every record on the books. What did you win, some three million in only two weeks? You even beat IBM's Watson, when Ken Jennings couldn't. And then you gave all your winnings to charity. It's so great to meet you. What's your IQ, honey, if I may ask?"

"Well, ah," stammered Suzy, pleased with the recognition of her brain, instead of the size of its container. But now she just wanted to be somewhere else.

"And what beautiful children you have," the woman continued, resisting the urge to touch them. "They don't look alien at all."

"For God's sake, Judith!" scolded her husband.

Chapter 42

The truth was, despite being the author of twelve books on UFOs and the publisher/editor of *Sightings Magazine*, Brady Leach didn't believe in extraterrestrials and UFOs. He had never un-covered one shred of solid evidence, yet his Photoshopped pho-tos and fictitious writings had made him a wealthy man, along with a high degree of notoriety in the ET-crazy community.

But now that the entire world knew aliens had been roaming the planet for almost a century—and none of them proved to look anything like his grainy facsimiles or artist's renditions—sales of his fabricated literature had crashed and burned. Science fiction had become science fact, and what the people wanted these days were genuine snaps and insights into both the Regg and Mejan alien nations.

The Reggs held their own special appeal, because they were original. Having never propagated with humans, they were a genetically untainted species. (The jury was still out on whether they ever mated with dogs or wolves.) Nothing else on the planet looked like and acted like them, what with their wolfman exteriors and carnivorous attitudes. Literally, these were earless, cat-eyed, man-sized, lupus erectus.

The Mejans, on the other hand, were far from pure. They had been interbreeding with humans for so many generations, the au-thenticity of the race had become diluted to where finding an entity with even half Mejan blood was almost impossible. In her interview with Bill Furman, Suzette Jackson had commented that a few fifty-fifties still existed. But they are so sequestered away in the good ship Mej-America, Brady Leach had no chance of ever interviewing them, let alone scoring a photo.

So, Brady had to embark on a new journalistic genre, one dealing with something totally foreign to his nature: Facts.

There were plenty of facts, to be sure...from hours of videos and audio recordings, to libraries of photographic stills. But the

major studios of Fox News and CNN owned the rights to virtually all of them. Brady's only hope was to snap a unique photo
of two Reggs copulating or maybe tearing at each other's throats.

So, for the first six months since the defeat of the Reggs,
Brady Leach rented an old duplex in Marble Rock, Iowa, every
day going out among the other paparazzi to the Regg sanctuary
with his thousand-dollar drone. He didn't dare fly it directly
over their airspace, for fear of it getting shot down within
minutes. The Reggs were allowed a modest armory, plus the
right to kill wild game and defend themselves if necessary. This
included drones and anyone foolish enough to find a way inside
the perimeter.

By systematically trying a different location each day, Brady
would fly his drone straight up to the allowable four hundred
feet, and use its sophisticated fifty-power zoom lens to observed
the hairy creatures in their daily routines. The best video he ever
got was a Regg turning the John Deere tractor too sharp and rolling in onto himself. An ambulance and firetruck wheeled out of
the mothership, and a pair of Reggs in whitecoats got the victim
onto a stretcher and back inside mother to the hospital. NBC
was so desperate for anything scooping CNN and Fox, they paid
Brady fifty thousand dollars for the video with five percent guar-
anteed on residuals.

That was three months ago. Since then the Reggs had become boring and unprofitable. Unlike their indigenous canine
counterparts—who could care less who watched them take a
dump or fornicate in the town square—these secretive wolf-peo-
ple were as sensitive about their love-making and misdemeanors
as most humans, apparently doing it only away from prying
eyes. So, good-paying photos were few and far between. His
last series of four Reggs acting like border collies as they herded
a dozen head of Holsteins into the mothership for slaughter,
brought only five hundred dollars from The National Enquirer.
The editor said they already had a stockpile of those, and to
please send no more.

So, when Brady Leach saw Suzette Jackson divulging there-
tofore secrets about herself and family on Bill Furman's Factor,
he left Marble Rock, Iowa in a cloud of dust and two months
owing on his rent. There she was, the very alien he had tried to

corner last summer on a tip from Jacob Marshall at The New York Times. But the Iowa City address he was given turned out to be bogus and a virtual dead end. So, with no other leads, he had abandoned the quest and gone back to Arizona.

Now he knew exactly where she lived, as did everyone on the globe. The multi-million-dollar spread on the outskirts of Iowa City was the most famous residence in southeast Iowa, and now maybe the world. It belonged to Patrick Bernard Jackson (Jax), one of the richest men in the Midwest. And Suzette was his wife, living there for ten years, right under everybody's nose. They even had two adolescents.

Brady Leach was in heaven. That is, until he discovered his million-dollar baby lived in a fortress fortified with an electrified front gate and a ten-foot-high chain-link fence running the entire perimeter. There was no way a Navy Seal could sneak inside, let alone an out-of-shape paparazzo with a stomach the size of a sofa sack.

His drone proved useless, too, as he learned on that warm summer day in June. Using a satellite print-out from Google Earth as a map of the premises, Brady Leach had snuck around to the back of the two hundred-acre estate to a hide in a stand of trees. He sent his drone southward across the property, only to find anything its inhabitants might use—like the tennis and basketball courts—were so perfectly canopied by a green forest of oak and maple trees, the only way he knew they even existed was from the satellite photo taken in winter when the trees were stripped of their leaves. The five-acre pond had no such cover, but no one was fishing or boating that day, so he flew on toward the mansion itself and its interconnected complex of buildings. But before the drone got within a hundred yards of the massive, retractable roof hiding the pool area, his aeronautical peeping Tom suddenly lost power along with its transmission, crashing on the roof of an outbuilding. The echo of gunfire was self-explanatory.

So, the following six months were as frustrating as the first six. Brady Leach hadn't gotten a single paycheck since the photo series he later did on the exterior of the Jackson estate itself from ground level. Because he was the first to submit what instantly became a cliché, Star Magazine paid him five thousand dollars, with the caveat to send no more after this.

So, what else was there? The Jacksons rarely left their mansion. And when they did it was via a dark windowed SUV with police escort to the airport. Laws forbid flying drones within five miles of any airport, so even if he and his Nikon camera with its 500 mm telephoto lens could get to the chain-link fence in time to shoot the person or persons boarding the private jet, he, she or they were always so cloaked in disguises there was no way to tell who they were. The rags allowed a lot of leeway on a story's content, but on photographs they required proof positive. And the technology of authenticating photographs had become so sophisticated, it was impossible for Brady to get away with his usual Photoshop tricks.

The pudgy, fifty-two-year-old man was sitting on the raised cedar deck of his apartment in nearby Coralville, seriously contemplating getting back into the business of fiction and fantasy. Perhaps the metaphysical. Brady Leach had read that fifty percent of the country believed in ghosts. He could move to New England and rent some old haunted mansion. He could rent a cabin in the north woods and look for Bigfoot. Or he could fly to the Scottish Highlands and dive for Nessie.

He was about to call Jacob Marshall at The Times to see if anything along these lines had come across his desk, when his police band scanner started squawking about a *164* (crowd or traffic control) being required at City Park on the other side of Iowa City. It wasn't until the name *Jacksons* was broadcasted that Brady's ears perked. Was it possible? Had Suzette Jackson actually come out from her ivory castle to walk among the unwashed in City Park? It had to be. Tabloid target that he was, Jax Jackson alone could never create this kind of commotion requiring the police, even though he hadn't been seen much since he and Suzette did the Furman show last summer.

In a frenzy, Brady Leach raced down the stairs to the parking lot. His two hundred pounds of pale flesh in plaid shorts and tie-dye T-shirt jumped on the rented Honda electric scooter, and whined off for City Park four miles away.

Brady Leach's mind was already there, way ahead of his body and bike. He realized the local press would probably have her surrounded by now. That was okay. They had no idea of the potential gold mine. The important thing was to beat any of his fellow paparazzi. So, time was of the essence. The word on the street was that a single face shot of Suzette Jackson in the flesh—meaning nothing covering her large head and especially those secretive eyes—could bring as much as half a million dollars. Video would pay upwards of a full million. Until now, Suzette had been seen only digitally recorded in a studio setting, with sunglasses hiding her eyes, and angled lighting to help diminish her abnormal head. No one had ever caught her face completely au natural. To get her answering the right questions on video could even up the ante to a Pulitzer in the mind of one Mr. Brady Leach.

Always planning ahead, still three miles from the park Brady pulled out his smartphone and called Gerald Lockhart, the managing editor at *Pictell*, an up-and-coming social network that went a step farther by publishing a hardcopy magazine, lately giving *People* a run for its money. The two had talked briefly six months ago when Brady was trying to get a feel for what some aerial snaps of the Jacksons lounging around their pool might bring in dollars. That, of course, was just before his first and only attempt to achieve said photographs was sadly concluded by the untimely and violent demise of his thousand-dollar drone.

Gerald Lockhart wasn't in at the moment, so Brady Leach asked to be connected to someone in Pictell's digital upload division. All Brady really needed for now anyway was to establish a direct link between it and his smartphone. That way, each and every photo he took from that moment on would cross cyberspace in milliseconds and land at Pictell.

The technician said no problem, and sent the link to Brady's smartphone. With one hand Brady snapped off a test photograph of a pickup passing him on the left. The Pictell technician verified it had come through just fine, and wished the photog luck on whatever celeb hunt he might be on.

The electric scooter was already going as fast as its little motor would take it, but Brady Leach twisted the throttle as hard as he could anyway. Everything was set. Now all he needed was to get to City Park and Suzette Jackson's unveiled alien face before any of his fellow maggot mob.

Chapter 43

In the weeks running up to this prospective *walk in the park*, many scenarios were considered. But none suggested the Jacksons would be given anywhere near the volume of attention that ultimately confronted them. When a person or couple were bold enough to step up and engage them, many others would gather around to listen...if not to gawk at Suzy's intriguing mixture of beauty and prodigious head. That would embolden others, until the building throngs frequently forced the Jacksons to excuse themselves, so the kids could get on this ride or that ride or get a snow cone or feed the ducks. Jax and Suzy would then patiently turn back into the salivating multitude and answer the questions the best they could.

Word traveled fast, and by twelve noon a reporter and photographer from the Iowa City Press Citizen were on them like puppies on a squeak toy. Soon followed both Cedar Rapids television stations, and then the three Des Moines metro stations arriving by Leer jet. By one o'clock a squad of Iowa City PD were directing traffic on all adjacent streets, while half a dozen other officers were inside the park itself for crowd control. Most of the latter, however, had surreptitiously positioned themselves for the best chance to see the famous Suzette Jackson in person, thereby mostly adding to the problem.

One thick-bodied man with thinning chestnut hair and a brightly-colored tie-dye T-shirt was particularly persistent. He had bulled his way through the crowd to get front and center to Suzy by the pool entrance. Unfortunately, he found himself being forced to remain in the second row, thanks to the entire defensive front line of the University of Iowa's football team, who didn't particularly like line crashers. So, Brady Leach had to do the best he could from behind the massive wall of Blutos.

"Missus Jackson," Brady yelled above the buzz, lifting his camera over his head and above the football players, "could you take off your sunglasses? We've heard your eyes are gorgeous."

Suzy ignored him, being presently engaged with a young couple, just one of many dying for a selfie with her. When she was finished, Brady yelled out his request again, catching her without recourse. This time the crowd murmured with some anticipation. They too would like to see that carefully-guarded alien feature hiding behind those oversized sunglasses.

Suzy shook her head, waving off the request. There was a limit to this honesty.

"Honey?" said Jax, nudging her.

The petite mother of two looked up at Jax. "I really don't want to," she whispered stubbornly.

Jax understood. But he also thought that maybe this was the time...to end the speculation...to take a giant step toward what Suzy and he had been wanting for the length of their entire marriage. "You've come this far, Suzy Q," he said. "Why not let them see the real you. Your eyes *are* beautiful."

Suzy looked tentatively at the crowd. A few just stood there in wide-eyed anticipation. Most of the women smiled and nodded their encouragement. Most of the men didn't seem to care one way or the other, keeping their gaze riveted on her shapely legs and perky breasts.

Suzy's gaze dropped to the ground. Her mind flashed back to the only other time she had exposed her eyes to the public: those two cops at the mall over a year ago. The thought of doing it again, especially in front of such a horde of salivating humans, made her stomach queasy. But there seemed no way out of this. Even her supportive husband wanted her to do it.

Truth be known, she secretly wanted to do it, too.

With a sigh of surrender, Suzy slowly raised a hand to the bow of her Prada sunglasses. The crowd fell silent. A dozen camera phones lifted into position. Brady Leach held his breath and looked up to the small screen of his smartphone to make sure she was perfectly in frame. But there was no image. The screen was black. He knew he hadn't turned it off. It was working fine on the way here. But now it was dead. The battery was dead. He realized he hadn't charged it in...hell, he couldn't remember the last time.

The one-eighth Mejan, seven-eighths human slowly pulled the sunglasses from her face and blinked her big, beautiful, copper-browns at the crowd. At first there were soft gasps of amazement, followed by nods and mumbles of approval. Mild applause morphed into clapping and shouted accolades, all the while dozens of cameras and smartphones snapping pictures and taking videos, some soon getting uploaded to the internet. Within minutes, millions of people on Facebook, Snapchat, YouTube and a hundred other social media were gawking in awe at the spectacle of Suzette Marie Brookfield-Jackson's unabridged alien eyes.

Groans and expletives rising up from behind them, a couple of the linemen turned around and looked down at the balding, beady-eyed, frumpy, middle-aged man, sitting cross-legged on the ground, beating his fist on the helpless Samsung smartphone. Finding this of no consequence, they quickly turned back to take more pictures of the gorgeous, five-foot-four Mejan phenomenon.

****

As the hours and expo worn on, the Jacksons wore out. Nathan and Nichole had wanted to go home for the past two hours. Jax thought a couple PBRs would hit the spot. Suzy relished the idea of working on her tan at the quiet privacy of their pool, the ceiling retracted, the overhead drones and helicopters be damned. But she had to admit it felt good to be accepted by the very people she had to hide her identity from for all those years. Today, here in a small city's park by the Iowa River, with dozens of people taking pictures, wanting her autograph, and asking to take selfies with her, it was beginning to look as though her dream was coming true. She was being accepted for who she was: a normal member of the community.

As they headed back to the car later that afternoon—leaving the dwindling crowd behind—the kids danced with the exuberance of school letting out for the summer, while Jax and Suzy walked holding each other up, literally exhausted.

"That went rather well," laughed Jax, kissing the top of his wife's brunette head. "I think the townspeople actually want you to stay around, rather than go back to Alpha Centauri in your flying saucer."

"It was almost too good," smiled Suzy, shaking her head. "We used to fear being exposed as husband and wife. Now we have to fear being trampled to death by well-wishers."

"It'll wear off," said Jax. "Give it time."

The call came from behind, as they were only a hundred yards from the seclusion of their parked SUV. "Please, Mister and Missus Jackson," called the man, obviously running to catch up, "just a quick word."

Without turning around, the whole family came to a slow-motion stop on the asphalt. Nichole's sigh was the loudest, but Nathan's "Shit!" was the most profound.

"Go on ahead to the car, you two," said Jax, handing the fob to Nichole. As the kids scampered off, he and Suzy turned to face one more exuberant fan, who turned out to be two. Both men were black, in their late-thirties, good-looking, and based on the single diamond in both right ears, openly gay.

"Oh, thank you!" puffed the taller one with a shiny bald head, pulling up to a stop.

"Yes, please forgive us," said the other, just as bald and just as out of breath. "We won't take but a moment of your time, if that's okay."

"Certainly," smiled Suzy patiently, tightening her grip on her husband's arm for physical and moral support. "What can we do for you?"

Jax couldn't help but size up the two men, mainly because both would be powerful adversaries if their intentions were less than cordial. So far, the people had been friendly. But the law of averages said the Jacksons' City Park excursion was overdue for a contrary opinion.

The one introducing himself as Peter was six-foot-one—an inch shorter than Jax—but definitely in better shape, his chiseled arms poking out from the pink wife-beater, while the white, satin running shorts hid very little of his equally-toned legs. He was the thinner of the two.

The other—named Jerry—wore virtually the same outfit, only the colors of the top and shorts were reversed. At five-nine, he was built like a bull dog, yet his effeminate voice and manner, combined with his cocker spaniel eyes, were a study in contrast.

"We just wanted to thank you with all our hearts," said Jerry, placing both hands over the aforementioned thumping organ, his brown eyes clearly on Suzy.

"For what?" she asked.

"For your bravery," said Peter, half bowing. "For standing up on TV and showing the world you are proud of who you are."

"Well," scoffed Suzy, "I was hardly brave. In fact, today was the first time in my life I've had the nerve to venture out into public like this without a disguise. All the rest of the time I was terrified."

"You sure didn't look afraid for those two weeks on Jeopardy," chuckled Peter. "You stood up there like a proud, bespectacled statue, rattling off the answers, while those so-called *comedians* (air quotes) were making fun of you every night on the late shows."

"Were they?" said Suzy, a little crestfallen. "I didn't know."

"Oh, God, yes!" said Jerry. "It was horrible the things they said. Sometimes they'd use fake videos, showing you finally removing your sunglasses to reveal everything from three bulbous eyes looking in three different directions to no eyes at all, just an extra mouth with hideous green teeth, eating an owl. And the jokes! Almost as bad as all that unfunny shit they keep throwing at our presidents."

"But I've read their ratings are dropping," pronounced Peter proudly. "People are getting sick of the constant bullying."

"Thanks to you, Mrs. Jackson," said Jerry. "You are our champion." He reached over and took his partner's hand. "We know all too well about prejudice."

"We know you do," smiled Suzy weakly, still stunned by the revelations she just heard. Jax nodded.

Assuming, if not hoping the accolades were over, the Jacksons turned to move on. But the gay couple had more to say.

"In some ways," said Jerry with a limp-wrist flip, "that whole Regg invasion thingy did a lot of good for the world."

"Yeah," said Peter, "having our way of life threatened like that kinda caused all of us to unite a little, common enemy, as it were."

246

"It's true," added Jerry, wrapping a thick arm around his taller mate's waist. "We definitely noticed people being kinder to us, like we weren't so out-of-the-ordinary after all. At least we didn't have hair all over our bodies and those gawd-awful yellow cat eyes."

"Yeah," chirped Peter. "Thanks to the Reggs, they had to change the definition of "queer" in the dictionary."

Everyone laughed. It felt good.

"Then your *coming out* (air quotes again) on Bill Furman's show," said Jerry quickly, as the Jacksons were once again turning to leave, "was *truly* the most fascinating and courageous thing we'd ever seen. I said to Peter that on so many levels the world desperately needed to see you in a conversational setting and hear your story. You showed everyone that looking a little different didn't mean you were a threat to anyone."

"I still hid behind my glasses," sighed Suzy. "I didn't want to scare the viewers."

"Oh, for Heaven's sakes, Missus Jackson," scolded Larry. "You're so pretty and petite, how could anyone be afraid of you?"

Suzy blushed. Jax pulled her close and quipped, "Oh, I don't know. You should have seen her when a cop pulled the floppy hat off her head a year ago."

More good-natured laughter before Peter continued, "You two were the perfect spokespersons. You, sir, proved we humans can marry people from another dimension and still have perfectly normal children...if not exceptional children. I'll bet your two kids are very intelligent."

"In some ways, too smart," said Suzy.

"But most of all," concluded Peter, "Missus Jackson, you have done more in the crusade against a whole list of phobias than anyone or anything in the past century. I mean it. You should get the Nobel Peace Prize."

With that, the same-sex couple shook the hands of the bi-dimensional couple and bid them God bless.

Pausing to watch them walk away, Jax gave Suzy a squeeze and sighed, "And the hits just keep coming."

"I am literally overwhelmed," she sighed. "I was just hoping people wouldn't point and stare at me. I never expected so many of them to be so nice."

"They love you, Suzy Q."

"I don't know about that," she laughed, turning them both toward the car. "I think they see me more as a novelty."

"Maybe so," said Jax. "But no one laughed at you today."

"I noticed a few were gawking," she said. "I could feel them saying *Look at that big head!*"

"Nah," scoffed Jax. "They were thinking, *Look at those great legs and tits! That guy sure is lucky to have a wife like that. Wonder where I can get me one of them sexy alien chicks.*"

Chapter 44

Just when they thought the afternoon was finally over…just when they thought there couldn't possibly be any more fans stopping them from their retreat, here came two young men on motorcycles, just now entering the park. Undoubtedly college students, both were dressed casually in jeans, U of I T-shirts, Nikes, and sunglasses. Despite the twin Harley-Davidson hawgs, they definitely were not the Hell's Angels types.

"Look! There she is," called one above the rumble, pointing at Suzy. Both throttled forward. Suzy and Jax dutifully paused to receive what they hoped would truly be the last pair of admirers.

Stopping ten feet from the Jacksons, the cyclists kept their motors running, while sticking out legs to remain upright. They smiled in youthful wonder.

"Wow!" roared one above his gurgling Harley. He had shaggy blond hair tied back in a ponytail, a ruddy complexion, and slender build. "That really is one ginormous head!"

"No shit," called the other, with closely-cropped brown hair, blue eyes and a stud through the side of his hook nose. He couldn't have weighed more than one-thirty. "But that thing looked even bigger on TV."

"Well, of course, numb nuts. Television adds ten pounds."

Jax was already stepping between his wife and the contentious duo. He glanced back down the parking lot where the two bald-headed gays had stopped to watch the commotion. Other people, including a pair of Iowa City PD, were also demonstrating interest, but staying where they were. Jax hoped none of them could hear this embarrassing confrontation. Things had been going so well up until now. But at least their presence should keep these bozos from getting physical.

"Buzz off, assholes," Jax hissed, fists clenched.

"Oh, look," chided the ponytail, "it's Mister *I Married a Monster from Meja*. How is that alien pussy? Out of this world?"

Suzy grabbed her red-faced, irate husband from behind, pinning his arms to his side. "Let it go, honey," she said sternly. "Let's just go get in the car."

Jax was livid. That adrenalin surge that comes along only when highly provoked was beginning to boil in his blood. He envisioned smashing his fist squarely into the face of that obnoxious punk, then neutering the other with a swift kick to the nads. But Suzy was right. They weren't worth it. It had been a good day until these misaligned millennials motored up. Let it go.

Despite the parting shout of "Catch ya later, freak show," Jax allowed his two hundred pounds to be manhandled toward the car by his one-hundred-ten-pound wife. Thankfully the kids were already inside and too busy with their game pads to be aware of anything. Without a word, Nathan and Nicole's parents slipped into the SUV and buckled up.

"Ready for home?" Suzy asked, turning toward the backseat. She was answered with a pair of distracted *Huh-uhs*. Good. They hadn't seen or heard a thing. She put her attention back on the profile of her seething husband. "You okay to drive, honey?" she asked. He just nodded.

After a moment of soul-calming, Jax backed the Lexus out of the parking spot and put the gearshift into drive. Telling himself he was checking for oncoming traffic, his glance in the rearview mirror was actually to see where the antagonists had gone. What he saw caused him to gently apply the brakes and put the car back into park. Curious why they had stopped, Suzy rechecked her husband's profile. Seeing his gaze was fixed on something in the mirror, she turned around to look back herself.

There were the two motorcyclists being roughly removed from their Harley-Davidsons by two black men with shiny bald heads. The smaller white boys were easily dragged away from the asphalt and thrown down on the grass. Cat-quick, each of the thirty-year-olds pinned his respective twenty-year-old with butt on chest and knees on arms. No blows were thrown, just what seemed to be stern lectures to a couple of clearly terrified academia racists.

250

Meanwhile, a half dozen men from the group of onlookers stepped up and began pushing the two motorcycles off the asphalt, over the grassy ground, and toward the Iowa River. Cheers and then applause rose up from the rest of the gathering crowd, as the two bikes rolled slowly down the river bank, into the water, catching the current before ultimately disappearing under the surface in a swirl of gurgling bubbles.

The two cops turned their backs on the scene and sauntered off in the opposite direction. Plausible deniability.

Jax turned his attention to his wife. Her lower lip was quivering. From under the huge pair of sunglasses trickled tears. Without asking, he tried to ascertain if those were tears of joy or sadness. He figured it was a combination of the two, maybe more. It had indeed been an emotional day.

Jax put the car in drive and eased forward toward City Park's exit. He took one last look in the rearview mirror to find the crowd of people waving goodbye.

"Like I said, "he grinned, throwing a thumb to the rear, "they love you, babe."

Suzy looked in the passenger's side outside mirror. She couldn't help but smile. She powered down her window and waved back without turning around.

"Thank you," she said softly to the people in the mirror. "Thank you so much."

With a literary career spanning decades and hundreds of feature articles, non-fiction books, and novels, Richard Douglas Taylor subject matter has ranged from astrophysics to aliens. His imaginative storylines have just the right touch of humor to make them a joy to read and difficult to put down.

Books by Richard Douglas Taylor:

Novels—
The Brookfield Daughter
The Brookfield Daughter—Sanctuary
Earth-Two
Earth-Two—Game-Changers

Non-Fiction—
Under the Solar/Lunar Influence
How to Know When to Go
Making Sense of It All

Web site: www.primetimes2.com/books.html
Email: rdtaylor@mediacombb.net

www.ingramcontent.com/pod-product-compliance
Lightning Source LLC
Chambersburg PA
CBHW020751250626
47155CB00003B/1022